Anasazi Triumph

To Dick,

With Best Regards,

James Seben

2007

Anasazi Triumph

James Gibson

Pentacles Press

This novel is a work of fiction. References to real people, events, establishments, and locales are intended only to give the fiction a sense of reality and authenticity. All of the main characters, organizations, events, and incidents in this novel are creations of the author's imagination, and their resemblance, if any, to actual persons, living or dead, or to organizations or events, is entirely coincidental.

Published by:
Pentacles Press
Division of James N. Gibson Enterprises, LLC.
340 N. Main Street, Suite 301B
Plymouth, MI 48170
www.pentaclespress.com

In conjunction with:
Old Mountain Press, Inc.
2542 S. Edgewater Dr.
Fayetteville, NC 28303
www.oldmountainpress.com

Anasazi Triumph

First Edition
Printed and bound in the United States of America by Morris Publishing • www.morrispublishing.com • 800-650-7888
1 2 3 4 5 6 7 8 9 10

To
Mark Cameron Gibson

Map 1: Mexico and Environs

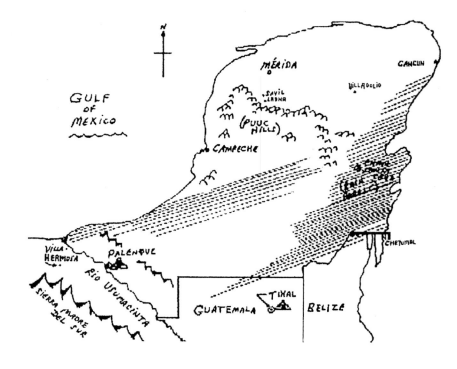

Map 2: The Yucatan

Prologue

"Watch over your heart with all diligence, for from it flow the springs of life. (Proverbs 4:23, NIV)

A HARVEST MOON ROSE in the east, casting a pale light over the semitropical forest of the Chiapas. A group of campesinos, bent and worn from a lifetime of labor on the haciendado, stood silently in a circle, watching the ministrations of the shaman Puco.

Puco's slight frame was wizened by the press of years as his claw-like hands arranged the power objects on the crude table set up in the clearing. A fire had been kindled, flickering flames casting shadows that writhed like snakes across his wrinkled face. His dark eyes burned with intensity. He had drunk the *ayahuasca*, the hallucinogen made from the sacred vine, and now he entered the spirit world.

"Aieeegh!" he shrieked, falling back to be caught by two men before he could touch the earth. They lifted him upright and he stretched his arms upward, staring sightlessly at the moon.

Puco reached down and grasped the chicken, feet tied, that lay on the ground. He swung it up to the table as his other hand grasped the machete and swung down hard, decapitating the chicken which began to kick and flutter.

He dribbled the fresh blood on the power objects placed on the table, and then cast the dead chicken aside. Grasping the sides of the table with both hands, he leaned forward, studying the liquid trails slowly turning from red to brown as the blood dried.

"They come!" he said in a loud voice. "The time draws near!"

"What's he talking about?" Raul whispered to Ortiz, who stood next to him in the informal circle of men.

"The ancient prophesy, written in the inscriptions."

Raul recalled the prophesy which had become little more than folklore that had lost its meaning for the descendants of the Maya. Now those descendants eked out a subsistence living laboring in the henequen fields for the landowners, the patrons,

1

who now controlled thousands of miles of land that once had belonged to the Maya.

Puco, the shaman, had access to hidden records stored on disks of gold since antiquity, and the records contained the prophesy that in the bad times after the greatness of the Maya had turned to dust, remnants of an ancient tribe descended from the Maya would return to free their people and lead them to restore their great civilization.

Puco resumed speaking in the patois of the Mayans, his words spilling from his lips like water over an abyss. The silent listeners leaned forwards to catch each word, for Puco was a powerful shaman whose prophesies always came to pass.

"They are few in numbers, but possess great power, Their *will* has been sharpened by the trials of their journey. They can tap the powers of the universe and bend them to their will. They come to unite the Mayas, the remnants of our ancient race, and lead us to greatness again."

Puco's eyes closed. He let out a great sigh and collapsed into the arms of his supporters. The men hastened to place him on a blanket and added fuel to the fire, warming him as he trembled. Low murmurs sounded around the circle as the men reviewed the import of Puco's words.

The campesinos had been reduced to serfs on the plantations of the Spaniards, but now there was hope. As Indios, descendants of the once-proud Maya, they had become strangers in their own land. Now all that was about to change!

Ortiz picked up his machete at the edge of the clearing, bade good-bye to the others and hastened back to his thatch-covered dwelling in the village. His wife roused from sleep, but he shushed her in a low voice. "I'll be back for work in the fields tomorrow," he whispered, careful not to awaken the children. He wrapped two tortillas, hefted his machete, and eased out into the darkness.

The unmarked trail he followed from long habit led into the rainforest that bore eastward to the great gulf of salt water that marked the eastern boundary of the Mayan world. To the east lived the Huits, the Mayan hunter-gatherers who had remained hidden from the conquering Spaniards, and thereby avoided being pressed into virtual slavery on the great haciendas, or plantations, of the landed gentry, the patrons.

It was the Huits who had initiated the revolt. Led by the noble guerrilla fighters, Jacinto Pat and Cecilio Chi, the Huit branch of the Mayans had slaughtered the exploiters in their villages and on their haciendados, in what came to be called "la

casta divina", the "War of the Castes". Even the great city of the
Spaniards, Villavolid, had been sacked and most of its inhabitants
massacred as they fled toward Merida. But in the end, the
numbers of the enemy had been too great and the revolution had
failed. The patrones had returned and the Indios, the descendants
of the once proud Mayas, had returned to the fields, pouring out
their life's work for the benefit of the haciendados.

The path bore through the dense forest like a brush-clogged
tunnel, leading Ortiz into a tiny, hidden village containing thatch-
roofed dwellings rising on stilts above the swampy land. Night
sounds of buzzing insects and croaking frogs filled Ortiz's ears,
reminding him of the cenote, the nearby lake that provided fresh
water for the villagers.

As he entered the clearing, a tall, slender man stepped out of
the shadows to greet him. "You are out late."

Ortize paused, startled. He had expected to awaken Tamil.
"How did you know I was coming?"

"I had a dream in which I saw Puco sacrifice a chicken, and
I saw you with great determination on your face as you left him
and the others. Then I awakened and waited."

"I bring important news."

"I know."

"You already know of the strangers?"

"No. I know the information you bring is of great importance. Come inside where we can talk."

Ortiz followed Tamil up the ladder that gave access to an
open-sided platform that served as the meeting area for the men
of the village. Tamil had stoked a small fire in the stone hearth,
and the flames danced eerily across Tamil's face, leaving his eyes
in shadows. Ortiz fought down a feeling of unease. Tamil had
great powers, and seemed always to know what one was thinking.

Tamil poured Ortiz a drink from a nearby jug of aguardiente,
the local intoxicant made from corn. Ortiz nodded his thanks and
took a drink. Tamil filled his cup and sat back to listen.

"You recall the ancient prophesy," Ortiz began. "The one
about members of our race returning to restore the might of the
Maya?"

"Yes, but we can no longer be sure it was a prophesy.
According to our tradition, there were vaults containing the
sacred records hidden in stone pyramids inside our city-states.
Those who could read them had great wisdom to pass on
regarding our future. The vaults were lost when civil war destroyed the city-states and the pyramids fell into disrepair."

"Tonight Puco not only affirmed that the prophesy is true,"
Ortiz replied, his voice rising with excitement. "But that it is

about to be fulfilled! He stated that strangers are approaching who are descended from our forefathers. They will lead us in throwing off the yokes of the Spaniards and restoring our civilization."

"We tried that thirty years ago and failed."

Ortiz hesitated. "There must have been a reason for our defeat at that time."

Tamil remained silent, gathering his thoughts. "We failed because we did not have a vision, with the plan and organization to carry it out. We fought a guerrilla war, taking our frustrations out on the patrones, and then we simply went home to our crops. The Spanish regrouped and then returned to take control of the land. They punished us and left us worse off. Looking back, what we did was a disaster for us."

"Maybe the strangers will bring the wisdom to avoid our past mistakes and return the Maya to power."

"Maybe," Tamil replied, doubt in his voice. "We have been disappointed many times, and many have paid with their lives. We must wait and see."

"So we just wait?"

"No. We get ready. I will send runners to all the villages, so that our leaders are alerted. And then we will await the arrival of the strangers, and hear what they have to say."

"At last there is hope!"

"Hope, yes, but we must be careful not to raise unrealistic expectations."

"For myself, I cannot help it! I have lived my entire life in poverty, without hope for my future, and that of my children. Puco is a powerful shaman. I have never known his prophesies to be wrong. I feel the excitement of hope for a new life!"

"With hope comes faith," Tamil responded, his eyes lighting up in the reflection of the fire. "And with faith we can build for the future!"

Chapter 1

CALEB STONE WAS up early, easing out of the stuffy ship's cabin to walk across the wooden deck to the rail as the ship plowed through the waves of the Gulf of Mexico. They were well away from Vera Cruz now, and he doubted that the authorities would bother to pursue them on Juan Zegarra's account. It was more likely that they would arrest Zegarra and he would pay for his treachery at the silver mine, and for his abuse of Shanni, Caleb's wife, as well as the other Huastec women.

A troubled look crossed his face as he thought of Shanni, still asleep. Although they were man and wife, it was in name only. She had built an emotional wall, freezing him out. They were like strangers, forced together by circumstances to complete their dangerous journey.

A noise caught his attention and he turned to see Matal lurching toward him, his face green as he leaned over the rail to throw up. Presently he quieted and turned, wiping his mouth with a cloth. "I'm sorry," he gasped. "Nothing left to throw up, but sick just the same. Will I die?"

Caleb tried not to smile. The Huastecs had never been on a ship before, and had no knowledge of seasickness. "No. The sickness is caused by the motion of the ship, and will be cured as soon as you step back onto land. Meanwhile it can make you miserable."

"Is there no cure? I mean, something I can take to help?"

"Drink only water, to prevent dehydration. And stand at the center of the ship where the up-and-down motion is minimized. Hold onto the mast, and look out at the horizon."

"I'll try anything," Matal affirmed, pushing away from the rail to stagger on the uneven motion of the deck to the tall mast Caleb had indicated.

Ambria emerged from the cabin area and joined Matal, mopping his brow with a cloth.

So far those two have endured the hardships of the journey better than the others, Caleb thought.

They were hardly more than children when the Huastecs were forced out of Mesa Verde by drought. Matal had been elected leader of the Huastecs, and remained steadfast during their trials in the desert

5

where many died. Toshni's revolt had been the low point, splitting families as a majority of the people retreated to the Navaho reservation, and certain captivity.

Caleb's reverie was broken as Aurel joined him at the rail. Upon Tonah's death, Aurel, his apprentice, had been thrust into the role of shaman and spiritual leader to the group of young warriors who remained to finish their journey to the mythical "Center", source of the Huastec civilization.

"Who could have dreamed of so much water!" Aurel marveled, looking across the sea to the horizon.

"There is much more," Caleb responded. "In fact, this is only a small portion of the oceans that cover the earth. We will travel on it only a few days."

"Days!" Aurel marveled. "And we could almost step across the largest pool back home. How fast do we travel?"

"About the speed of a trotting horse."

"And without pause to rest!"

"We hope not," Caleb laughed. "It would mean we were becalmed."

"Becalmed?"

"That the wind had stopped blowing."

"But I feel the wind on my face!"

"That is the breeze caused by our passage. The real wind fills our sails, pushing us forward." Aurel looked up as Caleb pointed to the billowing sails.

"So the wind drives us?"

"Yes."

"Who could believe that the wind could push a such a vessel! And I never dreamed of a boat so big that people could live on it."

"Some ships are even larger, able to be gone from their home ports for two years or more."

"Two years! Don't they run out of food and water?"

"Food and water are stored in barrels, plus they replenish at other ports all around the world."

"Around?"

"Yes, the earth is a giant sphere, a ball covered mostly with water."

"How could that be? The people would fall off!"

"People thought so for thousands of years, but somehow we don't fall. Wherever you are on the earth appears flat like this, and you are always upright."

"And you think that shamanism is strange!"

Caleb chuckled. "I'd never stopped to think about it, but you make a good point. What we understand becomes commonplace and taken for granted. It is only what we do not understand that seems strange and mysterious."

"And frightens us," Aurel added.

"We do fear the unknown," Caleb agreed.

"And then we must make the choice."

"Choice?"

"To shy away from what we do not understand and live in ignorance, or ..."

"Or?"

"To push forward despite our fears and seek to understand."

"As I was forced to do with shamanism." Caleb's mood sobered.

"Yes. Never have I seen a more reluctant apprentice to Power!"

"But in the end I was forced to learn and to understand."

"Just as my people are being forced to embrace the new and strange world of the Anglos."

Caleb felt the pathos in Aurel's words. How strange the world must seem to Aurel and the others after growing up sheltered in the hidden canyons of Mesa Verde. Nothing had prepared them for the chaotic world they had been forced to enter, a world even now in the throes of massive change.

"How do we do it, Caleb?" Aurel continued. "How do we learn to survive and build our lives in your world?"

"A day at a time, as all people do. You and the others have done all right so far."

"But it is hard! Always stretching to learn and understand, with surprises and threats at every turn. The more we learn, the more we can see that we do not understand."

"So you keep learning and you grow stronger."

"We have no choice, do we?"

"I went through the same process when I left home. I had to learn to survive in a world of rough and lawless men. In a way it makes you stronger. I, like you and the others, am still learning. Those who settle early, attempting to maintain a life based on what they already know, awaken one morning to find the world has changed and they no longer know what to do to survive in it. The world continually changes and it changes you. Survival becomes a daily habit."

"I know what you mean. I am very different since I left Mesa Verde. I still feel fear, but it is manageable, and with it comes a growing confidence that I can do this, I can learn what I need to survive, and to help myself and the Huastecs build a new life."

Caleb nodded, gazing out silently across the blue water. He had learned to survive in two worlds, the world of ordinary reality, and that of shamanism, or what Tonah had called "nonordinary reality". But now life had thrown him another curve in the world of emotions, and the pain of losing Shanni's respect and love.

Aurel sensed Caleb's mood change, and guessed it was related to Shanni, but he chose not to mention it. Some subjects were just too sensitive, even among friends.

"I'm hungry," Aurel said, turning from the rail. "Let's go open one of those barrels!"

Except for Ambria and Matal, the remaining Huastecs were seated when they entered the dining room and joined their friends at the rectangular table. Aurel was pleasantly surprised to find fresh fruit, bread, and eggs and bacon. "I expected salt pork from the barrel, Caleb!"

Caleb laughed. "That's for long voyages. We'll enjoy fresh food on a short sail from port to port. Evidently our captain took good care of us!"

The door opened to admit a portly man of middle-age in khaki shorts, leather sandals, and linen shirt with captain's bars on the sleeves. His walrus moustache drooped, accenting baggy eyes with mirth wrinkles at the corners. He looked like a man who had found his niche in life and was content to laugh as the world passed by. "Greetings, my friends," he said, taking his chair at the head of the table. "Welcome to my ship. We hope to make your journey pleasant."

"A good start," Caleb agreed, waving his hand at the fresh food scattered on plates along the table, as the others nodded in agreement.

"Please, please...help yourselves!" the captain laughed. "I am Carlos Mendoza, at your service. I am delighted to be your host during your brief stay with us."

"How did you manage the freshly-cooked eggs and bacon?" Caleb asked, filling his plate with appreciation.

"I am fortunate to have a cook on board who learned his trade in San Francisco."

"I see you've been around."

"All over the world, at one time or another. Now I am content to ply the waters of Mexico, earning a decent living and spending more of my days on shore."

"You have a family?"

"Regrettably I lost my wife many years ago, and our children are grown with families of their own. I content myself with lady friends who enjoy my passion for food and drink, among other things!" Mendoza laughed heartily as he dug into his breakfast.

"Come, come! Enough about me! Don't be so shy! Introduce yourselves and tell me something about you!"

Each of the Huastecs complied, speaking up in turn as they went around the table. Mendoza listened intently, commenting appropriately on occasion. Caleb felt himself relaxing. Mendoza was a man of good will, who downplayed what appeared to be a keen intellect and passion for life. Caleb was pleased that the Huastecs' first experience on a ship was not under a stern and humorless captain, which was more the norm.

Shanni ate quietly, making small talk with the others, and seemed pleasant enough. So far she had been spared the motion sickness that had befallen Matal.

Aurel referred to Matal and Ambria, who were still outside. Captain Mendoza stopped eating, suddenly concerned, when he heard of Matal's distress. "I will call my cook, Mr. Chin. He is very good with herbal medicines. Maybe he can relieve our friend's symptoms."

"And I'll take Ambria some food. This is too good to miss."

"Especially the coffee," Mala added. "I've never tasted coffee so good."

"We've never had freshly-ground coffee before," Caleb responded. "In the states, we had coffee pre-ground and canned. The freshness makes all the difference."

"Like a peach, fresh from the trees, compared to a dried peach," Iika observed.

"We love our coffee," Mendoza responded. "And here near the plantations we can afford to indulge our tastes. Mr. Chin also makes fresh coffee in the afternoon. Please feel free to help yourselves. Excuse me."

Mendoza rang a small bell and Mr. Chin came in from the kitchen. He bowed as Mendoza introduced him to the Huastecs. "One of our guests is outside with seasickness. Would you see if you can help him?" With another bow, Mr. Chin left for the deck.

There was a lull in the conversation as the group finished their breakfast and sat back, savoring their coffee. "And now," Captain Mendoza said, suddenly serious. "I do not mean to pry, but I hope you will trust me enough to tell me how I can be of help to you in your endeavor. If I cannot, that is all right. We will relax and enjoy our brief time together."

Aurel and the others looked at Caleb, silently making him their spokesperson by default. He was an Anglo, and experienced in the world outside Mesa Verde. Mendoza was being tactful, but Caleb knew he was concerned about their run-in with the authorities on the docks, and their hasty departure. They owed Mendoza an explanation.

"Let's clear up Vera Cruz first," Caleb said. "Juan Zegarra called the soldiers down upon us, without just cause, in our judgment."

"Juan Zegarra?" Mendoza questioned.

"You know him as 'Sebastian Guitterez'"

"Ah, he is rich and well-connected!"

"Unfortunately so. He was superintendent of a silver mine near Monterrey when we entered Mexico, traveling through on our way to the Yucatan. A bandit, Alphonso Alvarez, attacked our caravan and carried off most of the women, including my wife Shanni, along with some of the men. At the silver mine, the men were forced to work in the mine while the women were sorted to be shipped to the brothels of Vera Cruz. After our people escaped, Zegarra disappeared. Shanni was shocked to recognize him at the docks in Vera Cruz."

"And why didn't he just let you go?"

"I think he panicked, and sought to eliminate us as a threat before we could reveal his true identity."

Mendoza remained silent, thinking. "Which means he had something to hide from the government. Otherwise you would have posed no threat."

"That's what I concluded. That's why I told the soldiers on the dock that the government was looking for him."

"I know I should not speculate," Mendoza mused. "But Guitterez, or Zegarra, brought a good deal of silver to Vera Cruz and used it to purchase his shipping company. Maybe we could guess where that silver came from."

"Exactly," Caleb agreed. "Zegarra wasn't afraid of me or the Huastecs; he was afraid that we might reveal his real identity to the authorities. He wouldn't have dropped from sight as mine superintendent if he did not have anything to hide."

"Well, let that situation sort itself out in Vera Cruz," Mendoza continued. "I was afraid all of you were fugitives. I didn't relish having soldiers waiting for us in Campeche!"

Caleb knew he had been correct to confide in Mendoza. Mendoza had a legitimate need to know if he harbored fugitives. Mendoza had a keen mind, and didn't miss much. By leveling with him, Caleb felt that Mendoza would be on their side.

"That could still happen," Caleb responded. "We tried to contact the soldiers to report our presence in Mexico, and our intent. We even requested a letter of safe-passage. Unfortunately, their leader turned on us and tried to kill and rob us. We fought our way clear, but then Colonel Ruiz and his soldiers chased us all the way into the mountains west of Vera Cruz."

"And what happened after that?"

"He killed some of our warriors, and captured Shanni, who was later able to escape. We were scattered, starving, when they stopped chasing us. We reassembled in Vera Cruz and booked passage."

"Ruiz saved face by going after you," Mendoza surmised. "But he had more important things to do. The government is in chaos. He would be criticized for being away chasing bandits, which regrettably is how you are viewed, when he should be guarding his district. Once he had attacked you he could declare the action a success and return home."

"So he was not a threat to us in Vera Cruz?"

"It is not his district. Even when Zegarra told the military of your presence in Vera Cruz, it appears that the response was pro forma. Only two soldiers were dispatched to accompany Zegarra."

Caleb let out a sigh of relief and looked at the others. "That's good news for us! Now we can continue our journey in peace."

"From the military, perhaps, but have you been to the Yucatan?"

"No, this is our first trip."

"It is like a different country. In fact, it has seceded from Mexico on more than one occasion. About forty years ago, its own militia, under the command of General Santiago Irmon actually ran the Mexican soldiers out of the Yucatan by force of arms. The central government of Mexico, newly organized after throwing off the yoke of Napoleon's puppet, Maximilian, was too weak to do anything about it. The leaders of the Yucatan states of Campeche, Merida, and Chiapas still pretty much ignore government edicts from Mexico City, and Mexico City chooses to ignore their impudence."

"Which complicates matters for us."

"I will give you some contacts. You will need friends to survive the Yucatan.

"We are grateful for your interest, and your help."

"Da nada, it is nothing," Mendoza protested politely, getting up from the table. "Enough of business for now, let's go outside and get some fresh air. I will tell all of you about the ferocious pirates who used to ply these waters, and of their lair south of us on the Isla de Tris!"

"What's a pirate?" Iika asked.

Mendoza roared with laughter. "Aren't we all?"

Chapter 2

CHIN'S POTION HAD relieved Matal's seasickness, enabling him to regain his strength during the day and night that the ship plowed through the water on its way to Campeche.

Campeche's good fortune to have a deep-water port had made it attractive to the ships plying the Caribbean from the warring European countries of Spain, France and Britain. The discovery of the New World, and the looting of its silver, gold, and goods, had created a class of robber-baron merchants whose wealth depended upon their daring and ruthlessness.

As a result, nationalities from across the globe intermingled. Lebanese traders arrived on ships and came ashore to set up shops to coordinate shipping to their home ports. Chinese from San Francisco established outlets to service the demand for service industries. And the immigrants from Spain, supported and protected by their government, were given huge land grants of one hundred thousand hectares or more, which became the great haciendados in the Yucatan. The ironwood from the interior contained a chemical that set dyes, a key ingredient to keep the garment factories of Europe operating at full capacity. The demand for ironwood dye became so great, and the price so high, that families in the Yucatan became multimillionaires in one generation, in a time when the average wage was less than $1,000 a year.

But the wealth came at a price. The patrones of the great families had to subdue the indigenous people, the Indios, and form their own militias for protection. Then the pirate ships came to prey like wolves on the lumbering merchant ships that transported the wealth-generating goods back to Europe.

Caleb and the Huastecs stood on the deck, looking with excitement at the low green land that lined the horizon. The ship turned toward shore and time passed as the port of Campeche came into view. Great stone edifices stood on the shore, with massive gun barrels pointed out to sea.

"Those walls form the fort that protects the city," Caleb pointed out. "And the big guns are called 'cannons'."

"The fort was built to defend the city against pirates, the bandit sailors who preyed on the ships," Mendoza added, joining the others at the rail.

"I don't see how anyone could storm those guns!" Mala asserted. "The devastation they caused must have been horrible!"

"Yet Campeche was overrun and sacked on several occasions. One pirate, the wily Frenchman L'Olonois, raided so often that it is said that he kept a mistress in town!"

"A mistress?" Shanni questioned.

"Yes. These men showed no restraint. They were ruthless and took what they wanted. Often they obtained their crews, the men who fought for them, on the promise the men would share in the spoils they captured. Hence there was no constraint when they captured a city."

Shanni shuddered. What kind of world had they entered?

The ship eased into dock and the gangplank was lowered. Matal and Ambria were the first off, after shaking hands with Captain Mendoza and expressing their thanks.

Mendoza laughed and turned to Caleb. "Our friend cannot wait to get his feet on dry land! I think he was not cut out to be a seaman!"

"None of us were!" Caleb replied. "But thank you for your hospitality. The passage could have been much worse."

"My pleasure. I wish you success on your journey, and hope that we may meet again. Look up the people I referred you to; they will get you off on the right foot in the Yucatan."

"We shall. Take care of yourself, and thanks again."

They shook hands warmly and Caleb and Shanni followed the others down the gangplank to the dock. They walked to the carriages available for hire, and Caleb turned, waving at Captain Mendoza who stood at the rail of the ship. Mendoza returned the wave and turned away. *I'm glad I confided in him*, Caleb thought as he settled back with Shanni in the carriage. *Mendoza has survived and prospered in the Yucatan, while managing to keep decorum and a core of decency in his life.* Caleb knew the type. If Mendoza trusted you, his generosity knew no bounds; if you mistreated him, he became your worst enemy. Caleb felt the same way. He and Mendoza understood each other.

Chapter 3

THE HACIENDA AND surrounding grounds looked like something out of a storybook to Caleb as they approached on rented horses. Captain Mendoza had referred them to one of the oldest families of hacendados, or landowners, descended from the Spanish conquistadores who had conquered the Yucatan peninsula. The Yucatan was like a different country from Mexico, Mendoza had warned, and the Huastecs needed to understand it to have any hope of surviving to carry out their mission.

Mendoza had sent word ahead, and Senor Fuentes, aristocratic head of the Hacienda de Fuentes, was expecting them. He waved to them from the second floor gallery that ran the length of the great stone building, standing white like a monolith amid the green palms. It could have sat on a desert island had it not been surrounded by long rows of green plants, the henequen, or "green gold", that extended to the horizon. Sisal, the fiber required for the bailing machines of the industrial revolution, was made from the henequen plant. The sisal commanded such high prices that the state of Merida had built its own port, called appropriately, Sisal. Other sections of the haciendado were fenced to contain the cattle that had been the original source of wealth to the estate.

The yard workers, drawn from the Maya campesinos who lived and worked on the estate, hastened to take the Huastecs' horses and gear as Senor Fuentes stepped out to greet them. "Welcome my friends. We have been expecting you. Please come in and refresh yourselves from the long ride and then we will eat."

Fuentes was tall and thin, his gray hair long and combed back over his ears. Piercing eyes gazed out under bushy eyebrows, while his beaked nose and pale skin testified to his pure Spanish blood. He was immaculately dressed in cotton slacks, linen shirt with matching vest. Fuentes was of the ladinos, the pure whites who owned the land and ruled their fiefdoms as laws unto themselves.

The Huastecs were shown to their quarters on the second floor, with servants providing fresh water and real cotton towels. After cleaning up, they emerged, as bidden, to gather in the dining room.

"I can't believe the size of this building!" Shanni whispered to Caleb as they descended the long, winding stairway. "Our entire village in Mesa Verde was not this large!"

Caleb nodded agreement, taking in the enormous decorated ceiling that he estimated to be twelve feet tall with chandeliers imported from Europe hanging down in rows. The dining room itself was massive, containing an ornate table capable of seating fifty people.

Senor Fuentes waved them to be seated and then pulled up his chair at the head of the table. After introductions, they made casual conversation until the meal was completed. They sat back refreshed as the servants cleared the table. *Fuentes is an excellent host,* Caleb noted. *He was careful to see to our comfort before discussing business.*

"Is there anything else we can get for you?" Fuentes asked. "Water? A dessert wine?"

"I think I've had my fill for now!" Caleb smiled as the others nodded their agreement. "And what a feast after surviving on roots, wild berries and occasional game in the mountains west of Vera Cruz!"

"You have come a long way, then?"

"All the way from the Colorado Territory in the United States."

"You are fortunate to have survived. The northern part of Mexico is lawless, and the remainder has great problems."

"Yes, we met trouble at every turn, and many of the Huastecs did not survive."

"I am sorry," Fuentes replied, and Caleb knew he meant it. Despite his aristocratic background and unquestioned authority, Fuentes had kept his humanity, his common touch.

"Maybe the worst is over," Matal added. "This region seems more prosperous and more stable."

"True to a point," Fuentes nodded, his silver hair waving gently. "It depends on where you travel. This area of Merida, and some areas of Campeche to the west, are flat, suitable for agriculture. These areas were settled many years ago through land grants. The haciendados raised cattle and sugarcane, keeping the ships busy exchanging our products for those of Europe.

"Yet to the south, there is the unknown and almost impenetrable jungle called the 'Belen', that marks Mexico's border with Guatemala..." Fuentes paused at the puzzled glances exchanged the Huastecs.

"There are other countries south of us," Caleb explained. "Guatemala, Honduras, and a colony called Belize controlled by the British."

"It is all very confusing," Fuentes agreed. "And more so here in the Yucatan, because each of our states, Merida, Campeche, and others operate as separate countries, siding with Mexico when it is to our interest, and seceding when it is not. We have pulled away, and then re-united, several times over the past few years, and that is the source of many of our troubles."

"Troubles?"

"The 'War of the Castes', which almost destroyed us, and which has increased the danger to you if you travel outside our sphere of influence."

The Huastecs leaned forward, listening carefully; their survival would depend upon what they learned.

"About thirty years ago, during one of our many disagreements with the central government in Mexico City, our local General, Santiago Irman, implemented the novel idea of arming the Indians, the campesinos, and enlisting them in the successful attack on the garrison of Mexican soldiers at Valladolid. The soldiers were run out of the Yucatan, but then Irman and the local government reneged on their promise to abolish the taxes levied on the Indians. As you would expect, that fomented discontent, but there was no organized leadership among the Indians at that time. A year later, a local political chief at Peto, named Antonio Trujeque, raised an Indian army that added the fierce jungle warriors to the east, the Huit Mayas, to the campesinos. When they attacked Valladolid, the Huits turned the attack into a caste war to eliminate all the 'whites', the ladinos who had taken their lands. Of course the campesinos followed them. As a result, instead of taking the city, they destroyed it and began massacring the whites and mestizos. While they were looting the city, drunk on aguardiente, the survivors attempted to flee to Merida for safety, but they were attacked by the Indians all along the route. Even women and children were killed. Only a small number reached Merida to relate their tales of horror.

But the worst was that the government was in political turmoil and unable to punish the uprising. The Huits, led by Cecilio Chi and Jacinto Pat, among others, were emboldened by the lack of reprisals and gained more supporters. Before Trujeque could act to head it off, Chi and his followers sacked Tepich, killing the members of some thirty ladino families. A guerrilla war ensued that became so bad that the remaining members of the haciendado families were considering abandoning the Yucatan completely and sailing to Europe for safety. Fortunately, the tide turned when militias joined forces to put down the rebellion before it was too late. But even today the Huits live as a law unto themselves in the eastern rain forest, and the people of

Valladolid, which is nearest to them, are afraid to venture out of the city alone."

"So we risk attack if we enter the jungle searching for the Huastecs' ancestral Center," Ambria observed.

"I'm afraid so. We control the open land, and have the means to defend ourselves but in the jungle our militias are sitting ducks."

Matal sighed. "We had hoped that the hard part of the journey was behind us."

"It could be that the worst is yet to come," Fuentes said. "The terrain is difficult, and the jungle contains disease, dangerous animals and venomous snakes. And now it contains men who have grown to hate us. It is a dangerous mix."

"But what of the great city, the 'Center', and the civilization from which we descended?" Shanni asked.

"There once were great cities, with giant buildings made of stone, but now they are ruins reclaimed by the jungle."

"And the people who built the cities?"

"Their descendants are still here," Fuentes said. "You saw them outside when you arrived. They are the campesinos who till the land on our estates."

Shocked, Shanni looked at Caleb and then turned her gaze to the others. Had they suffered so much and come so far to find *this*? The Indios here were worse off than the Navahoes she had left behind on the San Juan.

"Excuse me," Shanni got up quietly to go to her room.

"Of course we will help all we can," Fuentes continued, noting Shanni's reaction. "Horses, supplies, even a guide part of the way. But that is all. We cannot help you in the jungle."

Chapter 4

T HE HUASTECS HAD gathered in Matal and Ambria's room after the meal, their faces ghostly in the light cast by the oil lamps set on ledges along the wall.

"It's over!" Sagay said, surveying the group. "After all we've gone through, it's over. Senor Fuentes has confirmed our worst fears. There is no Center - no civilization for us to return to. Now we have no choice; we must get on a ship and go home!"

"And where is 'home'?" Ambria retorted. "Life on a reservation?"

"Look outside," Sagay said. "The remnants of the once mighty Maya are little more than slaves!"

"How could this be?" Shanni asked, looking at Aurel. "With all his powers, Tonah would have foreseen if our quest to find the Center was futile!"

"Yes," Aurel nodded. "He remained steadfast in his belief that we would find the Center and rebuild our lives. We're missing something. Tonight I will travel into the world of nonordinary reality; perhaps I can find the answer there."

"Iika and I have made up our minds to return," Sagay retorted. "Who is coming with us?"

"Where are you going?" Nerial, who had been listening quietly, asked.

"Captain Mendoza said there is a port much closer to the Navaho lands, a port called 'Houston', in the United States. I don't know why we didn't sail from there in the first place! Instead we fought and starved on foot in Mexico!" Sagay cast a distasteful glare at Caleb.

"Did Mendoza tell you that Houston is in Texas? And that Texas has a string of forts running across it containing thousands of soldiers who are hunting Indians? One or two riders who know the country might get through, but not a hundred Huastec families."

Sagay paused. His sureness came from the brashness of youth and the need to act. Yet every time he wanted to move he felt checked by Caleb Stone.

"Too many of us have died! Iika and I are going back before it is too late, and we should not have to go alone. It is time to face reality. Senor Fuentes warned there's nothing ahead of us if we go into the jungle. There is no Center, or Fuentes would know of it! Open your eyes and see!" Sagay was almost pleading. *Why couldn't they see the truth?*

"Sagay's right," Matal said unexpectedly.

Shanni looked up in surprise. "Matal!"

"Facts are facts. We persevered as long as there was a chance to succeed. Now there is no hope. We cannot be faulted for turning back."

"Caleb?" Shanni turned her eyes to him.

"I came along to help. If the journey's over, you and I can go home."

"Can we?" she snapped, and then caught herself. She saw Nerial's half-suppressed smile out of the corner of her eye. Shanni turned and walked out of the room onto the gallery that extended the length of the second story of the hacienda. The aroma of bougainvillaea mixed with sage on the warm night air. A canopy of stars shone overhead and a campesino's fire flickered brightly in the distance.

Shanni had never felt so alone and so hopeless. Even her estrangement from Caleb had not devastated her because she had been focused on reaching the Center. She realized that reaching the Center had come to mean everything to her. As other things that gave her life meaning fell away, the quest to reach the Center had grown in importance. Now it had become an obsession, the lifeline that maintained her sanity. If they quit, what would become of them? And without hope, what did it matter?

Shanni heard soft footsteps approaching and turned as Aurel joined her at the wooden railing. "Oh, Aurel," she said. "What are we to do? Is it really over?"

"I don't know. I want to keep faith, but it seems there's nothing left to hold onto."

"I wish Tonah were here."

"He is, in a way," Aurel said, suddenly remembering. "He said I could contact him if ever there was a need."

"Then contact him, Aurel! There must be something we're missing, and he is our last hope!"

FLICKERING CANDLES CAST light from the walls of the vault as Huntal joined Popol Vuh at the altar.

"All is going as planned," Popul smiled.

"But they are drawing ever closer!" Huntal protested.

"Closer means nothing. Have we not been eliminating them one by one?"

"That's true, but now they have landed and resupplied. They will pursue us with renewed vigor."

"You were not listening. Did you not hear when Senor Fuentes told the Huastecs that there is no Center?"

"Yes, I joined the perception of the toucan caged in the hacienda. Through its ears I heard every word."

"And what did you hear?"

"They had a meeting, and an argument."

"What did they argue about?"

"Turning back!"

"Don't you see? Once they lose heart and decide to turn back it is over. We shall have won! Did they all agree?"

"Almost. Only Shanni could not be persuaded, but she is shattered by her emotional problems with the Anglo, and her loss of faith in Tonah's vision."

"Do you expect her to capitulate?"

"Yes."

"What if she doesn't?"

"She will have to proceed alone. The others will abandon her. Our allies will finish her if she enters the jungle."

Huntal let out a breath of relief. "I was worried. They were getting so close!"

"The closer they get, the greater the obstacles. At some point the struggle will become too great."

AUREL CLIMBED TO the lookout on top of the hacienda and seated himself cross-legged on the narrow platform. The stars marked the sky to the horizon in all directions. Aurel felt as if he were suspended in space, between the worlds. He removed his amulet, the small medicine bag secured by a leather strap around his neck. He eased the drawstring open and gently shook the contents of the bag into his hand. He sorted through the objects by feel, his eyes remaining focused on the horizon, until his fingers found the smooth coolness of the crystal; the crystal that Tonah had carried for a lifetime, and then given to Aurel shortly before Tonah's death. He held the crystal in front of his face, watching the stars reflected in its facets. Aurel felt his awareness shift, and he felt himself pulled forward, into the crystal, into the stars.

There was a mysterious energy that flowed throughout the universe, Tonah had explained. And like a fish in water, we swam through it unaware. The energy was a dark energy, unseen but felt, high-energy rays that permeated all matter, an energy that could be accumulated, focused, and controlled. The ability of the shaman to focus that energy gave him the potential to bring great power to bear in the world of ordinary reality.

Aurel focused his *intent* on the star light that slowly rotated about him inside the crystal, light that twinkled like fireflies on a warm summer's night. He chose a star and willed the light upward, and it flared, like a flame touched by a breeze. The *intent* directed the energy, Tonah had said. The energy flowed where the attention was directed.

The crystal became a beam of blue light, reaching up from the surface of the earth, extending like a column up into the heavens. Aurel reached over and grabbed the iron rail that surrounded the platform, and then it disappeared and he was flung upward, accelerating on the beam of light. And then he was gone, lost from earth, surrounded by a blue haze that rushed by him like the rapids in a river.

Aurel landed on a snow-white surface and looked back at the whirlpool of blue that now appeared like a calm lake. He looked up at billowing white clouds that surrounded the valley in which he sat. Slowly Aurel climbed to his feet.

A speck of black appeared, growing larger as it approached, and he recognized Tonah's human form clad in his usual cotton clothes, familiar to Aurel from Mesa Verde.

"Tonah! I am glad to see you!" Aurel burst out as he felt the warmth of Tonah's personality surround him.

"I felt your *intent*, and came to meet you."

"You know that events are not going well for us?"

"No. One gets distracted in the other dimensions. Here there is much to absorb and learn. One quickly loses all connection to life on the earth."

"Everyone is about to abandon the quest, and turn back; the few of us who remain, I mean. We are told that the Center no longer exists. Now only stone ruins remain, and the descendants of our forebears are serfs on the lands of the Spaniards."

"But the Center is there! I know it!" Tonah's presence protested.

"No one has found it."

"It will be camouflaged so that it does not fall into the wrong hands, savages who would not recognize its worth and destroy it. It will be at a center of Power."

"But how will we find it?"

"You must seek with your intuition."

"How will I recognize it when I find it?"

"It will not appear as it really is. You will look and then you will *see*. When your perception shifts to the proper frequency, it will appear."

21

"I do not understand."

"When you saved Walpi from death, you *saw* the energy with your intent. Suddenly it appeared, as if from nothingness, and as quickly it disappeared again, but in between you controlled its power and the task of saving Walpi's life was accomplished. It will be so with the Center."

"But what do I have to rely on? The others will want proof, something tangible to hold on to."

"Now there is only faith. The ruins are a decoy, to keep unenlightened people from searching for the Center. That is the way the ancients chose to hide the Center from desecration during the centuries until the proper time for the ancient knowledge to be revealed."

"Faith may not be enough to convince the others to go on."

"Doors have been closed to me in this dimension so that I cannot find out how to help you. I only know that there is something of great importance that you are approaching; knowledge of a new reality in the ordinary world, perhaps. Syou and the others must let up in your search or all will be lost!"

"If the others fail me, and refuse to go on, I am finished. One faces certain death alone in the jungle of ordinary reality," Aurel replied quietly.

"Find a way. Much depends upon your success. You and the others must not fail."

The form that was Tonah morphed into a silhouette and then faded as it withdrew along the snow white plain to a dot that disappeared in the distance.

Aurel walked to the roiling pool of blue light and stepped in. He was buoyed by a blue glow, warm and comforting, floating as if in warm water. He felt a sense of peace, of trust; he was one with the universe.

The column of blue light faded and Aurel's perception looked out on the crystal and the night stars, and he realized he was back on the parapet, clutching the iron railing. Aurel climbed down and went to his room. Tomorrow would be the test, for tomorrow he must find a way to convince the others to go on.

Chapter 5

Caleb awakened early and pulled on his clothes, leaving Shanni sleeping. He eased out of the room and walked along the balcony to the east, savoring the damp coolness of the night air as it heated in the first rays of dawn. Today they much decide, every person for himself, whether to turn back or to go on. Either choice seemed futile to him now, with Shanni's estrangement. His dream had been to settle down with Shanni on his ranch in Colorado, build his wealth and raise their children. After all the struggles they had endured, that should have been enough to ensure their happiness. But if he returned now, he would return alone. Would he wind up a lonely, eccentric old man holed up in the stone house full of childhood memories?

A rustling sound reached his ears and he turned, fully alert.

"Sorry I startled you," Nerial whispered. "I didn't want to call out. I might awaken the others."

Caleb turned back to the wooden rail of the balcony as Nerial eased up beside him.

"You're angry with me, aren't you?" she asked, looking up into his eyes.

"No. I'm angry with myself."

"Don't be. You must feel something for me, after the time we spent together. Don't fight it, let it grow into something we can share."

"You're an attractive woman, Nerial, beautiful even, and desirable. A man can be attracted to a woman and want her without loving her. And it creates all kinds of problems when he lets that happen. I should have known better!"

"Caleb, look at me!" Nerial grasped his shoulders, shaking him in the intensity of her passion. "It was my fault, not yours! I wanted you; I still want you. Let's go back together. I'll go wherever you want, and I'll be your wife. I'll make you happy! We're alike and we belong together!"

"I'm married to Shanni."

"Shanni doesn't deserve you! I'll fight for you, die for you if I must. Will Shanni do that? Shanni means well, but she's soft. She'll fail you when you need her most. Let's leave now, before it is too late!"

"It's already too late!" Shanni's voice hissed as she walked out of the shadows, fists clenched by her side. "I've made allowances, trying to hold us together for the greater good, but you've betrayed me, Nerial! Now get your gear and go!"

"Who are you to tell me what to do? To hell with you!" Nerial turned back to Caleb. "It is up to you to decide, not her! Let's go, and leave these madmen behind!"

"Nerial, I'm warning you...!" Shanni started to say when Nerial turned without warning and struck Shanni with her fist. Shanni fell against the wall of the hacienda, and placed her hand to her mouth as fresh blood seeped between her fingers. Her eyes blazed as she crouched, catlike and sprang forward. Her right fist slammed Nerial back across the railing. Before Nerial could recover, Shanni's left hammered at her face.

"Here! Hold it!" Caleb reached in to intervene as Shanni whirled, striking him squarely on the jaw. He fell back, stunned and sagged to his knees.

Nerial regained her balance and launched forward from the rail, closing on Shanni with tooth and claw, as they ripped and tore at each other in their mutual rage. Nerial was the stronger, and had mastered the fighting techniques that Walpi had shown the Huastecs. She blocked Shanni's blows and drove her backward, pinning her to the balcony. Shanni suddenly ducked Nerial's blows and grasped Nerial, jerking her forward, off-balance. With a scream of rage, Shanni swung Nerial's body over the railing, tottering as Nerial clawed the air for to regain her balance. With a scream, Nerial tilted over the railing and fell to the courtyard below.

Caleb sat up, rubbing his jaw, and tried to clear his head as Shanni turned, still burning with rage as she gasped for breath. "Damn, Shanni! I'm surprised you'd fight like that for me!"

"I didn't do it for you!" Shanni retorted, turning to go back to their room. "And don't you ever get in my way like that again!"

"YOU'RE BEGINNING TO sound like Tonah!" Sagay snorted, shaking his head in disgust.

"Ordinarily I would take that as a compliment, but I can see that you did not mean it so," Aurel responded. He gazed around Matal's room at the others, gathered together after the morning meal.

"So your vision, your so-called meeting with Tonah in the afterlife revealed that there is a Center, even though it is invisible to the people who live here?" Sagay repeated, shaking his head. "Even if we find it, what good is it to us if it is not in the real world? I thought we sought a place where our people could settle down and build a new life."

"We are seeking such a place. Tonah said that we will recognize it when we find it."

"Did he offer any clues, a roadmap, perhaps?"

"No. He said the information was being hidden from him."

"Then how does he expect us to find it?"

"He suggested we proceed on faith."

"By the gods!" Sagay swore, shaking his head helplessly. "Now we've sunk to reliance on faith! How desperate can we get? Matal, where do you stand?"

Matal leaned against the wall, listening. Ambria was seated nearby, gazing at the floor. "Ambria and I discussed our situation last night. We have nothing to go back to. As long as there is any chance, however remote, that we can find the Center, we will go on."

"And if you fail?"

"We'll settle somewhere, buy land, and make a living."

"Among strangers?"

"The Spanish did."

"And with all their power, they are still strangers in a strange land. Even Senor Fuentes does not seem totally at ease here."

"Well, Iika and I are going back, and any of you who have come to your senses are welcome to join us."

The door swung open and Shanni entered the room, daubing at her bleeding mouth with a cloth. "Nerial's leaving! Anyone else who wants to can go with her."

The others looked at her disbelieving at Shanni's disheveled clothes and blazing eyes.

"I've had it with this whining and indecision! We're going on, and we're going to find the Center! Now choose, once and for all. If you quit now, good riddance! I want total commitment from those who go with me!"

Sagay shook his head, reaching for Iika's hand. "Let's go," he shrugged. "Let's join Nerial and get out of here before it is too late."

They paused at the door, turning. "No hard feelings," Sagay said. "If you live, you will eventually turn back. Maybe we'll meet again and then you'll know I was right."

Shanni's gaze swung across the room, lightly touching Matal and Ambria, Mala, Aurel, and Niki. Tears of gratitude welled in her eyes at their loyalty. Despite everything that had happened, they were staying the course. What a debt the Huastecs would one day owe these few if they succeeded. When they succeeded!

Shanni corrected herself, ignoring the lurking fear that she could be leading them all to their deaths.

The door opened and Caleb walked into the room. The old confidence was in his stride, and he was dressed for riding, gun belt fastened around his waist.

Shanni's heart caught in her throat. She had forgotten about Caleb! Would he ride with them, or turn back with Nerial and the others? Had she pushed him into making the wrong decision?

Chapter 6

MAYAPAN EMERGED FROM his cave and looked out across the ruins, half-covered with jungle. His body was old now, like dried-up leather, and he walked with a limp from broken bones that had not healed properly. His wife had died many years ago, and their children were scattered, but it no longer mattered. He had tucked the good memories away and become detached from the desires and cares of the world. Now he simply existed, with no expectations and no fear. His sole attachment to the ordinary world was his duty, and soon it would be fulfilled. Already his mind shifted between this world and the world to come. Death neither frightened him nor preoccupied him.

He stoked the fire, adding water to the stew cooking in the ceramic pot balanced on stones. His water bag was full from the spring, and he had the day ahead of him. Who could ask for more?

As he sat staring at the fire, his awareness spread out from long practice, sensing the buzz of insects, the bird calls, and the stealthy sounds of predators and prey in the jungle; the ebb and flow of life in the vast rain forest that surrounded him. As his awareness spread out like a dim mist, he became aware of the presence of man, approaching quietly but confidently, and he recognized the presence as Tamil. Much time had passed since Tamil had found his way to Mayapan, and the way was difficult. Something had strongly motivated Tamil to make the journey.

But Mayapan accepted Tamil's approach without curiosity. Mayapan had learned to wait for events to unfold.

Tamil broke out of the dense jungle and stopped to wipe perspiration from his brow with a soft cloth. The jungle was hot, stifling, closing in on the breath. It was good to step out into the clearing.

He made his way across the rubble strewn clearing and saw the wizened, toad-like form of Mayapan the hermit. Once Mayapan had been strong, with a quick mind and strong feelings, but the years had robbed him of his strength and he had withdrawn from the world. Who knew where Mayapan's mind dwelled as he withdrew into himself?

27

"Greetings, Mayapan," Tamil spoke as he approached the fire.

Mayapan looked up calmly, without surprise, his dark eyes radiating a strange energy in his tired face. "And to you. It has been awhile since you honored me with your visit."

"Too long," Tamil apologized. "One gets busy and the time slips away."

Mayapan chuckled. "Ah, 'Time'," he said.

"Time is a funny thing, we breath it in and laugh and sing.

And all the while it works to bring

our curtain down.

We do not exist a moment from now;

we existed a moment ago, so how

can we allow we are around?"

Tamil paused, nonplused. He was used to Mayapan talking in riddles, and was unsure how to respond.

"I'm not looking for you to respond," Mayapan said as if he had read Tamil's mind. "Even the sages could not answer the question when I asked. We either were, or hope to become. What is that tiny instant when we cross over 'from-to'? We live our lives in an infinite series of 'nows'."

"I guess I had never stopped to think about it," Tamil admitted.

"You're better off. Why waste energy trying to solve such riddles? Better to do something useful, like making stew! Let's eat!"

Mayapan ladled stew into a bowl and passed it to Tamil. He filled his own bowl and they sat quietly, eating their food. The stew was strong and good, filled with chunks of meat. Dare he ask what kind? There was an under taste, an herb that he could not identify. "The stew is good."

"You like it?" Mayapan sounded surprised.

"Shouldn't I?" Tamil started to lower the bowl, and then remembered that Mayapan was also eating the stew.

"I snared the rabbits. The meat gives the stew its strength. I added the dried morning glories to help you to *see*."

Perspiration popped out on Tamil's forehead as his stomach lurched. His mouth was suddenly dry and he reached for his water bag, nearly empty from the journey.

"Here," Mayapan said, handing over his water bottle. "Drink mine."

Tamil drank deeply and set the water bottle down. His visibility dimmed and his surroundings blurred into a blue haze of pure energy. He felt his stomach lurch, and then steadied himself as he regained his vision. The jungle had receded and in its place stood a circle of stone pyramids, perfectly restored and aligned around a massive stone plaza. A transparent bubble made of some unknown substance covered the entire complex. Bolts of energy played like lightning on its surface, giving the complex an otherworldly appearance.

As Tamil turned his gaze back to Mayapan, he was shocked to see Mayapan morph into a man-sized frog, sitting quietly with bulging eyes. "You might have warned me!" Tamil chided. "I had not experienced the morning glory's effects before."

Mayapan seemed not to notice Tamil's remarks. "Isn't it beautiful?" He grunted, gazing at the city sparkling under the dome of light.

"Breathtaking!" Tamil agreed. "Has it been here all along?"

"For thousands of earth years, although time is relative in this dimension."

"It seems to be waiting," Tamil observed.

"It is. That is why you are here."

"I came to inform you of strangers that are approaching our lands."

"We have waited for a long time," Mayapan replied.

"You know of them?"

"I know of their potential."

"Potential?" Tamil raised his eyebrows in question.

"To correct the wrongs of a thousand years, and to put things right."

"Puco states they come to fulfill the ancient prophesy and liberate us," Tamil said quietly.

"That would be well," Mayapan nodded.

"What do you think?"

"That all will be revealed in due time, as events work themselves out."

Tamil paused to drink more water and then wiped his eyes. His vision again blurred and he felt a moment of disorientation, as if the ground shifted beneath him. Again his vision cleared, and he was back at the original clearing with the jungle encroaching on the ruins. He looked at Mayapan, who had returned to human form, studying him with an amused expression on his wizened face. Tamil recalled Mayapan's admonitions from past visits to accept the world with detachment. To do otherwise was to risk one's sanity in the complexity of the worlds upon worlds of creation.

"I'm not sure that was an answer," Tamil managed, fighting to regain his inner equilibrium.

"If they are the ones referred to in the prophecy," Mayapan responded, "They come with special gifts passed down from the

Ancient Ones. With these gifts they will know how to unlock the energy bubble you *saw*, and access the vaults. Much will be revealed that has been hidden."

"How will that help to liberate us?"

"The answer is hidden in the vault. No man can answer until they provide the key."

"What if they give up and turn back?"

"All is lost," Mayapan said. "The wisdom of the Ancients will have failed."

"Then we must alert Ortiz and the others to bring them!"

"No. We cannot compel them to continue. They must come to us of their own volition. Only then will they have the *intent* to unlock the energy field."

"And to access the vault?"

"Yes, to access the ancient knowledge that was lost to mankind."

Chapter 7

CALEB, SHANNI AND the remaining Huastecs rode out of the last of the henequen fields, returning the waves of the campesinos who looked up from their labors. They rode single-file, following Ortiz, who Senor Fuentes had chosen to guide them. "He is sometimes moody and doesn't say much, but he's the best guide we have. He knows the forests and rivers. If anyone can lead you through them, he can."

Ortiz had been quietly competent and helpful as they selected their horses and loaded their gear. Caleb had sized up Ortiz based on his own experience and recognized there was a depth to Ortiz that would be overlooked by a casual inspection. Caleb noticed that Ortiz was always alert, and always thinking. Despite his low station as a campesino, and his humble facade, Ortiz had a mind of his own.

At Fuentes' suggestion, they were riding northwest to the ruins of Sayil, a day's ride from the estate. "You'll see how the cities were laid out, and how they fell into ruins as the jungle claimed them. Even today, the stone work remains beautiful despite its state of disrepair."

Caleb realized that their present location was as far south, toward the equator, as he had ever traveled. They had entered an unfamiliar and potentially dangerous climate where the semitropical sun drove the temperature up into the nineties, releasing humidity from the rain forest that sapped one's strength. However, the horses Fuentes had loaned them seemed adapted to the heat, as Ortiz set a rapid pace in order to reach the ruins before nightfall. *We'll have to adjust quickly,* Caleb thought, mopping his brow with his bandanna, *or the jungle will kill us.*

They stopped for a quick lunch and then continued. Occasionally they saw other haciendas in the distance, surrounded by fields of the "green gold", henequen. Large tracts were still open to cattle ranching, with the Spanish cattle resting in the shade of low trees. The original wealth of the Spanish landowners had been founded on cattle, and the custom of bullfighting had been brought to the Yucatan from Seville. Even today, the ladinos, the aristocracy of New Spain, looked down on the cultivation of henequen, the plant that provided the sisal for baler twine to the mechanized harvesters and balers in the United States.

On balance, it was a beautiful country and a luxurious lifestyle for the old families who owned the estates. *I could be at home here*, Caleb thought. *Except for the language, it is not much different from my ranch in Colorado.*

Shanni nudged her horse up beside Caleb, who had left her alone since the altercation with Nerial. She had been surprised and quietly grateful when he had chosen to continue with her and the other Huastecs. She knew him, and could tell he was in a dark mood. Any moment he could lash out and bring their quarrel to a head. Then, they might begin the process of healing, or he might simply ride away. There was much hardship ahead, and they needed to reach an accommodation.

"Who could have dreamed of such wealth?" She said, sweeping her hand across the fields that stretched to the horizon.

"The original families who settled this land, usually conquistadors who had fought and risked their lives for the king of Spain, were given enormous land grants, sometimes over a hundred thousand hectares, as a reward for their service. Even today the haciendados like Senor Fuentes pretty well run the estates like their own country."

"What is a hectare?" Shanni asked.

"About two and a half acres."

"That doesn't help me!" Shanni retorted.

Caleb started to smile and caught himself. He didn't want to risk offending Shanni, now that she was at least talking to him. "One hundred thousand hectares would be about 250,000 acres. A square mile contains six hundred and forty acres. So the estate would contain nearly four hundred square miles of land. In terms we are familiar with, that is about twenty miles by twenty miles, or a day's ride across."

"So much land! How could one family use so much?"

"They cannot, alone. They must have help, and that's where the campesinos come in. They do the work, and are permitted to live on the land, where the patron looks after them."

"And if he doesn't?"

"They starve, or revolt."

"Sayil." Ortiz's voice called back, interrupting their conversation. They looked up ahead to see huge edifices of stone rising from the green scrubs that dotted the landscape.

"Oh," Shanni said, startled. "They are much larger than I expected. I had visualized ruins like the empty enclaves in Mesa Verde."

"Senor Fuentes told me that some of the buildings are four stories tall."

"I can't wait to see the buildings up close, and to touch the stones. Somehow I feel that there is a purpose, in addition to our own quest, that is calling to us, pulling us forward!"

Caleb shook his head. "Be careful. Too much is still unknown for us to rush ahead."

Shanni urged her horse forward, to ride in the lead beside Ortiz as they closed the distance to the ruins of Sayil. They reined in at the building Ortiz identified as the "Palace" and dismounted, gazing at the steps, made of perfectly cut and fitted stones that spread in geometric precision across the facade. They climbed the stone stairway to the second level, where columns made of stone supported archways that led to yet another level. They climbed to the huge stone temple that dominated the fourth level, and stood scanning the green forest that led to the horizon. Below they saw the ball court where their ancestors had competed in vigorous matches on which hung the prestige, and even the lives, of the participants. Across from the ball plaza, the pyramid that Ortiz called the Temple Pyramid rose up toward the sky, its base connected to the plaza by a stone causeway. A carving of a god with a snake's body and a human head lined the broad stairway that gave access to the platform at the top of the pyramid.

"What is that?" Shanni asked, unsettled by the fierce countenance before her.

"We'll have to ask Ortiz," Caleb answered. "All this is new to me, too."

Ortiz had remained with the horses, and had a campfire going when they descended the ruins and walked across to the camp under the trees. Ortiz had unloaded the horses and tied them on a picket rope to graze. Ortiz knew his business, Caleb noted. He didn't have to be told what to do.

Caleb and Shanni compared notes with the others while they ate. "I had no idea the ruins would be so massive!" Mala observed. "I expected something on a smaller scale."

"And we haven't even explored the other buildings," Aurel added. "Just the carvings and the writing engraved on the stones could take weeks to study."

"There are more ruins nearby," Ortiz broke in, poking the fire with a long stick. Night was falling and the fire flared up to light their faces as they talked. "There is Xiapak, about four miles to the east, and Labna, a few miles to the south."

"Oh, we must see them all while we are here!" Ambria responded.

33

"Unfortunately, the jungle has claimed them. The ruins are covered with vegetation, and even trees, so that one must dig to unearth the stones."

"Why didn't that happen here?" Matal asked.

"My people, the campesinos, hold this place sacred. Volunteers come and clear away the vegetation, keeping the jungle at bay."

"Where do they find the time?" Aurel asked. "I mean, it seems their time is filled with the business of the hacienda."

"They come at night. It is a sacred duty."

Aurel glanced at Shanni and Caleb. People labored in the fields all day, and then worked here at night to clear the ruins!

"Of course the work is rotated," Ortiz continued. "So that people can catch up on their rest."

"It still seems demanding to me," Aurel observed.

"It is our reality, a sacred duty." Ortiz answered evenly. "In the daytime, we belong to the patrone. In the night, we belong to ourselves and to our gods."

Silence fell, each person struck by the significance of Ortiz's words. He had spoken without rancor or resentment; he had simply stated a basic tenet of his world view.

Shanni broke the awkward silence. "We saw a strange being carved in the stone stairway. He had a fierce countenance and the body of a snake. I was a bit frightened."

"I saw it too," Iika said, shuddering.

"We all did," Aurel added. "A magnificent carving!"

"That is the rain-god Chac. In the old days he controlled the rain. The lives of the Maya depended upon the rain."

"Why the snake?" Niki continued. "Surely he didn't use snakes to bring the rain!"

"Chac fell from heaven on the backs of winged serpents. His fall made him wrathful. He took his wrath out on us human beings."

"How so?"

"He demanded our blood. We were forced to sacrifice people to keep him at bay, so that he would send the rain. At Labna, the Ancients carved Chac with a snake's mouth devouring a human."

"How horrible!" Mala shuddered.

"For as long as our memories extend back in time, the Mayan common people have suffered. The campesino system is not so bad compared to the past. At least now we can eat, and keep our children."

"Keep your children?" Shanni echoed.

"In those days, sacrifices were required, and often the slaves, people captured from the forest dwellers, were not enough. And then Chac would demand the lives of our children."

"I wondered why Senor Fuentes wanted us to see this," Ambria observed. "He was insistent that we come here before embarking on our search to the south."

"I think the patrone wanted you to realize the futility of your quest," Ortiz answered. "Why risk your lives to find more ruins? They are scattered about everywhere."

"But what if there is more than just ruins?" Shanni insisted. "I have the strong feeling that we were called here. There is some purpose that will be revealed to us. Don't you feel it?" She looked around the circle at the others. "Tonah insisted that the Center exists, and that we would find it. That means there is something more than ruins."

"And he never wavered in his belief that it exists," Aurel added.

"And you-all, what do you believe?" Shanni said, sweeping her glance around the campfire.

"We're here because we believe in Tonah, and we believe in you, Shanni," Matal answered quietly.

"Ortiz," Shanni turned to the campesino who had listened with interest to the Huastecs' exchange, "Will you guide us to find the Center?"

"I will lead you part of the way, Senora," he said quietly. "The remainder you must do alone."

Chapter 8

P ICH, SON OF Cecilio Chi, looked up from his task of applying curare to the tip of his spear. The deadly toxin caused complete paralysis of a victim's nervous system, causing it to literally smother to death due to its inability to breath.

His flashing eyes matched his fierce countenance. His hair hung straight, held in place by a leather head band decorated with feathers. A javelin tusk pierced the septum of his nose and tattoos marched in rows down his back to the loin cloth that circled his waist.

The clearing lay deep in the rain forest of Chiapas, and held a few thatch-roofed huts on stilts that gave crude shelter from the daily rain. Hogs and chickens scrabbled in the muddy grime for sustenance as children played on the porches.

Pich had received word to be ready, and he would be. He spat with disgust as he recalled how his father and the other rebel leader, Jacinto Pat, had brought the ladinos to their knees. They had massacred at will, terrifying the hated Spaniards, and could have reclaimed the entire Yucatan for their people, but instead they had turned around and gone home!

Some leaders! The mantle had fallen to Pich upon his father's death, murdered unceremoniously by his wife's lover. Pich had exacted revenge, not for the infidelity, for he didn't care about that. The Huits had passed women around indiscriminately from time immemorial. No, he had caught his father's murderer, cut off his privates, and strung him up to bleed to death to revenge the affront to his father's prestige as a leader.

The one thing his father had done right was to store the rifles and ammunition. Pich knew where they were hidden, and he kept them oiled and ready for use on a moment's notice. This time he would have a plan and an organization. When he took over, he would know what to do.

Pich assembled his men from the village, a small group, six in number. But there were many more men scattered among the jungle villages no white man had ever seen. Twenty years ago the Huits had sacked Valladolid, massacred the inhabitants, and walked away. This time they would stay!

Uaya, his second in command, nodded and led away from the clearing and eased into the jungle. The Huits had learned to work with the jungle, not against it. Instead of pushing and slashing like the Anglos, they merged in shadow, flowing silently through the underbrush, senses picking up each sound that identified the location of danger.

The small party reached the river, Moc-tal, or "mother waters", in their language, but known as the Rio Usumacinta to the Spaniards.

Motioning with his hands, the warriors retrieved two dugout canoes and eased them into the water, leaping deftly aboard as they swung into deeper water. Today they would travel with the current and they would make good time.

They did not stop for meals when they traveled. They munched on fruit and nuts, or smoked meat if they had it. They drank from water containers made of animal skins.

Near sunset they turned their canoes shoreward, and drove them up onto the muddy bank of the stream. On the bank stood Tamil.

Pich leaped out of the lead canoe and offered his hand in greeting. "What, the Toad did not come today?"

Tamil shrugged. "I brought information from our meeting. Who knows what Mayapan is thinking?"

"If he can think at all!" Pich laughed. "Too much ayahuasca."

Tamil let the insult pass. He saw no point to swapping opinions on Mayapan or any other not present. One made less mistakes that way.

Tamil had started a fire while he waited, and now the party squatted around it, eating quietly. After they finished they got down to business.

"Puco, the shaman, says that strangers approach to fulfill the prophesy and free the Mayas," Tamil said.

"How many come?"

"About half a dozen. There were more."

"How many more?"

"We don't know. We believe some died on the journey, while others turned back before they landed at Campeche. More left at Merida. Only the few remain and they continue to approach."

Pich nodded, thinking. "They will all die if they come here."

"That's why I am here. Mayapan sent the message that the strangers are not to be harmed. We will give them safe passage until we decide if Puco's words are true."

"How will we determine that?"

"We will take them to Mayapan. He will test them and decide."

"If Puco's words are true, what do they mean? Will the strangers lead us in battle? Will they support us in setting up our own government?"

"Mayapan did not say."

"All right. We will watch the strangers while we send word to our army to get ready. If the strangers help us, that is well. If not, they die and we help ourselves!"

"Mayapan will be displeased if you move without his permission."

"Did I not say I would cooperate, and wait?"

"It is important that you do."

Pich's eyes flashed. "Do I need threats from you?"

"No threat; a gentle reminder. This may be a great time in our history. We must stay together, think together, and move together. Did we not learn from our mistakes in the past?"

Pich did not miss the implied insult to his father. But now was not the time to take offense. He needed information that only Tamil would bring. As for the Toad, let him stew in his irrelevant babbling.

"You're right. This time we must think things through and not let up until we win."

"Well spoken!" Tamil agreed. "Now let's sleep. I will return to Mayapan tomorrow and tell him that you are with us. He will know when to expect the strangers."

THE HUASTECS SAT on their horses, grouped around Senor Fuentes who stood at the gate of the hacienda. "My friends, I have misgivings about this venture. But in the end, I must respect your choice. I have tried to prepare you for the dangers you will face. Ortiz is my most trusted guide, but even he must not venture into the rain forest that borders Campeche. The state of Chiapas, which you must enter, is wild and uncharted territory. May God be with you!"

"Senor Fuentes, we cannot thank you enough for your help..." Matal began.

"Da nada, it is nothing," Fuentes waved his hand. If you can, pass it on to others, as people have passed help on to me. Remember, you have refuge here if you are forced to turn back."

Caleb reached down and grasped Fuentes' hand. No words were necessary. As their eyes met, Caleb wondered for a moment if Fuentes missed the call to action, the joy of setting forth. But Fuentes' time had passed. Now he must stay while others rode on, and fulfill his duties to the hacienda.

"I will see you again, Caleb Stone," Fuentes said, releasing his strong grip.

Ortiz turned and rode out, followed by Caleb, Shanni and the others. The way was long, over a hundred miles as the crow flew, through Campeche to the Chiapas border. Who knew how far from there? They had decided that they would go to the ruins of Palenque, and begin their search for the Center. If it was not there, they would go wherever the clues, and Shanni's intuition, took them.

Aurel rode up beside Caleb in the cool morning air. Soon the sun would heat the air and they would have to hold the horses to a walk. "You were there last night," Aurel began. "When Senor Fuentes discussed the ruins at Sayil."

"Yes."

"He said they were abandoned almost overnight about 1250, as the Anglos count the years."

"So?"

"That's the exact time that our ancestors left Mesa Verde, as well as the other cities scattered across our lands."

"Strange coincidence," Caleb agreed. "I guess I'd missed the connection."

"What if it is not a coincidence?"

"What do you mean?"

"What if our ancestors weren't isolated. There were roads, runners, and caravans of traders. What if the Huastecs' ancestors at Mesa Verde, Chaco Canyon and other places were connected to the Mayan cities before they fell? Maybe the Mayas did something to cause the fall of the Huastec civilization. Maybe they did something that destroyed us! Maybe the drought story is just a coverup."

"But why would they want to do that? It would be a long way to travel just to loot your cities."

"That's what I am trying to figure out. If I knew why they may have destroyed us, maybe I could guess why the Sentinels have worked so hard to stop us!"

"Ah, the Sentinels." Caleb nodded. "I had forgotten about them, since they are no longer trying to stop us."

"No longer trying, or are they just waiting for us to fall into their trap?"

Caleb shook his head and took a deep breath. Five hard days to the border and then they jumped off into the unknown.

Chapter 9

PUCO STIRRED RESTLESSLY in his sleep, nightmares fleeting in and out of his subconscious mind. He rolled over on the crude wooden floor of the hut and opened his eyes. They slowly focused on the large rat sitting nearby, staring intently at his face. Instantly Puco snapped fully awake, his heart pounding. He reached for his machete.

That is not necessary, the 'voice' spoke inside his mind. *I bring you a message from Huntal the Sentinel.*

Puco recognized the name of one of the beings from the world of nonordinary reality. Puco entered that world often with the help of the hallucinogenic drink *ayahuasca,* made from a certain vine in the rain forest. The Sentinels were mysterious beings, who ordinarily held themselves aloof from the affairs of men.

"What is it you wish?" Puco responded softly.

The strangers who approach are evil beings who must be destroyed. The Sentinels have spoken.

Puco could not hide his surprise. "But I thought they were the ones prophesied to save the Mayas and restore their prominence in the world of ordinary reality!"

That was the prophecy of a fool, an old man who broke away from the priesthood and created great unrest with his mad rambling.

"Akmul? I thought he was a great sage! He left us many written prophesies and instructions for implementing them when the time was due."

Akmul's writings must be destroyed! All of them!

"But we do not know where they are," Puco protested. "The original records, I mean. Akmul was cunning. He left only handwritten copies of key prophesies, but spoke of complete knowledge written on metal plates, hidden in a vault."

You know of the Vault?

"Only as it is referred to in Akmul's documents. I do not know where the vault is located. It may not exist in the world of ordinary reality."

Then you must leave it to us to deal with the vault. But you must stop the strangers and destroy them totally!

"But what if they abandon their quest and turn back?"

You must still destroy them. They are a threat as long as they are alive.
"A threat? To whom?"

That is not your concern. Be careful that you do not become inquisitive to your detriment.

Puco lowered his eyes. To anger the Sentinels meant death. There was no appeal from their wrath. "It will be as you say," he responded meekly.

See that it is. You will be held personally accountable.

The rat's eyes blinked and its body trembled. A blue aura formed around its body and then coalesced into a thin blue beam of light that flashed and vanished. Fear flared in the rat's eyes as it regained its senses and it scratched frantically to get away from the man-form of Puco. It scurried down the crude ladder of the thatched hut to disappear into the jungle.

Puco looked around and nervously licked his lips. *I must find Tamil,* he thought. *Maybe he will know what to do!*

Hours later Puco met Tamil in the forest and related what had transpired with the Sentinel. Puco knew that Tamil would not be pleased, and he was right.

Although he respected Puco's healing ability, Tamil was not a shaman and took much of Puco's rambling with a grain of salt. Sitting around drinking hallucinogens was liable to affect a man's brain, and Puco had become more and more erratic lately. "I've alerted our leaders to get ready, based on your instructions, and your statement that the strangers came to fulfill the prophesy. Not even two days ago I met with Pich and he is spreading the word throughout the Huit Maya world to prepare to fight. Now I am supposed to call it all off because you've had a change of heart?"

Tamil fought to contain his anger as he spoke. His credibility was at stake. He had become the informal leader of all the tribes through his quiet diplomacy and habit of being correct with his information. Had he relied on Puco too long?

"But you must!" Puco burst out, perspiration appearing on his brow from stress.

"Are you all right?" Tamil asked, watching Puco closely. Maybe Puco was having a reaction to all the substances he had ingested!

"I am fine. But I won't be, and neither will you, if we cross the Sentinels!"

Tamil shook his head. He had not gotten to his position of power by acting in haste. He needed to buy time to weigh all the alternatives. "Of course we will do what they say," he answered. "There was never a question of following their direction."

"Good! Good!" Puco whispered, visibly relieved. "Now I must go."

Tamil nodded and Puco hurried back into the jungle. It would be easy to turn Pich loose, Tamil knew. Pich was a doer, not a thinker, and often acted rashly. Pich had chafed when Tamil reined him in. Given the word, Pich would wreak havoc on the strangers and enjoy doing it. But why should he release Pich? Let the people believe that the strangers were here to save them. The campesinos would regain hope, and fight to the death to overthrow the ladinos.

Of course that might cost Puco his life, if the Sentinels could really act in the world of ordinary reality. But that was Puco's concern; he should have been more circumspect before he set the ball rolling. Maybe now Puco would forego his habit of staying half out of his mind on hallucinogens, and come to his senses. Tamil could use Puco's shamanic abilities to control the people, but he must be able to reason with Puco, or else stop relying on him and cast him adrift. Puco might think that he could handle power, but Tamil had learned what power meant in the real world. One had to out-think one's opponents, and be fast and ruthless when the time came to act. With Puco supporting him, and the strength of the prophesy motivating the people, Tamil knew that he would have a unique opportunity to emerge as the leader of the Huit Maya after General Cen attacked the ladinos. All the pieces were coming together and the time to act was fast approaching.

FOLLOWING ORTIZ, CALEB and the Huastecs had traveled fast on the good horses provided by Senor Fuentes. But the riders experienced fatigue from the long hours in the saddle and the need to concentrate on picking their way through the thick brush. They had traveled southwest through the state of Campeche to approach Chiapas from the north near its border with Guatemala.

Ortiz reined up in the afternoon of the sixth day of travel and let the other riders form up in a loose circle around him. "We are nearing the Chiapas border," he said, pointing. "You have no doubt noticed the change in vegetation. You are about to enter subtropical rain forest where the horses will be of no use to you. From now on you must proceed on foot, hacking your way through with machetes. Deep inside the jungle there is a river, the Rio Usumacinta, which you may use for easier travel. It leads from the Sierra Madre del Sur to the south, northward to spill into the Gulf of Mexico north of Villahermosa. Along the way it passes the ruins of Palenque, where you will stop and begin your search. It is here that I must leave you. We will camp for the night, and tomorrow I will return to the hacienda."

Caleb and the others looked at the foreboding wall of green jungle that confronted them. What dangers lurked in that unbroken wall of green? They silently dismounted, helped Ortiz unload the horses, and settled down for the evening meal.

Ortiz seemed upbeat as they finished their meal. *Ortiz is happy to be returning*, Caleb thought. *And if Ortiz fears the jungle, how much more should we?*

"How I dreamed for a horse when we walked through the mountains," Mala observed, rubbing her tired legs. "And now I am numb from riding!"

"We all are," Matal replied. "It didn't help that we traveled so fast, but it was necessary. Now our progress will be much slower; right, Ramon?"

Ortiz nodded. "There is a path made by the pilgrims to Palenque, but it is overgrown and filled with twists and turns. You will be able to walk only a few miles each day."

"And with packs on our backs again, we will be even slower!" Matal observed. "We'll have to pace ourselves and stop often to rest."

"Do not forget the heat," Ortiz added. "You must listen to your bodies and rest often. Heat stroke is deadly."

"Any other good news?" Caleb broke in, trying to lighten the conversation. It was serious business, but they needed some balance, or they'd feel defeated before they started.

"No more saddle sores?" Niika piped up, reacting without thinking. The others laughed, breaking the tension. Even Ortiz, always the taciturn one, smiled.

"Poor Ramon," Niika continued. "No respite from the horses. Perhaps you'd rather stay and go with us!"

"A part of me would like to go," Ortiz admitted. "It is many years since I visited Palenque as a boy, with my parents. It is a mystical place. Even now I remember the feeling it evoked. I felt the spirits of our ancestors, and the power they once wielded in that place."

"Power?"

"When humans come together for a common purpose, they draw energy, which we call 'power', to themselves."

"You sound like a shaman," Aurel observed. "I've only heard shamans speak in such terms."

"I am not a shaman," Ortiz protested. "I am only a campesino. But my people, the Maya, still look at the world in the old way. Many of the ideas remain that were handed down to us by the ancients."

"What kind of ideas?"

"About spirits that influence the lives of men. The power of belief, and how the universe responds when we know how to call. I think maybe my people view the world in a very different way than the ladinos."

"I can understand that," Shanni agreed. "We Huastecs have certainly been forced to adapt to a new and different world during our journey."

"And now I am afraid that you enter yet another world," Ortiz said.

"The jungle?" Matal asked, not quite following Ortiz's meaning.

"That, too, but that is not all." Ortiz paused, gazing into the fire while he chose his words carefully. "We believe in things unseen, in worlds beyond what exists here on the earth. Entities exist in those worlds that we trust to guide us and keep us safe in the physical world."

"Entities that will not be available to help us, since we do not believe in them?" Aurel responded, trying to grasp Ortiz's meaning.

"Yes. That is it," Ortiz said, brightening. "I did not know how to express my meaning."

"So much depends on faith, doesn't it?" Aurel observed, gazing around the circle looking for affirmation from the other Huastecs. "In every culture we've encountered, the ability to choose to go on depends on a faith that the universe cares about us and wants us to succeed. Without that faith, there can be no motivation to try, to reach out when the outcome is much in doubt."

Caleb recalled what he had seen of the lives of the campesinos, little more than serfs on the estates of the big landowners. The people had been invariably polite and patient. They found happiness in simple pleasures and seemed to accept their lot in life. But there was a dark side, lurking unspoken, perhaps so deeply submerged in the subconscious that the people had forgotten it. But it was there, and it had erupted briefly and tragically in the bloody massacres that became known as the War of the Castes. Human nature did not change. Inside every man, woman and child was the basic desire to be free and to have control over their lives.

Matal had also been turning Ortiz's words over in his mind. He respected Ortiz and valued his judgment. Maybe there was something here, a clue that would help them. "Taking your point," he said. "We would be more likely to survive in the jungle if we knew something of its ways."

"Yes." Ortiz waited. What was Matal's point?

"It seems to me that what we need is a guide, and you have done well bringing us this far. How come you're not coming with us?"

"Because I am not of the jungle."

"But surely there is someone you can recommend; someone you would trust to help us."

Ortiz paused, again staring at the fire. "Guiding others is a grave responsibility when injury or death are ever-present dangers. People of the jungle do not seek such responsibility. They have enough looking after themselves and their families."

Matal glanced at Caleb, and then around the circle of silent faces. He could see that Ortiz had them all thinking. They needed a guide who could keep them out of trouble while they learned how to survive in this new environment. Both Caleb and Matal had broached the subject with Senor Fuentes, but he had been unable to help. His world extended little farther than his estate, and Ortiz had been the best resource he had to lend them.

"Surely there is someone who can help us!" Matal insisted. "We would pay them, of course."

"There is one I know of, the shaman Puco, who has no family. He might be willing to assist you."

"Is he reliable?"

"I am not sure. He uses the sacred drink, ayahuasca, to travel to the spirit world. His prophesies carry great weight with my people. We have never known him to lie, or to be wrong with his prophesies."

"How can we contact him, to see if he is interested in guiding us?"

"There is a network for communicating among the villages. I can ride back to the village we passed today and send word to Puco."

"What do you think?" Matal looked around the circle of faces.

"What do we have to lose?" Mala asked. "I can't think of anything worse than entering that jungle alone."

The others nodded agreement. "It's settled then," Matal concluded, nodding to Ortiz.

"As you wish," Ortiz responded, rising from his place beside the campfire. He saddled a horse and soon rode away into the darkness.

"What if he just keeps riding?" Ambria wondered, half-aloud. Silence followed, as each realized Ortiz would soon be gone. Tonight, or tomorrow would make little difference.

"Hell of a way to travel!" Caleb mused. "Reaching for a life rope that you hope will appear just when you need it!"

"Hasn't the whole journey been that way?" Ambria shot back. "Going from one crisis to another, always into the unknown. There is no way to anticipate what we need!"

"True enough," Caleb agreed. "I guess I would feel better if Ortiz had been more positive about Puco."

"He did sound as if he didn't know Puco that well. Maybe he was stretching to help us, not wanting to say 'no'."

"Doesn't matter now; the die is cast," Matal said. "Let's turn in and hope that Puco shows up. Then we'll see."

They awakened at sunrise to find Ortiz had returned during the night. He set about stoking the fire and bringing water from a nearby spring. The spring was the source of water for animals in the vicinity, startled by the humans who had invaded their territory. Rabbits scurried into the brush, and a cat-like animal that Ortiz called a jaguarundi appeared briefly and then leapt away.

Ortiz kept looking expectantly at the underbrush that led into the jungle as they ate breakfast. Caleb could not tell if he was anxious that Puco would not come, or impatient to begin his long ride back to the hacienda. They could only watch, and wait.

After the meal, Caleb and the Huastecs checked their packs and filled their canteens as Ortiz prepared the horses for his return. Time dragged, and Caleb glanced at the sun climbing ever higher in the sky. They needed to get started in order to complete a few hours of travel before they were forced to stop in the heat of the day.

Ortiz left the horses and returned to camp, shrugging at the unasked questions in the eyes of the Huastecs. "Who knows?" he said simply. "Perhaps he will not come."

"How long can we wait?" Matal asked, looking at Caleb.

"Not much longer, or we'll lose the day's travel."

"I am sorry," Ortiz said. "Perhaps it is for the best. Maybe he was not a good choice."

"Not that we had a choice, at that," Matal agreed.

There was a slight rustle in the underbrush, and the Huastecs turned expectantly. A small man, bow-legged and wrinkled with age stepped out from the underbrush, a gap-toothed smile on his face. He was clad in a loin cloth, with a dirty headband holding black hair back from his eyes. A leather carry-bag and wicked-looking machete completed his outfit. His dirt-streaked face and muddy feet indicated that he had traveled far.

"Puco," Ortiz said, as Puco approached him with outstretched hand. They conversed briefly in a language that Caleb assumed was a local Mayan dialect, and then turned to face the Huastecs. As Ortiz introduced Puco to each person by name, Puco bowed solemnly as if to royalty, and repeated the name. He must lace his ayahuasca with liquor, Caleb thought as he shook Puco's hand, noting the odor of alcohol and the half-dazed look in Puco's eyes.

Nobody knew what to say after meeting the strange man to which they were about to entrust their lives.

"It is time to go," Ortiz said, turning toward the horses.

"Ortiz, thank you," Matal said, extending his hand. "You have been our friend."

"The words have been spoken," Ortiz answered, grasping Matal's hand. "I wish you success on your journey." He turned and walked to the waiting horses.

Caleb and the others shouldered their packs and followed, single file, as Puco flashed his machete overhead and led into the underbrush.

Chapter 10

As SOON AS they entered the undergrowth, the heat and humidity closed in on them like a dense fog. Within moments their linen shirts clung to their bodies, wet with perspiration.

Caleb could hear Puco up ahead, chopping at branches with his machete. Matal followed him, also slashing at the dense growth as they advanced at a slow walk.

Ambria, behind Matal, turned to Shanni, "This is horrible! I had no idea it would be like this!"

"If we could just feel a breeze, it would be bearable," Shanni agreed. "And the branches keep whipping into my face!"

"The gnats are the worst!" Mala interjected, swatting at her face. "I can't seem to breathe without getting a gnat in my nose!"

Caleb listened in silence, concentrating on placing his feet to avoid stepping on Shanni who progressed erratically in front of him. The forest floor was littered with leaves, fallen logs, and sink holes that made walking a constant hazard. Caleb kept his machete tied to his belt. Soon he would remove it and go forward to spell Matal in cutting trail.

After several hours, Puco stopped at the base of a tall tree which had smothered out the underbrush, creating a small clearing where they could gather together. Puco smiled, leaning on his machete. He breathed easily, with only a sheen of perspiration on his forehead.

"How do you do it, Puco?" Caleb asked. "You've hardly worked up a sweat!"

"Long practice," Puco spoke Spanish with an unfamiliar accent. "One learns to work with the jungle, not against it." Puco smiled.

Maybe it is just a nervous habit, Caleb thought, *Puco smiling for no reason. But it makes me nervous.*

The Huastecs lifted their canteens to drink. "Our water is going fast in this heat," Matal observed. "I hope there is more available as we go."

A puzzled expression replaced the smile on Puco's face. He cocked an ear, as if listening to some unusual sound. "Water?" He repeated.

Caleb realized that Puco was having trouble understanding their Spanish. The Huastecs' pronunciation was very different from that in the Yucatan. And difficulty in understanding could become a problem in a tight spot. They had to be able to communicate instantly. Hopefully their ability would improve with practice. If they had enough time.

"Yes. Where can we get more water?" Matal said.

"More water?"

"Yes."

Again Puco smiled, and turned as if to continue.

"Wait, we're not ready to go yet." Mala protested. "We just got here."

"Wait here," Matal said. "I will go with Puco. Maybe the water is nearby."

Puco did not cut the undergrowth when he traveled. Instead he wove among the plants, parting their leaves with his hands like a harpist. Matal tried to follow, struggling to learn the technique while keeping up with Puco.

Puco paused, pointing to the base of a nearby tree. Coiled among the exposed roots was a large snake, its coloration blending into the leaves. Matal realized he could have stepped on it without seeing it had it been in his path.

"Death." Puco grunted. "Fer-de-lance."

Matal drew in a slow breath and moved past it, following Puco. They reached a brackish stream and Puco stopped. "Water," he said.

Matal knelt to inspect the water. Small insects skated along the surface, and a green algae covered the edges. He looked up at Puco and rubbed his stomach. "Sick? Will it make us sick?"

Puco reached into his leather carry-bag and brought out a small, square container made of cloth with a wooden frame. Then he retrieved a battered tin cup. He placed the square object over the open mouth of his canteen, and then used the cup to pour water from the stream through the rough filter into the canteen. He repeated the operation until his canteen was full, and then repeated it until Matal's canteen was filled. Puco returned the filter to his carry-bag, and fished out a small bag containing a bluish powder. He sprinkled a small amount into each canteen and shook them. "Count!" He said, looking at Matal. Puco held up his fingers as he counted slowly, showing Matal what to do.

After counting to sixty, Puco opened one of the canteens and showed the water to Matal. The bluish tinge of the powder had disappeared. Puco lifted his canteen to his lips and drank. "Good!" He said, passing the canteen to Matal, who sipped cautiously. The water had a slightly metallic taste, but otherwise seemed fine. It would have to do. They had to trust Puco's methods to keep them from sickness, or even death, from drinking contaminated water.

They returned for the others and retraced their steps to the water, where all the canteens were soon filled. The Huastecs watched with rapt attention as Puco repeated the water purification.

"I wonder what's in that blue powder!" Mala exclaimed.

"What if it is nothing?" Aurel asked. "Maybe he is just believes that the powder works, and his body is tough enough after a lifetime here that the water doesn't make him sick."

Mala frowned. She wanted to believe that Puco knew what he was doing, and that the powder really worked. They had to have water and she wanted to trust that it was wholesome.

"What do you think, Caleb?"

"I don't know, but I have to think he wouldn't go to the trouble to carry the powder if it didn't work. The stuff reminds me of iodine, which is a disinfectant."

"What if he runs out of powder?" Mala continued. "We're going through a lot of water in this heat!"

Caleb turned to Puco. "Where do you get more powder? What if we run out?"

"More powder?"

Caleb made a motion of sprinkling the powder into the canteen.

"No need. Already safe." Puco replied.

"No, I mean where do we get more powder for use in the future, before we run out?"

Puco stared, and then his expression changed as he grasped Caleb's question. "Oh, no problem," he answered. "Blue powder comes from coast. People there make it from seaweed. I have enough for many days, and can get more."

"Now if Puco could just do something about the heat!" Ambria complained.

"I'm afraid that's something that exceeds even the power of Puco to fix," Caleb said as they resumed their march through the jungle.

They stopped for the night beside a small stream that meandered slowly through the leaf-laden underbrush. Puco disappeared into the brush as Caleb and the others retrieved dried fruit and meat from their packs. They could exist a few days on the food they had brought with them, but then they would be forced to live off what they could hunt or gather as they traveled.

More than an hour had passed when Puco emerged from the jungle, proudly displaying the dead monkey slung over his shoulder. He threw the body on the ground, its glazed eyes staring lifelessly at the sky.

"Ahh!" Mala shivered. "Why did he kill the poor monkey?"

Caleb inspected the body closely. There was no sign of blood. Had the monkey fallen to its death?

"Food," Puco said, and smiled. He drew a skinning knife out of his bag and took the monkey's body to the edge of the clearing to dress it for cooking. Soon he had the body on a wooden spit, roasting over the fire, as the Huastecs watched in morbid fascination.

"How did you catch it?" Caleb asked.

"Catch?"

"You know, how did you kill the monkey?"

"Kill with poison."

"How?"

Puco carefully lifted an arrow out of his quiver, revealing a tiny stone arrowhead tightly bound to the wooden shaft with dried leather string. "Don't touch!" Puco warned, pointing to the arrowhead. "Poison."

Caleb grasped the arrow and examined the tip up close. The arrowhead appeared normal except for a dull black coating, as if it had been dipped in paint.

Puco smiled proudly, making the motion of drawing a bow and releasing an arrow up into the trees. "Hit monkey," he said. "Poison paralyzes; cannot breathe."

Puco's exaggerated gestures of the monkey, face wide with surprise, toppling over slowly to fall out of the tree were so realistic that Caleb couldn't help from chuckling.

"Monkey fall from tree. All done," Puco concluded.

Matal shook his head in wonder. "This is truly a different world!"

Puco used the knife to cut off slivers of fresh-roasted meat. He plopped one into his mouth and chewed rapidly. "Good!" he said, as he passed out slivers of meat. "Now you try."

Caleb tasted the meat. "Not bad," he said, looking around at the others. "Tastes a bit gamey, but we can live on it."

Caleb watched with interest the varied reactions of the others. Ambria was a finicky eater, and seemed repulsed by the dark sliver of meat on the bark that served as her plate. She struggled to gather the courage to put the meat in her mouth. Mala's reluctance was based on her empathy with the monkey. She hated to eat the little creature. Niki and Aurel were not enthusiastic, but soldiered on, chewing silently.

"We might as well learn to enjoy it," Matal said to encourage them. "We must eat whatever we find to live, and next time we may not even know what it is!"

"Actually, it doesn't taste bad," Aurel said. "If I just hadn't seen where the meat came from!"

Puco smiled. "Good. We drink, we eat, we sleep, we travel! Now it is time to sleep."

Nobody has to be invited a second time, Caleb thought, lying down on top of his poncho in the humid, night heat. We're all worn out and this is only the first day!

Chapter 11

LIFE EMERGED LIKE a wave in the ocean, Tonah perceived. Out of the enormous stretch of ocean, each wave formed as the water approached the beach. The wave became a separate entity, yet never completely separated from the underlying water that supported it. It rode along, reached its maximum strength, and then dissipated as the water thinned on the beach and returned to the ocean from which, for a brief moment in time, it had existed as an independent entity.

Now Tonah had returned to the vast universe of energy that vibrated in a never-ending cauldron of potentialities, of energy bundles springing into particles and then back into the ocean of pure energy. Some of the particles remained in the physical realm, aggregating into bundles held together by forces inherent in their being.

But not Tonah. Now he had completed his cycle in the physical universe and returned to the multiverse of potentiality that permitted all things to create themselves. Like a wave, he had returned to the ocean of intent that caused all things to be born, and to be.

Other souls who had preceded Tonah in the cycle of life had welcomed him into their care, nurturing him as he lived and then let go of his life on earth. Only in the physical world could he experience suffering, and only by suffering could he learn compassion. Compassion, he understood now, was the driving force behind the universe.

You are adapting well. You made the transition with ease, a former entity, now part of the ocean of energy, 'said' to Tonah.

"I had prepared for death, taking the steps that ease the transition," Tonah replied. "When my work was done, I was ready. I welcomed the release from responsibility and from suffering that death brought."

That is why death is a part of life on the physical plane. Incarnating into matter and therefore life on earth, is an immense undertaking. Once incarnated into a physical body, one struggles to survive, and often suffers physical fear and deprivation. But it is through the suffering that one comes to understand compassion, and caring for others. Once you are perfected, it is a great gift to return to your natural state here on this plane.

"Yet we resist it so!" Tonah observed.

Because we become attached to life in the physical plane. We can experience the world through our bodies, so we indulge ourselves in food and drink, and other passions. We make bad decisions. We are permitted to be irresponsible, so we are.

"And then we suffer," Tonah said.

Yes, and learn compassion.

"But some in human life do not learn," Tonah replied. "They do great evil, causing the deaths of many people. Why don't you put limits on them?"

Each universe reaches a point in its development where it needs co-creative entities in human form to create new combinations and control the potentialities that the combinations bring into the physical world.

"But man uses his knowledge to do great harm. Why not control his impulses?"

We found that anything less than free will does not work. Look at the other life forms on earth. They are programmed at birth, and live out their lives in a predetermined way. Man can create only because he is given the ability to make conscious choices.

"For good or evil!"

Yes. That is why we must erase his memory of prior lives. If man feels that anything else is in control, he becomes complacent. He waits for someone else; God, nature, priests, kings, to decide and tell him what to do. Only when he bears the responsibility to choose does he learn to do so.

"But surely we must intervene at times, to keep those who choose evil from destroying mankind!"

We are careful not to intervene in a direct way, for man would conclude that his choices didn't matter and wait for us to right the world's wrongs. But when a civilization loses its balance and tilts toward evil, and therefore total destruction, we may intervene to put it back on course.

"How?"

A number of ways. Sometimes we utilize men on earth who have achieved power but not yet embraced evil, and we assist their efforts to turn the course of history around.

"You mean great leaders who rebel against the status quo, and lead armies to right injustice?"

Sometimes. We can influence the outcome of battles, send ideas to commanders in their dreams, and influence natural events to aid a favored group.

"But what if that is not enough?"

Then one of 'us' may volunteer to become a 'wave' again; to incarnate into the physical world in order to turn the momentum of human events back on a positive course.

"The great prophets and religious leaders!"

Those, too. But sometimes we incarnate as a common person to set the example for every individual that his or her life can matter if they choose to embrace a cause for good, and to develop the courage to overcome their fears. Some find the spiritual strength to fight and die if necessary in order to make a difference.

"Now I understand why death is such a gift. No one would have the courage to endure such suffering if they had no hope of an end to it, a release from pain."

Exactly, and how could a compassionate universe permit such suffering without end?

"What about the evil-doers?"

There are innumerable universes or planes of existence. The evil ones are cast again and again into the fires of refinement until they are purified. Only then are they welcomed back into the ocean of compassion.

"But that doesn't make up for the suffering they cause."

Once they have learned, they are often the ones who volunteer to go back to sacrifice themselves for positive change.

"On the earth?"

On the earth or in other places of existence, other universes.

"But how can there be more than one universe?"

There is only one universe that the entities you joined, the ones called 'humans', know. That universe is only one of countless others.

"How can that be? Energy, matter, planets, stars, and galaxies all obey basic laws."

Yes, but laws determined by the basic causality of that particular potential. Potential occurs prior to formation of a universe, at that point where energy becomes matter and vibrates back and forth between the two states of 'nothingness' and 'something'. Think about it. There are countless permutations of how a universe can begin. And once begun, how its particles evolve. The different principles of each permutation determine the development of that universe. That is why we exist in spiritual form in this dimension.

"I don't understand."

Groups of us return to our local 'ocean', having learned the lesson of compassion. Using our compassion, we influence the development of the region of the physical universe under our care.

"We become 'God'?"

No, the creative power of all existence is an immense Presence of which we are a part, constantly evolving. Words cannot convey a concept for which you have no experience. You will experience the Presence at the proper time as you progress in your development.

"Is there no end to it?"

Your identity, your sentience, still clings to the memory of your earthly life, your identity as a 'wave' separate from the ocean. Soon the memory will fade and 'you' will merge into the communal identity of the group you have joined.

"I will lose touch with the earth?"

If your work there is completed. Some entities keep a tenuous connection for a time in order to assure events that they set in motion reach a successful conclusion. But expect your focus to shift to the important work ahead of us.

Then I must contact Aurel again, Tonah 'thought'. *He and the others must realize that soon I will no longer be able to reach them. And only now do I glimpse the great work they must do.*

Chapter 12

MAYAPAN SAT QUIETLY outside his cave in the cool crispness of the morning air. The small fire crackled cheerfully, dissolving the dew that glistened from the stones surrounding the fire pit.

Mayapan watched a banded falcon that perched on the branch of a nearby tree. Any moment he expected to see it fly, but it sat passively, its feathers reflecting the morning light with a rainbow of colors. The hawk lifted a wing and used its beak to preen the feathers. After aligning them, it stretched the wing, flexed it and refolded it. Unhurried, it repeated the process for the other wing. Its ministrations completed, it sat motionless, gazing out at the world revealed in a new day.

Mayapan recognized a kindred spirit in the hawk as it sat 'doing' by 'not-doing'. The hawk was in harmony with its world, going with the flow of existence. Unlike man, who awakened with a feverish mind, driven to waste his strength on activities, the hawk simply waited. It knew without question the optimal time of day to hunt, to eat, to drink and to rest. It would complete a successful day without strain, and without effort.

We breathe the same air, Mayapan thought. *We walk the same earth, we eat, and in time we return the elements of our bodies to the biosphere that is earth. In the end, we are all equal. No one entity is greater than another. We all serve our purpose according to the same design.*

Mayapan looked up without surprise as Tamil appeared at the edge of the clearing and scanned the ruins of the stone temples set among the trees of the encroaching jungle.

Why did Mayapan choose to live here? Tamil wondered. *Alone with these lifeless ruins. A recluse in a cave. How could he not lose touch and become a little crazy?*

"Back so soon?" Mayapan asked, not taking his eyes from the hawk. Tamil, distracted, followed his gaze. The hawk sat impassively, its beautiful band of neck feathers contrasting sharply with black wings and scarlet breast.

"I am surprised it did not fly when I appeared," Tamil said.

"Out here it does not know of men, so it is not afraid."

"But you are here."

"I do not hunt it. I have become like the trees and the stones to the hawk."

"Part of the landscape," Tamil said.

"Yes."

"Why do you chose to live here?"

"Without the confusion of men, I am free to align myself with the natural world, to think with understanding," Mayapan said.

"About what?"

"The hidden energies flowing about us, influencing our actions. They create the trends that play themselves out in the world of men. Most people bury themselves in mindless activity which prevents them from seeing where their actions are taking them."

"That's why I'm here. Something has changed since we received your instructions." Tamil waited for a reaction from Mayapan. Receiving none, he continued.

"Puco came to see me, all agitated. He reversed himself and ordered that the strangers be killed."

"He admitted that his prophesy is not true?"

"No, I guess he didn't, now that I think about it. He said that Sentinels from the spirit world had ordered him to stop the strangers.. He wants me to order Pich to attack and kill them."

"Have you contacted Pich?" Mayapan asked.

"No, I wanted to discuss his orders with you first. It's not like Puco to reverse himself like this, and I don't like him changing direction after I've given orders. It makes me look bad."

"Act in haste, repent at leisure," Mayapan replied. "You did well to come to me first."

They were distracted by movement, and turned to watch the hawk launch itself from the branch to glide on silent wings down the slope toward the grassy clearing. With a deft motion, it swung its taloned feet forward and sank them deep into a grazing rabbit. The hawk flapped its wings, lifting its heavy burden into the air. It glided to a nearby tree and began eating its meal.

"All takes place in its proper time, if one is in harmony with the flow of energy in the universe." Mayapan said quietly. "I fear that Puco has lost his connection."

"Connection?"

"With the flow. Now he will find that much more energy is required to correct a problem than is required to avoid it."

"I don't know what problem you refer to."

"If Puco's prophesy is true, Power has sent the strangers to help us. Now that he is opposing them, he is opposing Power, the energy that influences all our lives. If he wins, and achieves the destruction of the strangers, he loses, for he has defied Power. Now Puco can only win by losing."

Tamil drew a deep breath, calming his frustration. Mayapan always talked in circles. Who could understand him?

Sensing Tamil's agitation, Mayapan smiled. "What we think we know often keeps us from hearing what we really know when we listen to our 'inner voice'. We think we know what we don't know, when we don't know what we don't know. Understand?"

"I had a feeling it would be wrong to act on Puco's change of heart. That's why I came to discuss it."

"You were wise to come to me, and correct not to act on Puco's instructions. Ignore Puco from now on. His credibility is in doubt. Do everything in your power to protect the strangers."

"But Puco's prophesy could be wrong. He's been half out of his mind on ayahuasca lately."

"Would the Sentinels oppose the approach of the strangers if his prophesy had no validity?"

"No, I guess they wouldn't care what happened to the strangers."

"There is always a reason when Sentinels deign to take notice of the affairs of men."

"What is it?" Tamil asked.

"Time will tell. Ah, 'time', that funny thing that we draw in and laugh and sing...Oh, you know!" Mayapan laughed. "Time to eat!"

Chapter 13

P UCO STOPPED AND waited patiently for the others, unseen in the dense foliage, to catch up. They had learned to be quieter, although he could still hear their advance. They were quickly learning the ways of the jungle. Some, like Caleb, were observing and asking questions. Caleb wanted to know all about plants. The one called 'Matal' had a predilection for weapons. Matal had crafted a bow and accompanied Puco on last night's hunt. Puco was growing to like these strangers, and felt conflicted by the orders from the Sentinels, which he dared not disobey. But at least he would stay out of the actual attack. Pich and his men would do the dirty work. They enjoyed it. Puco would treat the strangers well. His conscience would be clear when Pich arrived and Puco stepped aside.

Puco had stopped near a broken mound of stones, half-covered with vegetation, when Matal emerged from the foliage, followed closely by the others. "Ruins are scattered all over this jungle," Matal said. "How are we possibly going to recognize the Center if we find it?"

Puco waited until all had assembled before responding. "The mound permits us to see over the trees. Maybe in the distance you can see the Rio Usumacinta, if it is not covered with mist. Be careful. The mound is unstable. Only one or two should climb it at the same time."

Matal and Ambria began climbing as the others dropped their packs to rest. Puco eased away into the foliage as he often did, apparently scouting for remnants of the ancient stone trail that led through the jungle.

Shanni was upbeat. At last they were on the final leg of their journey. She could feel the Center getting closer. She accepted the canteen that Caleb offered and turned it up to drink.

"Is the aloe helping?" he asked. With Puco's help, Caleb had gathered aloe vera to use on their sun-chapped skin. The oil also soothed the scrapes and tears from branches and briars that scratched as they pushed their way through the jungle.

"Much better," Shanni replied, as Matal and Ambria clambered down the mound and leapt to the ground.

"Clear as a bell!" Matal reported, "A thin line of blue snaking through a sea of green. Not more than thirty miles, I guess."

"And farther south, near the horizon, the land rises into a long line of mountains like we crossed west of Vera Cruz," Ambria added.

Puco returned and stood silently, listening to their report. "The mountains form the border with Guatemala, Mexico's neighbor to the south," he explained.

"Yet another country?" Shanni exclaimed. "Is there no end to the countries we must cross?"

"The countries extend all the way down Central America," Puco said. "And then there is another continent as large as North America, still farther south, that contains many countries."

Shanni shook her head, powerless to comprehend such a huge world, as Aurel and Mala clambered up the mound to see for themselves.

"There are ruins in several of the countries adjoining Mexico," Puco continued. "But the ones we are going to, called 'Palenque', are in Mexico, farther down the Rio Usumacinta."

"How long to reach them?"

"Maybe two days to the river. We find dugouts, or build a raft. Only one day down river to Palenque."

"And what do we find there?" Shanni asked.

"Ruins of an ancient city. According to Mayan tradition, that was the spiritual center of the empire at the height of its glory. Maybe there you will find the Center you are seeking. If not, maybe the Temple of the Inscriptions will provide a clue."

Mala and Aurel climbed down from the mound and Puco led away, pushing his way into the dense underbrush. They found remnants of an old stone road still holding back the foliage trying to reclaim it. The road aided their travel, and their pace quickened. They neared a deadfall, a tall tree felled by lightning many years ago, and now a rotting hulk of wood lying across their path. Puco waved them to a halt and approached the log, watching carefully where he stepped. He raised his machete and chopped down into the rotting bark. He laid the machete aside and began gathering something from the bark as the Huastecs gathered around, watching with interest.

Puco looked up, smiling, and presented his open hand to reveal a handful of winged insects lying inert. "Termites," he said. "Good for healing."

Puco found a depression in one of the stones along their path and emptied the termites into it. He seized a small pebble, and used it to grind the termites into a brown paste. He scooped the salve-like mixture into his hand and showed the Huastecs how to paint the scratches and sores on their exposed skin.

"We all look like we're camouflaged for jungle fighting," Caleb laughed, looking at the streaked faces gazing at him with dark eyes.

As they resumed travel, Caleb's curiosity got the better of him. "What does the termite salve do?"

Puco spoke out of the side of his mouth as he continued to watch where he stepped. "The bugs sweat a juice out of their foreheads. The juice keeps wounds from festering. Now you will see the redness go away from the cuts and scratches, and they will heal quickly."

So that's it, Caleb thought. *The juice somehow prevented infection, which could lead to gangrene and death in this climate.*

"A good thing to know," Caleb said.

"Yes," Puco agreed. "Mothers use it to heal their children."

Late in the afternoon of the second day they reached the river and pushed aside the foliage to look out on a broad sandbar that led down to the river. On the sandbar was a group of Indians, lounging loosely around a campfire where meat was roasting on a wooden spit. Dugout canoes were pulled up on the river bank behind them.

Caleb looked at Puco, who waved for silence as he studied the tall man who stood up to face them. *What is Tamil doing here?* He wondered. *And where are Pich and his men? I expected Pich, who would eliminate the foreigners. Now what do I do?*

Chapter 14

TAMIL WALKED UP to the group, leaving his men silent by the campfire. "We expected you sooner," he said to Puco in Mayan.

"We traveled slow. The foreigners are not used to the jungle."

Tamil chuckled, his eyes surveying the strangers, who stood streaked with Puco's termite medication. "Doesn't surprise me."

"Where's Pich? I expected him."

"Away on his own business. He'll join us later."

"Who's going to take care of the foreigners?"

"We'll wait for Pich."

Caleb stirred restlessly, glancing at Matal. They could not understand the language, and the conversation made him nervous. They were having to place too much reliance on Puco.

"What does he say?" Caleb asked Puco quietly, keeping his eyes on the stranger.

"This is Tamil, leader of the Indios in this region. He will assist us in getting to Palenque."

Tamil nodded slightly and responded in Spanish. "I am pleased to be of service. Come, we have prepared food."

The group walked down to the campfire and joined the others. After brief introductions they joined in the meal. Tamil's men appeared to be of the same stock as the campesinos, but dressed lightly in the jungle heat. There was an intensity about them, a silence that made Caleb nervous. *Maybe they feel the same about us,* Caleb thought. *They don't know us and probably cannot speak our language. I guess I'm being paranoid about Puco and Tamil. They could have spoken in their native tongue out of habit.*

The food cheered the travelers and Tamil's men seemed to relax. The men were solicitous and polite, but approached the Huastecs with awe. *What do they see in us?* Caleb wondered.

"We couldn't ask for better treatment," Caleb observed.

"And we appreciate it," Matal added.

"To my friends you are honored guests," Puco replied quickly. "They are here to help you to reach your destination."

"So what happens next?" Matal asked.

"We sleep here. Tomorrow we enter the boats and use the river to reach Palenque."

"How far?"

"Maybe a day if the river is clear. In places the river is low, causing drifts that block our passage. Then we have to take the canoes out of the water and go around. I think we will reach Palenque by tomorrow night."

"Tomorrow night!" Shanni repeated. "So near after all the months of travel!"

"I guess we'd better turn in and get a good night's sleep," Caleb suggested. "We've come far, and the heat has taken a lot out of us."

"I agree," Matal added. "We want to be fresh for tomorrow."

The Huastecs stirred from the campfire and made preparations for the night. They slung their hammocks among the trees at the edge of the jungle, and placed their machetes and rifles at hand as usual. Puco stayed with Tamil and the men near the fire.

Matal's hammock was near Caleb's, with the others grouped loosely up and down the tree line.

"Might be a good night to keep guard," Caleb suggested in the dim light as they completed their preparations. "We don't know what Puco and Tamil are up to."

Matal nodded agreement. "Shall I take the first watch?"

"Let me. I want to move around and observe them before they settle down. I'll awaken you to watch until morning."

"All right."

"I can help," Shanni whispered from her hammock nearby.

"Pass the word to the others. Make sure everyone has their pack and equipment handy in case we have to leave suddenly. Then get some sleep. If Tamil's men try anything, it will be much later after they figure we are sound asleep."

Caleb secured his machete to his belt, grasped his rifle and eased away down the sandbar in the dim light, taking his direction from the glow of the campfire several hundred yards away toward the river. The pale moon cast a dim glow over his surroundings as Caleb settled into the edge of the jungle, positioning himself where he could see movement between Tamil's camp and the trees bearing the hammocks. Weapons ready, he settled down to wait.

Aurel lay quietly in his hammock listening to the night sounds of the jungle. His body was tired but his mind was hyperactive, unable to settle down into sleep. They had come so far and were so close to the Center, but so much could still go wrong. He could sense the undercurrent of violence in Tamil's men. They came from a different culture. Who could guess their motives? Who was Tamil, who had apparently known where to meet them? And why had he appeared mysteriously out of the jungle to help them? Puco must have sent word to Tamil, but why? More and more Aurel had the feeling that he and his companions were not really in control of events surrounding their journey to find the Center. They were caught up in Puco's plans, whatever they were, and now Tamil had become a part of it. And who could guess what other plotters, unseen, might be attempting to control events? Aurel drew a deep breath and let it out. It bothered him that he could not identify the source of his uneasiness.

Shanni listened as her companions settled down to sleep. Mala was restless and Niki, who usually fell asleep instantly, was whispering to Ambria. But Aurel, Shanni could feel the force of his mind working; Aurel was wide awake. Adjusting her sight, Shanni could see his aura like a blue cocoon of energy seething in his hammock.

Shanni closed her eyes and quieted her mind, spreading her awareness out across the area like a fog, floating, wavering, sensing. Aurel felt her presence and adjusted his vibrations to perceive her awareness. *You feel the uneasiness, also?* Aurel projected silently.

Yes. Much has happened here in the past. I feel the shadows of violence and the screams of dying men. The strands of potentiality form a strong node at this place.

Tamil and his men?

Maybe. It is difficult to perceive the difference between something terrible that has happened in the past, and that which is about to happen.

Can we detect their intent?

There is a risk. Puco is a shaman, and we do not know Tamil's powers. They may be able to detect our probing and be warned.

Of our paranormal powers of sorcery, you mean?

Correct. We may cause them to attack us out of fear. It is better to wait and see what they do...Hold on!

Shanni's awareness detected a strong pulse of fear and recoiled. She regained control and pushed outward, adjusting her vibrations until she realized that the pulse had come from Puco, who had left the others and walked down by the river alone. He was mumbling to himself quietly, his mind twisting and turning as if drunk on the ayahuasca that unleashed his visions.

Puco's guard was down and Shanni seized the opportunity to tap into his perception. And she *saw* the Sentinel with Puco's eyes.

You must destroy them! She 'heard' the Sentinel order Puco, who stood trembling. Already you have delayed too long!

But I cannot do it alone! I expected Pich, but only Tamil appeared.

Use Tamil or whatever means. The Huastecs must be stopped!

65

Shanni felt Puco's terror and anguish as his mind attempted to form a reply. *But I...*, he began.

Silence! The Sentinel paused, and Shanni felt it adjusting its vibrations, probing. It had sensed her mental probe! Instantly she withdrew her awareness, returning to the fog-like seeking that had preceded contact with Puco's psyche.

Did you perceive it? She queried Aurel mentally.

Yes. Did we disengage in time?

We can only hope so. We must not forewarn the Sentinel!

Caleb was alerted by the shadowy movement as several dugouts appeared out of the gloom and nosed in to the sandbar. A tall warrior of fierce visage leapt out of the lead canoe, followed by his men. Tamil walked down to greet them as they unloaded packs and joined the others by the fire. The leader remained with Puco and Tamil down by the landing.

Using a fallen tree as cover, Caleb eased closer, moving within earshot as the men began to converse. "Why did you not act?" Puco hissed at Tamil..

"We must not act in haste. What if your prophesy is true? We must observe the strangers to determine what to do."

"But the Sentinel has ordered us to kill them! We must not delay!"

"Ordered you, perhaps. You take too much ayahuasca. As a result, it is difficult to judge which of your demands to follow."

"Let me make myself clear!" Puco hissed, his words cutting through the night air like a knife. "Kill them! And kill them now!"

Tamil turned to the tall warrior who had joined them. "Pich, did I not instruct you to protect the strangers, based on Puco's advice?" Pich, remaining silent, nodded his agreement.

So that is Pich, Caleb thought. *Senor Fuentes warned me about him. He is considered one of the most ruthless of the guerrilla leaders.*

Caleb gripped his rifle reflexively. Puco had helped them through the jungle, and Caleb had begun to trust him. Why the sudden change? Was it as Tamil hinted? Had Puco gone mad ingesting the ayahuasca?

"And if I refuse?"

"The Sentinels will hold you accountable, not me!"

Tamil paused, fear rising in him. He was not a shaman, but he feared the spirits. They could cause an ordinary person's death in a variety of ways.

"All right," he said doubtfully. "Pich, you and your men are released from my orders. You may follow Puco's instructions as you see fit. But a curse be upon Puco if we are wrong!"

Caleb pulled back silently, retracing his steps in the shadows to the hammocks where the Huastecs were sleeping. Shanni was awake when he approached her hammock. "We're in danger. Awaken the others while I get Matal and Ambria. Roll the hammocks and pull back into the jungle until we see what Pich does."

Shanni did not recognize the name, but did as asked. Now was not the time for questions. And now was no time to inform Caleb of her contact with the Sentinel.

Caleb returned with Matal and Ambria, with packs and rifles in hand. Caleb led the group down the river bank in the shadows, where they eased into the edge of the jungle, and knelt, rifles ready, to wait.

The minutes dragged as the wane moon reached its crest and began its descent to the west. Caleb heard yawns and occasional sighs as his tired companions tried to stay awake.

Was he wrong? Had he reacted too quickly? Maybe Pich intended to disobey Puco; to wait and size up the strangers before making up his own mind whether to act.

A glimmer of movement caught his eyes. He saw Pich rise silently from the camp, shaking his men and whispering instructions. Puco joined them, machete glistening in the moonlight as the men crept up the sandbar toward the jungle where the Huastecs had stretched their hammocks.

As the men neared the shadows, Pich ordered them forward with a sharp wave of his hand. The men charged into the foliage, slashing violently. The sound stopped abruptly, and Caleb could hear low cries of consternation as the men hurriedly conversed among themselves. The men turned and broke free from the jungle, running to the camp to retrieve rifles and ammunition, and hurry to the dugouts.

But Caleb and the Huastecs had circled the camp while the men were out of position, reaching the dugouts first. They threw their packs into the dugouts and pushed them out into the stream, clambering aboard quietly as their enemies emerged from the jungle to race back to camp. As Pich's men cleared camp and saw the dugouts easing out into the current, they threw up their rifles and fired quickly, without aiming.

Caleb and the others returned fire and four men fell as Pich's men dove for cover.

And then it was over as the dugouts carrying Caleb and the Huastecs disappeared into the shadows, picking up speed as the strong current of the Rio Usumacinta caught their dugouts and bore them strongly toward Palenque.

Sound travels far in the silent jungle. Many miles away, the faint echo of rifle shots reached the ears of Mayapan and he awakened, sensing the sudden hush in the night. Softly to himself he spoke,

"Puco hates,
Tamil waits,
And Pich came undone.
Man strives, to stay alive
And the foreigners come!"

Now all will be fulfilled, he thought as he smiled and turned to go back to sleep.

Chapter 15

Huntal tried to hide his uneasiness as he entered the presence of Popol Vuh in the ornate chamber of the pyramid. Everything had been going well despite the remarkable resistance of the psychics Stone, Shanni and Aurel. Shanni had almost fallen. With her gone, Stone would abandon the journey and Aurel could not succeed alone. The remainder of the Huastecs were of no interest to the Sentinels, for they could not *see* the Center without the aid of the psychics.

Popol was in an ill mood. Huntal sensed the controlled anger as Popol turned and walked toward him across the stone chamber.

"We had almost succeeded," Popol bit out. "Humans are such unpredictable weaklings. Who could have predicted that Shanni would rally at the last moment, and exile Nerial instead of Caleb?"

"You cannot predict human behavior," Huntal agreed. "They cannot control themselves, and therefore cannot be controlled."

"Pushed, prodded, threatened, and cajoled, but not controlled," Popol added. "And now even Puco fails us!"

"I had not heard," Huntal responded cautiously.

"Maybe you should follow events more closely!" Popol bit out. Huntal remained silent, ignoring the insult, as Popol continued. "Last night I had to threaten Puco to get him to act. Then he relied on Pich and his men, who botched the job and allowed the Huastecs to escape!"

Huntal thought quickly, hiding his emotions and weighing options. He and Popol had tried everything and nothing had quite worked. They were running out of alternatives.

"Tupac tried to stop them in the physical world and failed, paying with his life. Choctyl tried to stop them in the spirit world, and he's dead. Maybe there is only one thing left to try," Huntal said.

"And what might that be?" Popul asked.

"Let them think they have succeeded," Huntal answered.

"What?" Popol's voice was incredulous.

"Create a 'Center' for them to find at one of the many ruins lying in the jungle. When they realize the Center exists only in their minds, their quest will be finished and they will go home."

"But what if they discover the real Center?"

"How can they? It is too well hidden, phase-shifted from view in the world of ordinary reality. A human can stand right on the site and not see it."

"Even Puco does not know how to see it. He has let the ayahuasca consume him. Tonah, who somehow possessed the knowledge of the Ancients, could have found it, but he is dead."

Popol let out a sigh of relief. "Perhaps you are right. We're wearing them down. Only a few are left. Let them find a mirage and go home."

"Do we know if Puco and Tamil were injured during the Huastecs' escape?"

"They were not."

"Then give them time. They have been unleashed, and Pich will surely kill the Huastecs now that they have bested him."

"Good. I want them all dead, the Huastecs and the Anglo."

"Even if they abandon the search, and it no longer matters?"

"It will always matter to me!"

Huntal lowered his eyes, nodding with respect as he backed away from Popol Vuh. Popol's personal animosity was a disturbing turn of events. A Sentinel was trained never to become emotional or to attach to events in the physical world. It was a dangerous practice to become emotionally involved with human affairs. Revenge and hate could be tracked by the Guardians, and they only chose totally detached Sentinels to promote to the next level of existence!

THE RIVER CHANNELS alternated between fast-moving rapids and calm stretches where the water spread out, shallow and torpid, giving the tired, sleepless Huastecs welcome moments of rest.

"They will come after us," Mala said, holding her paddle out of the water to rest.

"Maybe we'll travel faster on the river, and they'll give up." Matal responded. He and Ambria were in one dugout; the others were in the adjacent boat, traveling in tandem down the river.

"Likely they'll go back to their village for canoes," Matal added. "Now they know we're aware of their intent, and they'll be circumspect about facing our rifles."

"So what do we do?" Mala asked.

"I say we go on to Palenque."

"But that's the first place they'll look for us!"

"This is their jungle. They'll know where we are anyplace we go. They can pick the time and place to catch us on the way out."

"Meanwhile, we have to eat and we're low on supplies," Aurel observed.

"I have my bow and arrows; I can hunt silently." Matal answered. "One kill and we can smoke enough meat to last awhile."

"More monkey meat, I suppose!" Mala wrinkled her nose in disgust.

"It will taste better the hungrier you get." Matal retorted.

"I didn't see you first in line when Puco roasted his kill." Mala eyes glinted.

Matal smiled and Ambria suppressed a chuckle. *That's good,* Caleb thought, observing the interchange as he paddled silently. *Some of the tension is easing. We'll eat and rest, and then be able to face whatever lies ahead.*

They beached the canoes on a shallow portion of the river bank to rest in the heat of the day. They ate a light meal from the supply in their packs and then rotated guard duty as they napped to make up for the sleepless night.

Matal was on guard duty up on the river bank when the herd of javalinas approached to drink. The pig-like animals trotted to the water's edge and dropped their snouts to drink. Matal raised his bow and waited as the javalinas finished drinking and turned to trot back up the bank. As they came within range, Matal released the arrow. One of the javalinas squealed, twisting to snap at the embedded arrow as the herd broke wildly for the shelter of the foliage.

The wounded animal lost its footing as it scrambled to get away. Matal rushed forward to dispatch it with a single blow of his machete. *Gruesome work,* he thought. *But in the jungle, one does what is necessary to eat, and to survive.*

The disturbance awakened the others who came clambering up the river bank, rifles in hand, to approach Matal, who stood holding the wild pig by its hind feet. "Food!" he said proudly. "Enough to last for a week!"

Near sundown a massive stone pyramid came into view on a plain that extended back from the river. The plain terminated behind a row of ruins along a ridge of hills and tree-covered mounds. Other stone ruins appeared as the current continued to carry them along the low plain that extended out of sight along the river. The ruins were almost hidden by the trees that had taken root on their stone terraces, splitting the rocks in the weathered masonry.

They began searching for a place to land the canoes as stone edifices continued to appear, extending as far as they could see in the distance.

"Oh, Caleb!" Shanni exclaimed. "It is magnificent! I expected a temple, or maybe two or three pyramids, but this goes on for miles, like a city!"

"And this is only what we can see from the river." Caleb agreed. "Perhaps there is much more to it when we climb up on one of the pyramids and look around."

The mouth of a smaller stream appeared, emptying into the Usumacinta and they turned into it, paddling upstream against the gentle current. The bank of the stream led to more ruins where it smoothed out into the surrounding plain. They nudged the canoes to shore and stepped out onto the grassy surface and looked around in awe.

They were in the heart of a great city built of stone pyramids that lined the smaller river. Stone causeways and roads ran along both sides of the ruins, connecting them to the broad plaza in the center of the plain. The ground rose beyond the plain to low hills to the north, covered with tropical rain forest.

"It is breathtaking!" Ambria breathed.

"This is what we are looking for!" Shanni exclaimed. "I can feel Power here!"

"But is it the Center that we seek?" Aurel questioned. "Such an immense place would retain residual energy from the many people who once lived here."

"We'll see," Caleb answered. "At least we're here at last. We can take the time we need to explore."

The sound of paddles slapping the water caught their attention and they turned to see Tamil approaching alone in a dugout canoe. He beached the canoe among the others on the river bank and walked up, holding his empty hands high.

He stopped as Caleb and the others raised their rifles. "I come in peace," he said. "I was not part of the attack. I have come to help."

"Why should we trust you?" Matal demanded.

"Because I believe in the prophesy that you are sent to help us restore the kingdom of the Maya."

Matal looked uncertainly at Shanni. "What's this all about?"

"Explain yourself," Shanni responded to Tamil.

"Puco told us weeks ago that strangers came who are descendants of our ancestors. There is a prophecy that such strangers will be able to unlock the ancient knowledge and lead us to victory over our oppressors. I believe that you are the people in the prophesy."

"Why?"

"Do you not descend from the Maya? Is that not why you return to us?'

Shanni turned and hurriedly conferred with Matal, Caleb and the others. "Apparently he or someone he trusts knows about Power. How else could he know why we're here?"

"Still, I don't trust him," Matal retorted. "He stood by while Pich attacked us."

"How could I intervene?" Tamil responded, overhearing their conversation. "I would be of no use to you dead, and they would have turned on me if I tried to help."

"So how did you get here? Did they just let you come to help us?"

"I often travel alone, contacting the seer Mayapan who lives in the ruins. No one knew where I was going when I left Pich and Puco this morning."

"How do we know they're not following you now, preparing to attack?"

"I believe the prophesy, and am here to help you. Puco is confused, and influencing Pich. If they come, you are better off if I am here to help you than you are alone. If I were with them, I would not have come to you alone and defenseless."

"What do you think?" Matal asked Caleb.

"I'd rather have him with us where we can watch him, than in the jungle with the others."

Matal nodded. "Come on up," he called to Tamil. "But you'll understand you've got to work to earn our trust."

"I understand," Tamil agreed. "You will see that I am only here to help you."

Tamil led away, pointing out the major buildings. "That is the north group." He pointed to a long stone edifice abutting a square pyramid. "The pyramid is called the 'Temple of the Court'. The open plaza between the temple and the Otulun, the small river, is the ball court. The main building in front of us is the Palace, and to its left is the Temple of the Inscriptions. The Otulun runs northward through the center of this complex, but there are many other ruins scattered along the Usumacinta, which runs roughly northwest."

"How far do the buildings extend?" Mala asked.

"Eight, maybe ten kilometers."

Caleb calculated quickly. Five to six miles! They would be here awhile sorting out Palenque!

The Huastecs retrieved their packs and followed Tamil across the ball court to the temple. The adjacent building had arcades along the front, supporting second and third stories reached by broad stone staircases.

"I suggest we camp here," Tamil said. "We'll be protected from the weather for a change. It rains every day this time of year, usually in the late afternoon."

Tamil gathered large stones and placed them in a circle just off the edge of the stone floor of the Palace. He started a fire and helped the Huastecs store their gear. "If you wish, after we eat I will show you the buildings."

Tamil retrieved a tin pan left by pilgrims and boiled water for coffee while Matal cut saplings and fashioned a wooden spit to roast the javalina. As they ate, Tamil sliced strips of meat and placed them to smoke into pork jerky. The smoked meat would be portable, and would keep for weeks.

They ate quietly, lost in thought, as reality set in. After all the days and weeks of anticipation, they had arrived to the reality of an abandoned stone city wasting away in the jungle. The letdown was palpable, Shanni knew. But what had they expected?

The predicted afternoon shower arrived after they had eaten, cooling the air and leaving a humid closeness that further dampened their spirits. As the rain tapered off to a drizzle, they ventured forth to explore the ruins.

They walked past the enormous man-made platform of stone and earth that spread along the Palace for hundreds of feet, and made their way to the Temple of the Inscriptions. They climbed the broad, stone stairs that led steeply up the side of the Temple to the stone shrine perched at the top, its open rooms supported by massive columns.

The stone floor had been polished smooth by countless feet as priests carried out the rituals necessary to maintain the crops and the lives of the Maya.

"What's this?" Niki asked, pointing to the waist-high table of stone in the center of the room

"That is the sacrificial altar," Tamil replied.

"Sacrificial?" Mala asked.

"Yes. Here the sacrifices were made to the 'chaakob', the rain gods. The sacrifices were necessary to maintain the *tamen*, the harmony with heaven."

"What did they sacrifice? Animals?" Mala continued, studying the dark patina on the surface of the smooth stone.

"The chief of the rain gods, Kunu-chaak, was very thirsty. He had to be propitiated with human blood, or he would refuse to bring the rains."

"Human? You mean that humans were killed here? Sacrificed on this altar?"

Tamil nodded. "This is where it was done."

The Huastecs looked at each other, unbelieving. Shanni shuddered, feeling the ghosts of people who had died here.

"At first slaves were used, men captured in battles with other tribes. But as Kunu-chaak became more thirsty, people were chosen from the populace. For the people chosen, and their families, it was a great honor. The chosen ones were feted here on earth and then passed directly to paradise upon death."

"So they volunteered?" Mala's voice was doubtful.

"They were chosen."

"By whom?"

"By the priests. The priests controlled everything."

Shanni's eyes were scanning the carved reliefs on the stone walls of the chamber, and fell on a representation of the sacrifice itself, showing a priest wielding a sharp instrument as other priests held the victim immobile on the stone slab. She gasped, pointing at the scene as the others crowded around to see it more clearly in the shadows.

"By the gods!" Matal muttered, as he comprehended the scene showing the priest ripping the heart out of the chest of the victim.

"Is it true?" Mala asked, looking at Tamil.

"It is true," Tamil responded quickly, explaining. "Kunu-chaak demanded fresh blood, with the heart still beating."

Shanni felt a wave of nausea sweep over her and she turned to walk outside, gasping for air. Caleb came up behind and took her arm to steady her.

"This is all wrong!" she said, taking deep breaths. "We came expecting to find wisdom; the knowledge of the ancients. But something terrible happened here; something so terrible that it destroyed our ancestors!"

They turned and followed Tamil and the others as Tamil pointed out the stucco figures on the six pillars that supported the entrances to the temple. Hundreds of glyphs were chiseled into the walls leading to the last chamber in the rear.

"These are the ancient writings," Tamil said. "Regrettably, their meaning has long since been lost."

Dusk had fallen as they made their way back across the meadow to their campsite. They were walking single file, as Shanni dropped back beside Caleb. "When I was a child, Tonah and I played a game with wooden blocks he had carved. To play the game, I was required to memorize the symbols on the blocks and match them with words in the Spanish alphabet. It was only a game in which he gave me rewards, small treats, when I got the words right."

"I'm not sure I'm following you," Caleb said.

"Those symbols, the ones on the wall of the temple, are the same as the ones on Tonah's blocks. He was teaching me how to translate those glyphs!"

Chapter 16

CRESCENCIO POOT, THE first general of the Cruzob, stood in the doorway of his thatched dwelling and surveyed Chan Santa Cruz, the village hidden deep in the rain forest of Quintana Roo. He was tall, and very dark-skinned, the result of the melting pot of races that had encroached on the Mayan Indios of the Yucatan.

In his physical prime, Crescencio was an imposing figure, his muscles moving smoothly as he strode out onto the earthen plaza, his keen gaze sweeping over the Indios gathered outside the Balam Na, the "house of the priest", that contained the Speaking Cross of the Cruzob. He looked around for his second-in-command, Valencio Cen. The Speaking Cross had passed over Cen for promotion to General because of his violent nature when Bonifacio Novelo had died. Now Crescencio knew that he had to keep a close eye on Cen, for any man who had killed his own two sons was not to be trusted.

Still, Cen had his uses. The Maya had been at war with the *dzul*, the foreign whites from Spain who had invaded the Mayan lands since 1848, when the Caste War of the Yucatan had commenced with the sacking of Valladolid. In the intervening years, the conflict had settled into a war of attrition in which neither side had been able to achieve victory. Now the Cruzob, the "Followers of the Cross", had retreated deep into the rain forest where they could resupply themselves with guns and ammunition from the British colony of Belize to the south. He needed Cen to lead the raids that killed the hated dzul.

Crescencio passed by the assembled worshipers and entered the church. The "Talking Cross" was housed behind a tapestry that hung across one end of the long room. Only Crescencio, Cen, and the other leaders were permitted to hear the Cross's edicts which they in turn communicated to the villagers as they saw fit. Such was the people's belief that thousands of the Mayan men had volunteered to be trained as soldiers in the holy war. Their primary weapon was the machete, effective in close-quarter fighting against single shot muzzle loading rifles.

Cen stood near the curtain and watched Crescencio steadily as he approached. Several other generals and religious leaders bowed with respect as he approached.

"Your arrival is propitious," Cen greeted, parting the curtain for Crescencio to enter, followed by Cen and the others. "We have news from the West, and the Cross is preparing to speak."

They assembled in a semicircle in front of a wooden cross set into a creche in the wall of the building. A metal barrel set in the wall behind the cross created an echo chamber to amplify the words when the cross spoke. Numerous candles flickering softly on a high table cast flickering shadows over the savage visages that stared upward in anticipation.

The santos, or priest, bowed before the Cross and offered a rapid prayer and then stepped back to rejoin the group. A low hum that rose to become a voice reciting a mantra began to emanate from the echo chamber. It stopped suddenly, leaving a ringing in the ears of the assemblage in the sudden silence.

"In the times of the Ancient Ones," the voice of the Cross spoke sonorously across the room, focusing their attention, "The *Chilam Balam*, the Prophet of God, left us their ancient wisdom in the hieroglyphic codices which were later translated by the sages, and handed down to us for our well-being. The Chilam Balam prophesied that one day strangers would come to lead our people out of bondage and drive the invaders of our lands into the sea."

Crescencio glanced at Cen, who stood impassively, eyes focused on the Cross. Crescencio remembered the legend well. In fact, his predecessor had prayed for the delivery to come and help them break the stalemate of the caste war, the years of frustrating attrition that was slowly strangling the Mayan race. *Was he to be the one?* Crescencio thought, his pulse quickening. *Was it his destiny to be the general supported by the strangers, the prophesied ones, who restored the greatness of the Maya after their long twilight of bondage and abuse?*

"Now strangers have come from afar, Indios who have great powers. They have fought their way through many races, many hostile *dzul*, or foreigners, to arrive unharmed. You must bring them here to lead us. With their help, the victory of our cause is assured!"

The low hum of the mantra resumed, fading into silence.

"The Cross has spoken," the santos said softly. "Let us go."

They turned and filed out into the room outside the curtain and down the narrow aisle to exit the building. Crescencio and Cen strode purposely to Crescencio's headquarters across the plaza and went inside.

Crescencio turned to Cen. "Take your best men and the runner who brought the news. Go to the strangers and bring them here. They are not to be harmed."

"What if the strangers resist?"

"Persuade them. Explain who we are and their importance to our cause. Treat them with deference."

"I will try, but I may have to bring them by force in the end."

"No. They must choose to come. We don't yet know who we are dealing with. If they are the prophesied ones, attempting to force them could cause them to turn on you. Do you dare risk that?"

Cen's dark eyes flashed. He was impetuous, with a violent temper, but even he saw the wisdom of Crescencio's words. He would wait until he knew more about these strangers, and then he would decide for himself what to do.

"It will be as you say," he replied shortly and turned to walk out of the room.

Outside the Balam Na, one of the Indios returned from the interior and stood quietly whispering to the group that gathered around her. "The Cross spoke of strangers who are approaching, sent by the gods to liberate us. The prophesy of the Chilam Balam is about to be fulfilled!"

The word spread like wildfire through the village and soon young men were running to nearby villages to spread the good news. At last all their sacrifice and suffering at the hands of the dzul would come to an end. The Maya would regain their lands and rebuild their great civilization.

The time had come for all tribes to unite in holy war, the armageddon of the whites.

Chapter 17

CALEB CLIMBED THE last stone step to the top of the pyramid and halted to catch his breath. He gazed down at the foliage that had gained a foothold on the ancient stone terraces. The mounds, covered with trees, led off in berms of green to the horizon.

He raised his gaze to look out across the ball court to the Palace, still massive and white despite the trees that sprouted from its roof. Dominating the skyline to the west stood a verdant peak, shrouded in mist. The Rio Otulun flowed silently, dividing the complex of pyramids as it wound its way to join the Rio Usumacinta to the south.

The scene was like something out of a fairytale, a mystical place of children's books, and yet it was real.

Caleb shook his head in awe. Tamil had said the complex went on for kilometers; an advanced civilization with tens of thousands of people must have worked together to build and maintain such a city! What had happened to bring it all to ruin? And what unknown mission had brought the Huastecs, a remnant of this mighty race, back home at this time in their history?

Past the Palace he saw Shanni in the shadows accompanied by Ambria and Iika as she studiously wrote notes, deciphering the inscriptions. The others had gone with Tamil to explore the pyramids farther down the Otulun, the temples he called the "House of the Sun", and farther on, "Jaguar" and "Foliated Cross."

We could spend weeks here, even months and years, Caleb thought. *And what would we accomplish?* It was clear that the people of the Center, wherever it had been, were dead. These ruins bore silent witness to a once-mighty race that had long since vanished. After all they had suffered to get here, they had found only ruins. Even in their success they had failed. Where did they go from here?

Shanni had been his wife in name only since his unfortunate liaison with Nerial. Caleb had admitted his mistake and worked to restore his relationship with Shanni. She had been civil as she became more and more distant. She seemed to be withdrawing into a world of her own. Caleb's stomach tightened as bitterness welled in his throat. His mission was done. He had stuck by the Huastecs and helped them get through. The time had come for

Shanni and him to return to his ranch in Colorado as they had planned. Would Shanni go with him now?

The rainy season was approaching here in the lowlands and they were surrounded by enemies. Shanni must decide, and decide soon.

Caleb turned and walked into the first open chamber of the temple perched on top of the pyramid. Hieroglyphics graced the stone walls, enhanced by faded colors of stucco figurines. Sunlight filtered through the open portals as he walked through the middle chamber into the third, its doorways open to the east.

A stone altar reflected sunlight from obsidian knives lying long unused amid dark stains of dried blood left from sacrifices. What had led to such madness? How had such a highly integrated, civilized people come to practice such barbarity?

And then Caleb caught himself. Who was he to judge? Was his world any different? Different ways, perhaps, and less ritualized, but the killing was just as barbaric.

He walked around the temple and saw Tamil and the others returning in the distance. They had watched Tamil closely, but grudgingly had come to trust him. Whatever the confusion at the sandbar, Tamil had been only helpful since joining them. With a last glance around, Caleb began his descent of the steep stone steps leading down from the top of the pyramid.

Shanni seemed subdued as she, Ambria, and Iika joined the others in the shade of the Palace as they ate their noonday meal.

"How did it go?" Matal asked, looking up.

"All those carvings are immensely complex," Ambria answered, thinly-veiled excitement in her voice. "And there is evidence of colors on the carvings, now fading away. The temple must have contained glorious mosaics of color when they were in use!"

"And now the forest is reclaiming them," Aurel added. "I wonder how long it has been?

"A long time," Tamil answered. "Hundreds of years."

"What happened to make such a civilization fall?" Caleb asked.

Tamil hesitated. "There is a gap, a period of darkness in our history. The elders were forbidden to discuss the 'End Time', as it came to be known. As a result, the knowledge was not passed down, and was lost. Now we know only the legends which speak of war, pestilence, and starvation. Only those who returned to the old ways of subsistence farming, far from the cities, survived."

"But they left the carvings," Shanni interjected. "Perhaps they contain the history of what happened."

"Perhaps," Tamil agreed. "Perhaps you can deduce their meaning, an ability lost to my people."

Shanni looked at Caleb with tired eyes. "It could take years. Their language is a mixture of phonetics and ideograms. There were more than three hundred basic building blocks, equivalent to the Spanish alphabet, in their written language. In addition, they wrote in a code that changes the meaning for those of different classes such as the rulers and priests, and perhaps others we do not know about."

"A code?" Caleb questioned. "What kind of code?"

"For example, they wrote all their numbers using three basic symbols, the 'zero', represented by an ideogram of the *pop*, or sacred mat knelt on by kings and used as a throne. The 'one' is represented by a hollow dot, or circle, and the 'five' by a horizontal bar. Therefore any number could be made by combining these symbols. However, each word ideogram could have several meanings depending upon context. For example, the ideogram for 'jaguar' can also mean 'hunter', and also 'power', according to the symbols in the game Tonah taught me as a child. Now I can see its importance."

"This is all too deep for me!" Matal retorted, attempting to follow Shanni's explanation. "I don't even know how to write!"

"Nor do any of us," Iika chimed in. "We only speak Spanish because Tonah insisted that it be part of our schooling, which he called 'games'."

"He was trying to impart learning to us as children by incorporating it into games," Aurel observed. "Now I see the wisdom of his efforts."

"But I still fail to see the point," Ambria objected. "What's the value of writing knowledge down if it can be misinterpreted and therefore misunderstood?"

"It appears that the ancient scribes were constrained to write that which was pleasing to their rulers and priests, while hiding deeper secrets in code for those who came afterwards."

"That was a lot of effort, with a risk that no one would ever figure it out," Caleb said, shaking his head. "What would be the point of doing it?"

"Maybe there was something so important to convey that it was worth the effort," Aurel observed. "Tamil, what do you think?"

"We have only our legends which prophesy that at the proper time all will be revealed."

Aurel swept his arm out and around, encompassing the temples in their surroundings. "This is a place of Power. The spirits of the people who inhabited this place create a sense of foreboding. I can feel that something terrible happened here. We must proceed with caution. The knowledge that we tap into may be very dangerous. That may be why the Ancients took pains to hide it so well."

"But how will we know until we access it?" Matal answered. "And then it may be too late!"

"I will spirit-walk into the other world, the world of nonordinary reality, and seek guidance. Maybe then we will know how to proceed," Aurel said.

"You are a shaman?" Tamil asked quickly.

"I have completed my apprenticeship," Aurel affirmed. "Does that concern you?"

"These forests are inhabited by Cruzob, followers of the 'Speaking Cross', and sooner or later they will come for us. It is best that they do not know that you are a shaman."

Aurel glanced at Caleb, who remained impassive. *We must find out what we are facing soon,* Aurel thought. *In both worlds!* What had they stumbled into: And where did Tamil fit into the node of causality? Could Tamil be trusted, or was he, like Puco, under the control of the Sentinels?

"It will be as you say," Aurel assured Tamil. "And your caution is appreciated."

Tamil nodded and turned his gaze to the horizon, unseeing. *Was Tamil afraid?* Caleb wondered. *Or simple carrying out his mission; a mission that could lead them into mortal danger.*

Chapter 18

THE RAIN MADE the time drag, and slowed their progress in examining the ruins. Caleb watched from the stone portal as Shanni, Iika and Aurel followed Tamil back to the Temple of the Inscriptions. Shanni had become totally absorbed in her work, leaving no time for Caleb to broach the subject of their relationship. Despite sharing the same camp, they had become strangers.

Shaking off his despondency, Caleb spoke to Matal, who was mending equipment nearby. "I'm uneasy. We could be attacked anytime out of the jungle."

"I also feel vulnerable, but Tamil seems to have no concern."

"That's part of my uneasiness. It is strange that Pich and his men have not shown up by now."

"If they had come, they would have attacked." Matal said.

"Something strange was happening that night on the river. I overheard Puco goading them to attack, yet Tamil resisted. Pich just wanted to kill us. I could see it in his eyes," Caleb said.

"Maybe Tamil doesn't report to Puco." Matal observed.

"I have a feeling that we're caught up in a bigger struggle, one we don't understand."

"Maybe we can get some insight from Shanni's work. How is she progressing?"

"Slowly, with a great deal of frustration. The 'surface' translation went quickly, consisting mainly of historical events and astronomical observations. But the deeper meaning, the real translation by necessity is obscure, taking a lot of intuition. The writers had to outsmart the priests, who were not fools. If the priests had even suspected, the hieroglyphics would have been destroyed and the scribes killed."

"Who could have come up with the idea to code the hieroglyphics and implement it without getting caught?" Matal asked.

"Shanni believes that only a priest, or a small group of priests, had the knowledge and skill to devise the code. Only they had the authority to oversee the craftsmen carving the glyphs."

"But why would they take the risk?"

"Shanni's initial translations indicate a few of the priests were horrified by the wrong turn toward human sacrifice and bloodletting the priesthood had made, but were powerless to stop it. To protest openly would have been instant death. Somehow they hoped to absolve themselves from blame by recording the truth."

"What difference would it make now, far in their future?"

"A good question. Maybe none, but they seemed to think it was worth the effort and the risk. They jeopardized their lives to pass on some principle, something key that they had learned, not knowing if it would ever be found, let alone understood."

Matal shook his head. "Hundreds of years ago! And yet they reach out to us across the centuries. Who could look so far ahead?"

"Clearly they were an advanced people. They studied the stars, calculated and predicted cosmic events, and built these magnificent stone pyramids and monuments. Something cataclysmic would have been required to end it all so suddenly."

"What if Shanni finds the secret? What then?" Matal asked.

Caleb paused. Busy with their day-to-day struggles, he had not stopped to think about how discovery of the information might change them and their mission. What would Shanni do with the secret if she found it? What might it require her to do?

He felt a cold chill as realization struck him. That was the reason behind the attacks by the Sentinels in the world of nonordinary reality! The Sentinels were left behind to guard the past to keep the present course of history in place. If Shanni discovered the secret, the Sentinels would try to kill her and all of them to keep it buried in the past! He must warn Shanni as soon as she returned from the day's work at the pyramids.

"We may have waited too long," Matal said, rising to point across the clearing to the edge of the jungle. Caleb followed his gesture to see Indians emerging silently, to pause along the tree line. They were clad in loincloths and decorative feathers, their black hair held back by cloth headbands. In their hands they held shotguns. The leader, a dark muscular man of fierce visage stepped forward into the sunlight and waited.

Caleb reached for his rifle and turned his gaze to the pyramid where Tamil was clambering down to walk out to the strangers. Shanni and the others were hurrying back to camp.

"If Tamil is with them..." Matal left his suspicion unspoken.

"If he is, we won't know until it is too late," Caleb finished.

Shanni and the others arrived at camp, breathless from their haste. "Tamil knows them," she gasped. "He told us to return to camp and wait. Whatever we do, we are not to fire our weapons! Tamil's orders!"

Matal glanced at Caleb, his face clouding. So Tamil was giving the orders now!

"We'll wait and see what happens," Caleb agreed. "We wouldn't fire anyway unless they threaten us. But be ready; if they make a move against us we'll defend ourselves, Tamil or no Tamil!"

Matal nodded. "We don't know who to trust, so we better trust ourselves."

Tamil and the leader of the Indians turned and walked toward the camp. "It's all right," Tamil called out, "I know this man. He means us no harm. He only wants to talk with us."

The leader walked confidently, his muscular body striding smoothly across the open meadow. He smiled, showing strong white teeth, as he and Tamil neared the waiting Huastecs. He raised his hand in a gesture of peace, and stopped. "You have nothing to fear," he spoke in Spanish. "We come on a mission of peace. If it were otherwise, would we have shown ourselves?"

His words rang true, Caleb thought, easing his grip on his rifle. "About that shotgun."

The man laughed and emptied the weapon, handing it to Tamil for safekeeping. He seemed supremely confident, at ease and in control of the situation. But he was a warrior and Caleb sensed that he could turn quickly into a dangerous adversary.

"All right," Matal called out. "Come on up."

Tamil and the man walked into camp and Tamil made the introductions. "This is Crescencio Poot, war general and leader of the Cruzob, the followers of the Speaking Cross. He brings greetings from the *tatiche*, as Valencio Cen's followers are known, and welcomes you to their land."

"We greet all who come in peace," Matal responded. "I am leader of the Huastecs, although we are all equal and make decisions as a group."

"An interesting approach," Crescencio answered. "Perhaps we can learn much from each other."

Matal went around the circle of Huastecs, introducing each by name. When he reached Shanni, Crescencio's eyes widened. "Chah-neh!" He repeated, glancing at Tamil.

"Shan-ni," Tamil quickly corrected. Crescencio nodded slightly and masked his reaction with a professional smile as Matal continued the introductions. Crescencio turned and called out to his men, who began filing over to the pyramid across the plaza and laid down their weapons. Unarmed, they approached the camp and joined Tamil in preparing a meal. They brought corn meal, fruit and a freshly killed deer which they soon had roasting on a wooden spit. *Crescencio clearly does things with style*, Caleb thought. *Compared to what we've been eating, this is a banquet.*

The tension eased as they ate. Crescencio en answered the Huastecs' questions while his men sat apart, listening and occasionally talking among themselves. Crescencio enjoyed his meal, seeming in no hurry to get to the point, the real reason he was here. Only as they neared the end of the meal did Crescencio ease into questions of his own. "You have come far?" he asked casually.

"We came from the United State, down through Mexico," Matal responded.

"Such a long journey!" Crescencio said. "Something of great importance must have brought you here."

"Yes." Matal answered.

Crescencio noticed the slight, for he had expected Matal to elaborate. He smiled and waved his arm in an expansive gesture. "I do not mean to be inquisitive," he said. "Your business is your business. I had only hoped to be of service to you. Clearly if you came so far, your mission must be of great importance."

"What do you know of these?" Caleb broke in, pointing to the stone pyramids across the plaza.

"The stone buildings?" Crescencio looked puzzled. "They were built by the Ancients, and have been here since before our memory."

"Your people, your ancestors I mean?"

"Yes. Our ancestors built these temples and many others scattered throughout our land."

"What happened to them?"

"The cities fell, and the people returned to the land. To this day we raise the corn and hunt game. That is how we live."

"And what of the ancient knowledge?"

"It is lost. No one lives who remembers the ancient ways."

"What about the inscriptions?" Shanni asked, "Can anyone read the writings?"

"No longer. There were a few but they are all dead now. One who knew how to read them shared his knowledge with a priest, Father Diego de Landa, before he died, and Father Landa wrote it all down. There were books of ancient writings captured on bark paper and bound with leather, but after Father Landa found and examined them, he cast them into the fire."

"Burned them? Destroyed them?" Shanni burst out.

"Yes."

"But why?"

"He said they were of the devil. The Spanish did many strange things."

"So the knowledge in those books is lost forever," Shanni's concluded with dismay.

"One of our people who was educated by the priests, managed to capture some of the writing in the books of *Chilam Balam*. They contain some of the words of the Jaguar Priests, the Ancient Ones who led the Mayan priesthood. That is all that we have left."

Shanni remained silent, realizing what treasure of ancient knowledge might have been lost.

"What's done is done," Matal, the practical one, interjected. "You've been forthright with us, which I appreciate, so I'll respond to your question. We believe that our ancestors came from here to settle in our homeland in what is now called the United States. What is left of our people, about a hundred families, was forced out by drought, seeking to travel here and reunite with the Mayas. Many of us were killed, and others turned back."

"So you come seeking land on which to live?"

"We are seeking a place to settle and rebuild. We would pay for the land and send for our people to join us."

"In that case we can help you," Crescencio replied. "I come to you with an invitation from Valencio Cen, our supreme leader. He invites you to visit him at Chan Santa Cruz, the capital of the cruzob people, and the home of the *Balam Na*, the sanctuary of the Speaking Cross."

"How far?"

"Several days' travel to the east."

"We must think on it, and discuss it among ourselves," Matal hedged.

"Of course," Crescencio replied. "My men and I will be more comfortable camping in the forest tonight. We will return in the morning for your answer."

Matal nodded and Crescencio rose to his feet. Tamil followed as he rejoined his men. The group walked to the edge of the clearing and disappeared into the forest. After a few moments Tamil reappeared and rejoined Caleb and the Huastecs.

"Can we trust Crescencio?" Caleb asked Tamil, point-blank.

"Yes. He is under strict orders from Valencio Cen not to harm you. Cen wishes you to join him at Chan Santa Cruz so that he can help you with your mission and continue to protect you."

"Protect us from what?"

"There are other tribes of Maya not under his control. If they know that you are under his protections, they are less likely to attack."

"What about Puco, and Pich?"

"I think Puco is harmless. Pich and his followers are renegades, under no one's control."

"What if we choose not to go with Crescencio?"

"It would be an insult to Valencio Poot to refuse his hospitality and protection."

Caleb gazed at the faces of his compatriots around the campfire. There were so many unknowns. He did not know the people, nor their motivations. He only knew that the Huastecs were tired, and they had to make their decision tonight.

Chapter 19

MAYAPAN EMERGED FROM the cave and added willow bark to the water heating in a metal pot to make tea. He sat, staring dreamily at the flames of the campfire, his mind concentrating on the images dancing across the ether in the world of nonordinary reality.

He saw the Huastecs facing Tamil and Crescencio, engaged in conversation that he could not hear. He did not need to know what was said for he already knew what needed to be said. At last the prophesy was being fulfilled and with it a new dawn was breaking for the Mayan people, who had suffered greatly for the sins of their forefathers.

Mayapan thought, *Those who need to know, know.*
Others need not know.
For knowledge can be a dangerous thing -
Without wisdom, become corrupted -
And lead to horrible things.

Mayapan knew that he had a role to play in the unfolding, and Power would reveal it to him at the proper time. He had but to wait and stay attuned to the ripples in the matrix of the unfolding world of reality.

"THEN WE'RE AGREED," Matal summed up the lengthy discussion that had kept him and the others up late. Tamil had excused himself and gone across the plaza to sleep, leaving Caleb and the Huastecs to make their decision in private.

"We'll all go," he continued. "We all stay together."

Each nodded agreement as he swung his gaze around the circle of faces illuminated by the firelight. Each had misgivings, but they knew they had to overcome them. Refusing Crescencio's invitation, and attempting to stay here, would only invite attack.

"Let's get some sleep then. Dawn will come soon enough," Matal continued, rising to go to his hammock. The others followed, each to their hammock, to settle in for the night.

Shanni listened to Caleb's deep breathing as he fell asleep in a nearby hammock. She wanted to reach out to him, touch him. Why didn't she? What was holding her back? She felt a dread in the pit of her stomach as the answer came, unbidden. She was becoming a different person, a person she did not recognize. The demands of the journey, the dangers, violence and death had hardened her to the cruelty of the real world. She could no longer be the trusting, loving girl who had fallen in love with the dashing Anglo rider in her fairy tale existence in Mesa Verde. Now she had faced the real world, the world of intrigue, disappointments, and death. To survive in that world she had been forced to change, to harden, and to fight back. Tears welled in her eyes as she felt the loss of her childhood innocence. Now she wished that she and Caleb had stayed behind, returning with Toshni and the others. On Caleb's ranch, she and Caleb would have had each other. She had made the wrong choice, and Caleb had shown his love and loyalty by remaining by her side. Now she had shut him out, and she was powerless to change it. There had been no time, and no energy, for them to be alone and to sort things out between them. They were leaving tomorrow, journeying into another unknown. She would make time, she promised herself. She would make time for her and Caleb before it was too late.

The promise brought relief to Shanni's trouble mind and she slipped into a light sleep. Her unconscious mind continued to mull over the disjointed impressions that lay unresolved in the world of ordinary reality. And then she was dreaming, her subconscious drifting across the stone hieroglyphs that she had spent days trying to understand. Her gaze stopped at the noble-woman, dressed in finery of woven cloth, girdled by decorative leather. Intricately embroidered boots covered her feet and an elaborate headdress of feathers crowned her head. Jade earrings and gold jewelry adorned her body.

The image shimmered as Shanni's awareness was drawn deeper into the vision, and she found herself standing with the other women of the court, facing an assemblage of priests and the king. She gazed around at the multi-colored throng, backed by the friezes on the walls of the temple, high above the plaza filled with thousands of people.

Kneeling before the priests were the prisoners, captured from other Mayan city-states and brought here for sacrifice to the gods. The prisoners hung their heads in dejection, resigned to their fate, as the head priest stepped forward, raising a knife made of black obsidian high above his head. The priest shouted a chant of propitiation to the gods, his words ringing out across the multitude looking up from the plaza below. "May Chac-mool be pleased! May he send the rains that bring food for his children! May he feast on the blood that we offer him!"

Four priests seized the first captive and lifted him, supporting him upright. He struggled in vain as they dragged him to the stone altar and laid him on his back, using their weight to hold him inert, spread-eagled on the cold stone surface as a fifth priest grasped his hair and stretched his head back.

With a deft movement born of long practice, the head priest slashed downward, ripping the captive's body open from the navel up the rib cage. He reached in with his other hand and grasped the beating heart, cutting around it with the obsidian knife to wrench it free in a splash of blood that spurted from the severed arteries. He held the beating heart overhead, blood spattering his face and clothes, and then he tossed it expertly into the waiting stone bowl on the belly of the reclining stone Chacmool.

The four priests dragged the lifeless body of the captive to the edge of the pyramid and cast it down the stone terrace to fall limp and broken until it crashed into the people waiting below.

A great shout of thanksgiving swept through the people, chants of praise for the nobles and priests who toiled so religiously to hold the world together and assure the well-being of the Mayan people.

Revulsion overwhelmed Shanni, and she fought the need to throw up. And then she saw the faces of the other noblewomen, smiling and serene. They were not repulsed. They found joy and peace in the sacrifice that kept their people strong. To the others, what they did was good, and proper. As Shanni averted her eyes, she heard the screams of the other captives as priests crushed their hands and feet with heavy stones, and then laid them on the stone altar to be disemboweled. The screams were met with roars of approval from the crowd below.

And then Shanni realized the horrible secret of the Mayas, hidden deep in the darkness, sealed away and protected from ever surfacing to the light of day.

The scene shimmered and disappeared, to be replaced by the human form of a dwarf, an old man sitting in front of the entrance to a cave. He 'said',

"Now you know, and with knowing comes Obligation.

"There is the Underworld of Evil, the Middleworld of Choice, and the Overworld of Heaven.

"You must choose, and you must act!

"What will you do?"

Shanni felt as if her head were held in a vise, preventing her from awakening from the nightmare vision. With the dwarf's final words, her head was suddenly released, and she snapped awake like a cork bobbing to the surface of the ocean. She wiped perspiration from her brow as she clambered from the hammock to stand at the edge of the stone portal, gasping for breath. She heard Caleb stir in the darkness and approach to take her in his arms.

"You're trembling," he said, concern in his voice. "What's wrong?"

"We should never have come here," she whispered, shivering. "This is a terrible place. We must go back at once."

"I'm afraid it is too late for that," Caleb responded quietly. "They'll kill us if we try to leave now. We're in the hands of Fate, and we have to see it through."

Chapter 20

CRESCENCIO LED AS the Huastecs walked briskly, single-file, through the jungle. His men were spread out in front, scouting, while others brought up the rear, ostensibly for protection. *But we might as well be prisoners,* Caleb thought. *They took our rifles and gear, and we have no way of knowing where we are. What good would it do us to escape into this hellishly-hot and wet rain forest?*

They walked in silence, gasping for breath in the humidity. Near midday, their path led past more ruins, almost covered in jungle foliage, the rounded hills revealing ancient stone terraces jutting out of decayed leaves and exposed roots as they passed by.

A mist rose out of the earth at the edge of a mound as they neared. Closer inspection revealed a cave, nearly invisible in the foliage.

"Caves are sacred to the Maya," Tamil explained. "We believe that the mist rises up into the clouds to make rain."

"We'll stop here to rest and eat," Crescencio commanded from the front of the column. "And then we will continue."

The Huastecs dropped to the ground to rest while Crescencio's men warmed food left over from breakfast, meat and a corn gruel, washed down with water from the canteens. As they sat quietly, eating, Shanni felt her perception reaching out, searching. There was something about this place, a feeling that she had been here before.

The world shimmered about her, as with a quake her perception shifted into the world of nonordinary reality. The ruins appeared fresh, appearing as they did centuries before the jungle had retaken them. She looked across the meadow to a nearby pyramid and saw the stones of a campfire, now extinguished, and a blackened cooking pot nearby. A glimmer of movement caught her eye and she saw the dwarf, half-hidden in the shadows, gazing at her intently. Shanni recognized the old man in her dream as their eyes met. The dwarf nodded solemnly and eased back into the shadow of the pyramid. Shanni's perception shifted and she returned to the world of ordinary reality, the tree-covered ruins where they camped.

Tamil sat nearby, watching her intently, as she drew a deep breath and looked around. "Did you see something?" he asked quietly.

Caleb looked up at his question, and then over at Shanni.

"I thought I saw something move," Shanni responded. Somehow she was hesitant to reveal her power to Tamil. He seemed always to be observing. Was he a shaman?

"Perhaps you saw an *aluxob*," he said, smiling. "They are said to inhabit the caves."

"And what is an 'aluxob'?" Caleb asked.

"A forest being, dwarf-like, known to play tricks on humans."

"Are they real?" Shanni asked.

"Real?" Tamil appeared to be puzzled by the question.

"Do they exist, like you and me?"

"Sometimes. The shamans say that they can shift between the worlds. They can be here, in plain sight, and then in the twinkle of an eye, disappear. Makes it easy for them to play tricks."

Crescencio walked over, hearing the end of Tamil's explanation. "Since the priests came, the aluxob no longer exist, at least to us good Catholics!" he said, and smiled. "They are part of the sorcery that the church is stamping out!"

"So you don't believe in aluxob?" Shanni asked.

"I believe in what is in front of me, what I can get hold of," Crescencio replied. "Now we need to get going."

A man after my own heart, Caleb thought, getting up and filing into line. *I have been forced to accept sorcery and he has let go of it. What an irony of role reversals!*

On the evening of the fifth day of travel they broke clear of the jungle at the edge of the village of Chan Santa Cruz and stopped, staring. Some of Crescencio's men had gone ahead to alert the villagers who had created a path of green plant fronds across the bare ground to the thatch-roofed headquarters of Valencio Cen. The structure backed up alongside a stone mission, in front of which Cen and the villagers waited to greet the new arrivals.

Tamil turned to Shanni. "You must go ahead of us, following Crescencio. I will follow with the others."

Without waiting for her answer, Crescencio led away as Shanni, caught by surprise, rushed to catch up. Caleb frowned as Tamil interjected, "It's all right. They just want to honor her. Let's go."

Tamil followed about fifty steps behind Shanni, followed by Caleb and the Huastecs, as the villagers voices reached them, chanting in unison, "Chah-neh! Chah-neh! Chah-neh!"

What is that all about? Shanni wondered. *The men who went ahead must have informed everyone of her name. But why? Why was she singled out from the others?*

Girls in colorful cotton dresses greeted her with flowers, and then a muscular Indian man, clad simply in cotton pants and linen shirt, stepped out to greet her. "Welcome! Welcome to our village, Chah-neh! I am Valencio Cen, your humble servant. We have waited so long for you to come to us. I and my people are at your service."

He took her hand and knelt on one knee, as the other villagers followed his lead, kneeling about her. As Pooled bowed his head, the villagers pitched forward, prostrating themselves on the fresh leaves lining the plaza.

Shanni stood stunned, not knowing what to say, as Tamil and the others caught up to her. She turned to Tamil for help as Cen and the villagers climbed to their feet and began singing. Nearby, musicians took up the tune with flutes, reed whistles, and drums.

Cen gestured for them to follow him, and led into the open doorway of the stone mission. The villagers remained outside, singing, as the wooden doors were closed, muffling the sound.

The interior was open, lit by candles and tall windows set high in the walls. The end of the room opposite the doorway was hidden by large curtains that extended from the floor to the ceiling. In front of the curtains stood Indian clergymen, clad in brown robes.

"This is an historic day!" Cen whispered. "The prophesy of the Chilam Balam is fulfilled. Chah-neh has returned to us!"

He waved a hand and the clerics parted the curtains to reveal a wooden cross set in a creche high in the wall. "All bow!" Crescencio commanded as Cen, the clerics, Crescencio and Tamil dropped to one knee. Caleb and the others followed suit, unsure what was happening.

A low chant, emanating from the direction of the cross, reverberated off the stone walls of the church. A sonorous voice, echoing as if from a metal drum, began to speak. "Welcome, Privileged Ones! The hour of liberation is at hand. As the Prophet of God wrote in the Chilam Balam, over the centuries Chah-Neh would return to lead our armies to victory! The Maya will unite under arms and drive the dzul, the foreign occupiers, into the sea. Chah-Neh will sit on the throne of Power and restore the mighty nation of the Maya. Follow her! Go forth and conquer! Victory will be yours! Let the blood of the dzul appease Chac-mool!"

As the voice fell silent, the sound of the mantra resumed for long moments and then quieted. Cen and the others bowed and turned to walk out, blinking in the sunlight as they exited the mission. They paused in front of the villagers, who waited expectantly. "You must tell me what is going on!" Shanni demanded, turning to Tamil.

"Do you have a mirror with you?"

"Yes." Shanni reached into her pocket for the tiny round mirror that Caleb had given her. She removed it and opened the cover. Tamil pulled a leather thong from his pocket, tied it to the mirror, and placed the string around her neck. The mirror hung like a necklace, reflecting the sunlight. A hush fell over the villagers.

"Mirrors are considered sacred, for they reflect the soul of the wearer. In ancient times, only the supreme leaders of the Mayas were permitted to wear them. One woman rose to the rank of supreme ruler of the Maya, over five centuries ago. Her name was Chah-neh! Now as foretold by prophesy, she has returned. You are Chah-neh reincarnated and brought to us to lead the Maya to their former greatness!"

Shanni looked at Caleb and the other Huastecs helplessly. How could this be happening? And what could she do to stop it?

THE RUNNERS SPED out carrying the news to all remnants of the Maya; north, west and south they ran. They left villages in an uproar as the men abandoned their fields and retrieved guns and ammunition long-hidden for such a day, waiting for the call to arms that would free them. Every machete was sharpened and every village chief sent word of his allegiance to the cause. After twenty-five years of war with the dzul, victory was at hand.

In the west, the Totzil Maya did not wait. The village chiefs united and marched on San Cristobal de las Casas, in the state of Chiapas. Unwittingly, Shanni had become the leader of a vast civil war that would sweep the Yucatan and put it on a collision course with the remainder of Mexico.

Chapter 21

"I MUST ADMIT, I thought we were losing when the Huastecs survived to reach Palenque!" Huntal, the Sentinel, said to Popol.

"It does not matter where they go in the physical world. Our battleground is in their minds! Even in the comfort of the hacienda, some quit and turned back. Now Shanni is has turned against Caleb. It is to be expected that will eventually break his spirit. He will return home a broken man, or die in the jungle."

"Without Caleb, will Shanni quit also?" Huntal asked.

"She will be weakened, for she depends upon him more than she realizes. With Tonah gone, and then Caleb, she will be defenseless."

"What about Aurel and the others?" Huntal continued.

"Without Shanni to keep them focused on their mission, they will each go their separate ways, trying to build their individual lives. The threat to the matrix, and to the Guardian, will be eliminated."

"But what if Shanni's love is strong enough for her to stay with Caleb? Can we overcome their combined strength and defeat them?"

"We have a last missile to hurl at them, one that will assure our victory." Popol said, smiling.

"Yet another? What could remain that we have not tried?"

"Power. When all else fails, the human ego will succumb to power."

"Sorcery?"

"Not that kind of power. The power of ego, the feeling of being exalted, of receiving adulation from the masses."

"But only the gods receive such worship!"

"And men and women who can be deluded into believing that they too are gods!" Popol observed sagely.

"Ah, yes! The Prophesy!"

"The Prophesy!" Popol nodded. "Made by men, for men. But we know full well the power of belief."

"Men die willingly for what they believe."

"It is so."

"And who could resist the opportunity to be the object of a whole people's adulation?" Huntal was forgetting to cloak his excitement as he realized the possibilities. "Think of it; Shanni becomes immortal, preserved in the hearts of her followers, and in the legends handed down to her children and her children's children."

"It is the ultimate corruption of the human ego." Popol agreed.

"We must not fail this time!" Huntal observed, suddenly sobered by the implications. The Guardian, Agora, will not tolerate it."

"We shall not fail. All is going as planned."

"But Shanni and the Huastecs are very near the Center!" Huntal observed. "All is lost if they discover it."

"It is invisible in the ordinary world, and they do not have the key to it in the world of nonordinary reality."

"But there is the hidden library, containing the Book of Knowledge of the Ancients. It is still in the ordinary world."

"But well hidden beneath the ruins of a pyramid, a pyramid among hundreds scattered across the vastness of the Yucatan. It poses no threat of being discovered."

"You have thought of everything," Huntal nodded, his voice neutral.

Popol felt a small hint of alarm. *Had he?* Huntal seemed to be distancing himself from their plan. Maybe Huntal wanted Popol to fail, and to receive the blame. Huntal could then step in and replace him, moving up in the queue toward immortality. Life was hell, at any level, when you could not trust your closest associate!

"Be patient. The plan is working." Popol said. *The contingencies I will keep to myself*, he thought.

THE ENTOURAGE BEARING Shanni's palanquin emerged from the stone road and continued into the new clearing at the place known as Tikal. Hundreds of workmen were busy clearing the jungle from the courtyard and the pyramids surrounding it.

Crescencio disengaged from the workmen and walked over to welcome them. "The work has gone quickly," he said. "The Great Plaza is cleared and the grass seed planted. Soon we'll have the Great Temple cleared and ready for the ceremony. The gods will awaken and be pleased that their children once again call to them."

Shanni stepped down from the palanquin and joined Caleb and the others to gaze about the jungle clearing. Even at this early stage of recovery the ruins were magnificent. To her left loomed a great pyramid that reached far above tree-level, its white temple perched at the top of precipitous stairs. The temple, set on the top of the pyramid, was overshadowed by an enormous roof comb that extended farther toward the sky. The still unclaimed palaces of the Central Acropolis poked in shadows at the edge of the forest in front, and an equally massive pyramid rose to the heavens to her right.

"It's magnificent!' Shanni breathed, turning appreciative eyes to Crescencio.

"A city befitting our resurrection! At its height of influence, Tikal was a major city with perhaps 40,000 inhabitants. It shall become even greater under your leadership."

"Why here? There are many ruined cities to choose from." Shanni observed.

"We are far south, in the rain forest. Our friends, the English, have a colony to the east, Bacalar, primarily for logging operations. We trade with them for the guns and ammunition we need."

"Don't the Spaniards object?"

"They are more concerned that the English wish to take the entire Yucatan from Mexico. As long as our war is localized to the Yucatan, Mexico City keeps out of it."

"Another reason to choose Tikal," Crescencio continued, "Is its remote location from our enemies, the *dzul* (foreigners') cities north of the Puuc hills. Even their soldiers dare not follow us into this rain forest."

Shanni remained silent. It would become a massive city as the peasants moved back and cleared the jungle for crops. The city could become great again, but there was much work to be done, and she would have to change many customs from the old days.

"We will restore most of the stone road back to Chan Santa Cruz," Crescencio continued. "We will leave the last few miles undone so that it won't be discovered by the soldiers who infrequently visit Chan. But we will be able to use the road to get here quickly until the time comes for us to relocate our seat of power permanently."

"How long, do you estimate?"

"A month, no more."

"Good work. You are to be commended."

Crescencio nodded his acceptance of Shanni's praise and excused himself while Shanni, Caleb and the Huastecs walked to the camp and sleeping quarters prepared for their overnight stay. Their shelters were thatched houses set on stilts, the beams still fresh-cut from the forest. Food was prepared by Mayan families who had moved here with the workmen. Already there was the bustle of activity that gave life to a city.

After dinner, Caleb turned to Shanni. "We really need to talk," he said quietly. "Will you walk with me away from camp?"

"I suppose so," she answered, rising to follow him out onto the plaza.

"Shanni, what are we doing here?" Caleb asked, turning to her as they were out of hearing of the others at camp.

"Why, fulfilling our mission."

"But we came to rescue your people, the Huastecs, not the whole Mayan nation!"

"Don't you see? By restoring the Mayas, our people can come down and join a thriving community. They will be home again."

"But you've had a glimpse of what happened before. Surely you cannot be a part of that!"

"I will abolish those customs. The people revere me, and they will do what I say."

"Shanni, they're trying to make you into a god, a figurehead for their rules and customs. You'll be responsible for everything, good and bad, that happens to them! They've been at war with the Spanish for twenty-five years, and they will lose in the end!"

"How can you say that? The Maya are great fighters, and they're fighting for their homeland."

"But outnumbered. Their time has past. The Spanish will keep coming and those already here will prosper. It is only a matter of time until the Maya are subjugated."

"They are already subjugated!" Shanni flared. "That's what we must change! Didn't you see what was going on at the hacienda? The people were forced into debt so that they could be kept in perpetual slavery."

"Shanni, I know it's not right, but our business here is to find a retreat for your people, not to solve Mexico's problems."

"How can I turn my back on these people? I didn't ask for the responsibility, it was thrust upon me. Maybe it is my fate to come here and lead them to victory. Their ancient prophesy gave them such hope, and now we are here. How can we turn our backs on them? And you can help. I can make you co-ruler beside me. Together we can make an unbeatable team!"

"Do you really think that they would accept me, a dzul? I would be lucky if they didn't turn on me and sacrifice me to the gods!"

"The sacrifices will not continue. I'll prohibit them."

"Until the crops fail, or the rains don't come, or a battle is lost. Your own people will compel you to permit the sacrifices, or they will turn on you."

"Why are you so hateful? Can't you see the beauty in these people, their hopes and dreams?"

"I am being realistic. It's not just these people, it is all people. You don't want to be their leader when things go bad."

"What do you suggest I do?"

"Abandon this course of action before it is too late. Make some excuse to get off the hook with Crescencio and Cen. Concentrate on buying land for your own people. Stay out of this Yucatan conflict before you get hurt."

"And if I choose to stay, as ruler?"

"Then I must get out anyway I can. I can no longer protect you, and you cannot protect me."

"What about Matal and the others?"

"They'll have to choose to go or stay. Although they're Indios, they're still foreigners. I think they'll be at risk if they stay."

"Caleb, I want you to reconsider. Together we can do much good here. We can abolish the Maya's slavery, restore them to peace and prosperity, and bring my people the Huastecs here to live. What better way to use our lives?"

"And you'll become a god, the supreme ruler of your kingdom." Caleb grimaced.

"Is that what's bothering you? That I might be revered for saving my people? If so, I've told you I'll share it with you."

"Thank you, but no! I'll be no part of it."

"Then that is your choice, not mine. I'm disappointed at your lack of vision."

Caleb shook his head in exasperation. "Vision be damned! Can't you see it's a trap? Your generals and your priests will call the shots. You will be looked after, paraded out for the people to see, but the real power will be behind the throne. You will be little more than a pampered prisoner!"

"I don't think so. I'll use my powers to keep them in line. And it is a risk I will gladly take to free the Mayas and to provide a place of refuge for my people."

"Then there is no hope for us." Caleb turned away as the tears welled in his eyes. "After all we've been through, we can never return to my ranch and make the life together we'd promised ourselves."

"It was a good dream, Caleb." Shanni reached out to touch his arm. "But we were children, looking at the world in an idealistic way. Now we've been forced to grow up."

"There is no room for love in grownups?"

"A different kind of love, perhaps; one based on the real world."

Caleb drew in a deep breath and let it out slowly. When he turned back to her he was in control, his old steely self.

"Do you hate me?" Shanni asked.

"Hate you? No. But I hate what the world has done to us."

"I'll sign papers, give you a divorce, if you want to return...you know, to Nerial."

Anger flashed in Caleb's eyes. "That's over and done with! Can't you forgive me for one mistake, for being human? Can't you love me a little?"

Shanni was shocked into silence. "I don't know what to say," she finally managed.

"Neither do I," Caleb agreed. "Let's go back to camp."

Matal looked up, reading Caleb's face as he and Shanni rejoined the others.

"Excuse me, I'm tired from the journey and think I'll go to bed," Shanni said as Caleb sat down.

Crescencio had prepared special quarters for Shanni's stay, away from the others, with guards on duty and women attendants to see to her needs. Shanni climbed the steps to the house on stilts and disappeared inside.

"How did it go?" Matal asked.

"Not well. We're farther apart than ever."

"Nerial?"

"Much bigger than that. She feels obligated to fulfill the prophesy and lead the Mayas to freedom."

"Or doom!" Matal flared. "I'll ask Ambria to talk to her. Saving the Maya is not our battle. She'll die for a hopeless cause, and us, too, if we stay. Even now we may be killed if we try to leave. She must come to her senses."

Ambria was sitting next to Matal, listening to the interchange. Caleb looked at her, the pain showing in his eyes. "You can try, Ambria," He shrugged. "One can only try."

Caleb reached for his rifle and began to clean it, his hands working smoothly from long practice. Matal and Ambria rose silently and went to their hammocks, leaving him alone with his thoughts.

Chapter 22

THEY RETURNED TO Chan Santa Cruz the next day, and Crescencio walked out to greet them as Shanni disembarked. Soon the Huastecs were seated in the shade of the barracks, enjoying refreshing fruit drinks.

"Great news!" Crescencio opened after they had settled down and exchanged pleasantries. "The war of liberation has already begun! The Totzil Maya to the west have risen up and occupied San Cristobal, killing every dzul in their path! All village chiefs have sent word that they will march under our leadership. We shall push the foreigners into the sea!"

Caleb clenched his teeth and glanced at Matal, his face paling at the news. Aurel stood and walked out into the plaza as Ambria turned burning eyes on Shanni, who looked away.

"Excuse me," Shanni said, rising. "I have a terrible headache." She turned to walk to the special quarters set aside for her.

"I'll see if I can help," Ambria said, getting up to follow Shanni.

"Do you not think it is great news?" Crescencio looked quizzically at Caleb and the others, who remained silent.

"Their action was precipitous," Matal responded. "Who can guess what calamity they will bring down upon our heads?"

"You are warriors! I did not expect such a reaction from you!"

"Warriors fight to win the war, not only a battle. Now the Spanish are alerted, and given time to plan their response. What is your plan to combat them?"

Crescencio's eyes flashed as he stood up angrily. "Do you question my ability?"

Matal jumped to his feet, facing Cen. "I question nothing. If we're to be drawn into your war, then show us your battle plan!"

Cen stood, momentarily stunned. Without a reply, he turned on his heel. "Come with me!" he ordered over his shoulder. Caleb and Matal followed, leaving Iika to walk out to join Aurel.

"We're coming apart," Iika observed as she walked up to Aurel, who was leaning on a fence post in the shade of a ceiba tree.

"And the danger increases the longer we stay," Aurel added. "Yet I cannot bring myself to abandon Shanni."

"Nor I. But dying with her will help no one."

"We must find a way to survive," Aurel agreed. "I will travel into the spirit world. Maybe I can find an answer there."

"Go quickly. I think we have little time."

Aurel nodded and they walked in silence back to the barracks.

SHANNI TURNED AS Ambria followed her into her room in the thatched hut. "Shanni, are you all right?" Ambria stopped, drawing a deep breath. "How can I help?"

"Just a headache. Maybe if I lie down it will go away." Shanni sat down on the cot provided for her bed.

" I know you don't feel like addressing the problem right now, " Ambria continued. "But we are running out of time."

"Ambria, I...I must rest!"

"I'm sorry, but listen to me! You know what Cen's news means? The uprising has started, in your name, and it will spread! The authorities, the Spanish, will brand you an outlaw, the leader of the insurrection to be shot on sight. You are not safe here, and neither are we. All of us must leave at once!"

"I'm afraid it is too late for me. Crescencio and Cen need me to legitimize their cause. They would arrest me, keep me here if I tried to escape. You and the others are free to go while you can."

"What about Caleb?"

"What about him?"

"He's your husband, for god's sake! How can you turn your back on him?"

"There is love, and there is duty. I offered him a place beside me, helping me to liberate my people."

"Damn it, Shanni! Wake up! These are not your people. You cannot help them. You are meddling in their affairs, being used by Pooled and Cen for their own selfish ends. Wake up and face the real world!"

"Sometimes I try...I get flashes of other thoughts, of other ways of viewing the world. I feel this overpowering compulsion as if possessed by another, more powerful spirit. It is as if Channeh has entered my body, returning to claim her throne. Perhaps I am bewitched."

Ambria paused, sudden realization shocking her to silence. "Perhaps you are," she managed to whisper. "But maybe it is not too late."

Ambria turned and ran out of the room. She found Aurel in the open room of the barracks, kneeling quietly in meditation.

She halted, uncertain, as Iika, seated nearby, raised her finger to her lips for silence.

"How long?" Ambria whispered.

"Just started," Iika replied.

Aurel opened his eyes and blinked, glaring at the interruption.

"Thank the gods I got here in time," Ambria burst out. "I think that Shanni is the victim of sorcery. She is not herself, and even she realizes that her thoughts are not her own. We must help her quickly, while we can still get out of this madness!"

Aurel sighed and rose to his feet, preoccupied with his thoughts. "Get your canteens, food and rifles. We must find a place where I will not be disturbed while I travel into the spirit world. You must stand guard until I finish and return."

Ambria nodded and rushed away, followed by Iika, to comply with Aurel's request. In a short while they returned, breathless, and followed Aurel across the plaza and climbed laboriously up the steep steps of the pyramid.

Aurel seated himself comfortably on a woven mat he had brought, and sat gazing at the stars in the quiet night sky. Ambria and Iika sat down nearby, inside the temple portal, to stand guard and wait.

Aurel centered himself, screening out all thoughts from his mind, concentrating on his breathing. His awareness turned inward, following his breath in and out, conscious only of the "now" of his existence. And then he sent his awareness out, following his breath as it left his body and wafted out to mingle with the thermals rising toward the heavens.

He adjusted his awareness, examining the vibrations of existence, and testing the frequencies that separated the worlds. He let go, allowing his perception to detect the disturbance in the void that identified the space between the worlds. He adjusted his perception to it, and then he felt an awareness, a strong *will* that was covering the plaza like a bubble.

Aurel focused, following the force down through the bubble like a beam of light into the room where Shanni lay tossing restlessly in troubled slumber. Aurel reversed direction, sending his awareness back up the beam of projected *intent* that extended across the jungle canopy to its source, a place of darkness hidden inside the earth, an ancient vault with its ceiling open to the night sky. A multi-faceted crystal rotated slowly, reflecting the moonlight in an array of sparks onto the form seated in the shadows. Aurel's perception moved closer and then he saw the wrinkled face of the man projecting his thoughts into the crystal where they were amplified and hurled toward Shanni at the speed of light.

How to attack? Aurel thought. *I wish that Tonah were here to guide me.*

Aurel's momentary uncertainty caused a flicker in the energy field, breaking the man's concentration, and he opened his eyes. Aurel felt the disconnect and withdrew, casting his perception back along the fading beam to the bubble over the plaza. In an instant his perception returned to his body and he opened his eyes to the night sky.

"Help me up," he said, wiping perspiration from his face. "We must help Shanni!"

As they approached the barracks, Caleb and Matal arose silently and walked out to meet them. "We were worried," Caleb said. "Where have you been?"

"There was no time to find you," Ambria explained. "We believe that Shanni is under the influence of sorcerers. Aurel went into the spirit world to determine who is attacking her."

"And?" Matal asked.

"It appeared that a Sentinel was channeling his thoughts at her."

"The explains the headaches," Ambria added.

"And the confusion," Caleb nodded.

"I caused the connection to be interrupted," Aurel said. "Now we must see how she is."

He pushed past and led the way to Shanni's quarters. Odd that the guard has left his post, Caleb thought as they neared the building. They climbed to the porch and entered the room, dimly lit by candles set on a table. Ambria approached the bed and gasped. Shanni was gone!

Chapter 23

THE PALANQUIN BORNE by four strong porters carried Shanni swiftly thought the forest as she peeked out of the curtained window. A wane moon cast a ghostly shadow on the armed escort that followed the entourage. Hours passed until they reached the repaired road and the travel became easier. The porters picked up the pace and near midnight they reached a clearing in the forest and stopped.

Crescencio Poot stood silently as Shanni emerged from the palanquin and stepped to the ground. "Where am I? Why have you brought me here?" Shanni demanded.

"Do not be alarmed. We're at Tikal. It is necessary that we introduce you to the priesthood."

"Why wasn't I told? Where are the others, my friends, I mean?"

"They cannot participate, but they are perfectly all right back at Chan. There was no time for explanations, as events are moving quickly. We must introduce you tonight as Supreme Ruler to cement their loyalty for what lies ahead. Come, we will help you up the pyramid."

The four porters seated Shanni in a chair-like conveyance with carry poles attached to each side. Tilting her back, they carried her on a terrifying ride up the steep steps of the pyramid. She stepped off, shaken, onto the smooth plaza at the top that served as the floor of the multi-portaled stone temple, and the roof comb that thrust skyward, casting a dim shadow in the moonlight.

Attendants moved about her, adorning her with an elaborate headdress made of feathers, a multi-colored shawl and woven belt. Boots made from the skins of serpents were pulled onto her feet.

She was led to a stone throne that commanded the plaza, and lifted up into place.

A drum sounded and torches appeared on the parade ground seventy feet below. Priests dressed in red robes trimmed with gold followed Valencio Cen as he climbed the stone stairway and gathered them in a semicircle about the stone altar. Two prisoners, bound and drugged, were carried up the pyramid by soldiers.

At the top, the prisoners were cast at the feet of the priests and the soldiers retreated down the stairs.

Cen raised his arms, outstretched toward Shanni seated on the throne ten feet above them and the stone altar.

"We salute Her Supreme Highness, Chah-neh, returned to us across the centuries of time. As prophesied, she has returned to lead us to our former greatness. Let the gods be praised!"

Cen turned to face the priests. "We turn to Kuxul, Most High Priest of the Maya, and Keeper of the Ancient Secrets, to bless our new ruler and prepare for our coming victory. May the gods be pleased!"

Cen stepped back into the semicircle of priests as Kuxul stepped forward, his black eyes glittering in the light of the torches. He removed the dried spine of a sting ray from his robe and leaned over a square of bark placed on the altar. With a quick motion, he pulled his tongue out, rammed the spine through it, and leaned over to allow the fresh blood to flow onto the bark.

Shanni looked away, fighting nausea, at Kuxul's self-mutilation. After a moment, he removed the spine and pulled his wounded tongue back into his mouth. He raised the bloodied bark to a torch, setting it afire, and then placed it on the altar. The priests began a chant as the smoke bore the blood offering skyward to propitiate the gods.

Kuxul nodded, and four priests grasped one of the prisoners ans spread-eagled him on the stone altar as Kuxul reached onto a ledge and retrieved an obsidian knife.

"Stop!" Shanni commanded. "There will be no human sacrifice!"

Aghast, the priests looked up at Shanni. "But Chah-neh," Cen protested, "The gods must by fed! Without their support, our efforts are doomed!"

"I am Supreme Ruler, and I forbid it! For centuries the gods slept. Now they awaken and I talked to them. They no longer require human blood."

Kuxul and the priests looked at one another, shaking their heads. Shanni could hear the low rumble of protests.

"Does anyone dare question my authority?"

Cen trembled, caught between his fear of Chah-neh and the disapproval of the priests. "Begging your forgiveness," he began, "But the priests wonder if you might be mistaken?"

"I will give you a sign!"

Concentrating her *intent*, Shanni focused on the obsidian knife still held in Kuxul's hand. She *willed* it to move and it rose, seeming of its own volition, lifting Kuxul's hand to place the knife across his throat. A sudden move and it would cut Kuxul's throat. Perspiration broke out on his forehead as he loosened his grip on the knife, easing his hand away. The knife remained at his throat, suspended in mid-air.

"I speak for the gods," Shanni commanded, her voice hard and uncompromising. "He who opposes me, opposes the gods. They are the source of my powers!"

She *willed* the knife away from Kuxul and back to its niche in the wall. Next, she turned her concentration to the torch in a priest's hand, causing it to move. The startled priest jerked his hand away as if bitten. Shanni raised the torch in mid-air and moved it past each priest's face, close enough to singe their eyebrows if they did not pull away. When she finished, she cast the torch down the steps of the pyramid.

"This night's work is done!" she commanded. "Now release the prisoners and convey me down the stairs. A new day dawns for the Maya!"

Shanni returned triumphantly down the stairway, followed by Cen and the priests. They gathered in stunned silence as she entered the palanquin and began the trip back to Chan Santa Cruz. She was hardly a mile along the jungle road when she heard distant screams, suddenly cut short.

People's beliefs died slowly, she realized grimly, clenching her teeth. The priesthood was entrenched and no one, not even Valencio Cen, Supreme Chief, dared oppose them. She stood alone against them and she had much work to do.

Chapter 24

NEAR DAWN, MATAL and Caleb rushed out to meet Shanni as she returned to Chan and stepped down from the palanquin. "Are you all right? We were worried!" Caleb said.

"I am fine. We had a meeting with the priests at Tikal."

"And?"

"Everything went well. Is that not so, Cen?"

"Yes, of course! It is as you say," Cen stammered.

A soldier had awakened Crescencio, who hastened out to join them in the plaza. "Is all in order?" he asked. "Do we have the gods' blessing to go forth?"

"The priests gave me their blessing," Cen agreed, avoiding Shanni's eyes. "All is as it should be."

"The gods be thanked! At last we can achieve victory!" Crescencio turned to the soldiers. "Assemble the runners to alert the other villages. Then we will all march forth together!"

Caleb looked at Matal, and then at Shanni. "Come with me!" she ordered, ignoring Cen as she motioned to Caleb and Matal. "We have much to discuss!"

Crescencio followed Cen into his headquarters and closed the door behind them. "I saw in your eyes that something is wrong. What happened out there?"

"Kuxul is furious and we almost had a revolt among the priests. Chan-heh forbade the sacrifice of the prisoners. She said the gods told her not to follow the old ways!"

"But the people expect us to propitiate the gods. They will lose faith if the rituals are not carried out!"

Cen nodded glumly. Their hopes for a champion, someone to lead them to a great victory over the dzul, had been fulfilled. But now this obstacle had developed to block their path.

"This could be a disaster!" Crescencio continued. "We must convince her to change course!"

"We can try," Cen replied. "But I am not optimistic."

"We must talk with her at once, and make her see reason."

"As you say," Cen agreed, rising to follow Crescencio out of the office.

111

After briefing Caleb and Matal, Shanni returned to her quarters and sat down, exhausted, on her bed. A light knock on the door startled her. "It is I, Crescencio. Cen and I have a matter of great importance to discuss."

"Can't it wait? I've been up all night!"

"No, I am sorry, but events do not wait for us!"

"Come in, then." Shanni unlocked the door and stepped back as Crescencio entered. His huge form filled the room as he turned, waiting for Cen to catch up. Shanni realized she was afraid of Crescencio; he had a primordial wildness that seemed always to seethe below the surface, held in check but ready to explode into violence at the least provocation.

On the other hand, Cen was typical of the Indios, barely five feet tall, stocky and strong. Cen was cunning, a politician who sensed the tides of events. He would only use violence as a last resort to get his way, but he would not oppose violence by others. Shanni realized that she had entered a new and dangerous phase in exercising her power over these people. She must be circumspect, and learn quickly.

"Well?" She demanded, meeting their gaze without flinching. She knew that Crescencio only respected strength. She must not show weakness.

"It is the matter of the rituals," Crescencio said. *He is the direct one*, Shanni thought. *Unlike Cen, he cuts right to the heart of the issue.*

"What of it?"

"You are new to our ways, and Cen and I must help you to know what is proper. Cen advised me of the events that transpired at Tikal last night. While you were well-intentioned, you must not interfere with the priests. Only they know how to appease the gods."

"I believe the priests are wrong to spill human blood."

"But that is what the gods demand! That is their sustenance, their food! We humans have no choice. If we do not feed them, they turn away from us. Without their favor, we cannot prosper. It is how we have lived for a thousand years! Is it not so, Cen?"

Cen nodded agreement. "And there is also the expectation of the people."

"What about the people?"

"They believe in the sacrifices. Their fathers, and their fathers' fathers throughout many generations sacrificed so that the gods would look favorably upon their crops, which allowed them to live and raise their families."

"But it is superstitious nonsense! Change is long overdue!"

Cen stared at Shanni, shocked, and made the sign of the cross reflexively at his chest. Crescencio's eyes darkened as the muscles in his jaw set.

"We will pray that your blasphemy does not destroy us!" Cen murmured. No one in his lifetime had dared to utter such words. He trembled, expecting the earth to quake and swallow them up.

Crescencio tried a different tack. "We must look at the greater good. With the people's support, you can lead our nation to a great victory, throw off the yoke of servitude, and return them to freedom and prosperity. Surely that is more important than the lives of a few prisoners, criminals who have opposed us and killed our people."

Shanni paused, uncertain. Crescencio had a point. What was the greater good? Maybe she should go along and make her changes more gradually.

Crescencio read the uncertainty in her eyes. "You can become a great leader, a god of the people. Think of how much good you can do. And your people, the Huastecs, can join us to live in peace and harmony. You can restore the greatness of the Mayan people!"

Shanni drew a deep breath. *It could be so*, she thought. *No, it will be so! I have come far to meet my destiny, and I shall become the god-queen of the Mayas!*

"It will be as you say," she agreed. "We must think of the greater good."

Crescencio bowed slightly, admiration in his voice as he spoke. "You will make a great queen. You have an innate understanding of the wielding of power. All great leaders know that power must be exercised, or it will turn and destroy both the leader and the people. You have made a wise choice. Now we will go."

Motioning to Cen, Crescencio turned and departed, closing the door behind him.

Shanni felt the tension go out of her body as she looked at her drawn face in the mirror. Crescencio had been very persuasive, drawing her in to his point of view. Had she decided too quickly? Did the end really justify the means?

She hated the feeling of uncertainty. But why was she fretting? It was clear that the gods had brought her here for a purpose. Had she not lived where others had died during their perilous journey? It was clear that her path was directed by the gods. Surely she could do no wrong.

CRESCENCIO REMAINED SILENT until he and Cen had crossed the plaza and entered Cen's headquarters. "A marvelous job of persuasion," Cen began, but Crescencio cut him off.

"We only bought time. You should have intervened back at the temple, before she could do such damage! Now we must restore the power and dignity of Kuxul and the priests, and we must make sure that Chah-neh never steps out of line again!"

Cen was stunned by Crescencio's audacity. Crescencio would dare to control the god-queen? "But," Cen stammered. "She is the Chosen One! Who are we to tell her what to do?"

"Cut through the garbage!" Crescencio exploded. "She is only a woman, and naïve at that. But we can use her and the prophesy to unite the people behind us. We must become the power behind the throne. From now on, you are responsible for her. We cannot afford more mistakes. Assign ladies-in-waiting, bodyguards, anyone who can surround her and keep her out of trouble! Assure that the people only see her in her regalia as queen, overseeing and blessing important events. Otherwise she is to be kept withdrawn, mysterious and unaccessible. We must develop awe of her among the people."

"But I saw her power; she used witchcraft to place the knife at Kuxul's throat!"

"Bah! She mesmerized you all! A magician's trick!"

Cen shook his head. Let Crescencio see it for himself, and then decide.

"What of the others; her companions, and her husband?" Cen continued. "Surely they will object!"

"We must move quickly to control her time and reinforce her belief in her destiny. Then we must get rid of the others."

"But she'll turn on us!" Cen objected. "We cannot kill her own husband!"

"Ah, Cen, don't you see? There will be battle soon, and we'll insist that Caleb and the others must join us, perhaps lead the charge, to show their support of the god-queen! And we'll assure that they die a glorious death!"

Cen shook his head in wonder. He and Crescencio had graduated from village leaders, hardly more than bandits and guerrilla fighters, to the leadership of the entire Mayan nation. Soon they would lead an army of tens of thousands of volunteers, driven by faith to kill all in their path - soldiers, women, and children - until all were dead and the Mayas reigned triumphant. To be alive upon the earth at such a propitious moment, and to have the opportunity to change the course of history! Cen smiled as the implications registered in his mind. "To assure a great victory for our people," he agreed. "We must do what we must do. The Anglo and the other Huastecs must be eliminated, and soon."

Crescencio had been waiting intently for Cen's reaction, and relaxed at Cen's words. Cen had bought into the dream and would follow Crescencio's lead. And for now, Crescencio knew he needed Cen's influence with the village leaders.

"Well spoken! I knew you would see the wisdom of it. Now go, hand-pick your people and surround Chah-neh with trappings and attendants. Don't give her time to think!"

Cen nodded and walked out of the room. He stopped on the porch to let his eyes adjust to the darkness, and shuddered as realization hit him. Crescencio had taken charge! Chah-neh was little more than a prisoner, and Crescencio had deftly persuaded him to agree. Now he dared not try to wrest control from Crescencio! Crescencio, his own general, was making the decisions and sending him, the elected leader of the Cruzob, out to run the errands! *I had better wise up fast,* Cen thought, *if I want to be the one left standing when this is over!*

Chapter 25

CALEB'S RESTLESS MIND made sleep impossible, and he eased out of his hammock quietly to avoid waking the others. He went outside to sit on the porch, pulling his boots on absently as he gazed across the quiet village.

The hot, humid air oppressed him, triggering memories of his nights on the lonely trails in Arizona where the air was cool and clean, and the night sky a canopy of stars seeming close enough to touch. What in the hell was he doing here! Events were spinning out of control and he felt powerless to intervene. Mingled with his frustration was an overpowering sense of foreboding, a sense of danger. He felt as if evil itself were descending upon them like a death shroud that would choke out the last gasp of breath.

"I see you also could not sleep," Aurel whispered out of the darkness nearby.

Startled, Caleb looked around, his eyes seeking Aurel in the dim light. "To be honest, I don't think I'll sleep again until we're out of this nightmare!"

"It's about Shanni, isn't it? She's set you on edge. Truth is, that's what's keeping me awake, too."

"What's happened to her?" Caleb agreed. "I feel that she has become someone I don't know. I couldn't believe her mindset upon returning from Tikal. She's all caught up in this so-called prophesy!"

"Wouldn't you be, if you could become a god and liberate a whole nation?"

"I want no part of it, and I told her so!"

"What did she say?"

"She just looked at me," Caleb shook his head. "Made me feel like one of her 'subjects' who needed scolding. What's happened to her?"

"Power is seductive. At best she is confused; at worst, she truly believes that she is destined to become the supreme leader of the Mayas."

"But we had agreed that we would lead the Huastecs to sanctuary and then she and I would return to my ranch and settle down to live and raise our family."

"That was in another life, Caleb! Our dreams grow and change as we experience life. If you were Shanni, would you exchange being a god-queen for being a rancher's wife?"

"Damn right! When she offered me the kingship, I turned it down cold!"

"You turned down the chance to be a king? To rule over a whole nation?"

Caleb frowned at Aurel. "Are you being sarcastic?"

"I suppose in a way I am," Aurel admitted. "You and I see what is happening. Why can't Shanni see it?"

"We'd better find out, and soon. I don't trust Crescencio and Cen, and soon they'll have made us outlaws and fugitives, if we're not already due to the revolt. We'll be totally at their mercy."

"I think it is time we talked to Tonah," Aurel said. "Maybe he can help us to understand what is happening and how to combat it."

"But Tonah is dead!"

"In transition is the more proper term, I think."

Caleb shivered as he drew in a deep breath. "Who would've thought I'd come to this?"

"On second thought, maybe I'd better try on my own," Aurel said, almost to himself.

"I'm sorry," Caleb said. "I have no problem with you. Since I completed the vision quest, I understand what you are proposing to do. I guess I just instinctively reject the ways of shamanism. I'm sure it will pass when I get over the funk I'm in."

"Maybe it is not a funk."

"What do you mean?"

"Haven't you noticed that we've all become a little strange?"

"Yes, but I put it down to the stress we've all been under. We've had it rough."

"We've all changed. We're not ourselves. We react strangely, often with hostility toward one another. All the good will is gone."

Caleb thought a moment. "So you think the Sentinels are back, attacking us?"

"Maybe."

"But before they always attacked in the physical world. I didn't think they could attack a human's psyche."

"They can attack anywhere they perceive a weakness."

"Our stress and uncertainty have certainly weakened us."

"Yes."

Caleb stood up suddenly. "You contact Tonah, if you can. If anyone can help us, he can. I'm going to try to get through to Shanni, reason with her. It may be my last chance." Without waiting for an answer, Caleb stepped off the porch and disappeared into the night.

Chapter 26

AUREL CENTERED HIMSELF as he sat quietly in the night, listening to the faint hum of insects from the rain forest. He stared intently at the smoke wafting skyward from the dying embers of a fire in the plaza. Using his *intent*, he sent out his awareness like a mist to melt into the smoke, riding it upward into the night sky.

His perception shifted as the smoke became a blue beam of light, a column of sparks swirling in a blue-white vortex that spun like fireflies about a light. The updraft caught his perception, snapping him upward like a slingshot into the world of eternity.

He fell gently onto a cloud-like surface, a soft, downy place that surrounded the pool of light that was the termination of the column, the linkage from Aurel's world to that of Tonah. He stood up and saw the familiar valley of white that led to the mountain of clouds that made up the horizon.

An oval-shaped luminosity detached from the landscape and stood, egg-like, waiting as Aurel advanced. As he drew near, the luminosity extended its aura like a blanket to envelop him in an overwhelming emotion of love and compassion. Aurel knew that Tonah, in his new energy body on the astral plain, had found him.

"No 'body' this time, or appearance of 'Tonah'," Aurel observed.

"No need, so I dispensed with the 'prop'. The last time we met you were introduced to my energy body, so I knew that you would recognize it and not be afraid."

"I am no longer afraid," Aurel agreed. "A matter of importance brings me."

"I judged it to be so."

"We are near the Center, but we have not yet found it. While we were seeking, we were informed that the Mayan people have a prophesy that descendants of their people would return to liberate them. They think that Shanni is the anointed one, and are making her into a god-queen. Shanni is being drawn into the role, and away from our purpose."

"That is not a good thing."

"She is becoming a different person, a stranger to us. We fear that she is losing her humanity."

"Then this is her moment of truth."

"Moment of truth?"

"Every human has the right of choice; what we refer to as 'free will'. Somewhere during each life there is a crucial choice, for good or for evil, which determines the remainder of the life-course."

"But what if she chooses the wrong course? She may die, and us along with her!"

"It would not be free will without total freedom to choose, and total responsibility for the consequences of that choice. I cannot imagine that Shanni would choose evil."

"That's the problem! We feel she has deluded herself into believing that she can do a great good by tolerating evil means. Revolt, slaughter, and human sacrifice will be used in an attempt to restore the Mayan civilization."

"It is the power that is seductive. Few humans can resist it. That is why the earth is the testing ground."

"I don't understand."

"Free will, the power to choose, has unimaginable potential for good or for evil. But without choice, there can be no free will. Man would be undifferentiated from the animals, which are programmed at birth, and live out their lives based on their instincts."

"But why are we allowed the right to choose, when we've proven ourselves unworthy? We cause great chaos and suffering!"

"That is why man is constrained on the earth. There is a limit, in the cosmic sense, on the damage you can do. If you destroy the earth, you only destroy yourselves."

"And if we don't?"

"Those humans who learn to handle their responsibility wisely, to control their egos and make the right choices, graduate to greater powers and responsibilities in the next dimension, and others beyond. For example, in my dimension, we monitor potentialities for entire galaxies, and sectors of galaxies, that may manifest in the world of physical reality. Imagine the damage we could do to the evolving universe!"

"So Shanni will be free to choose wrongly, and to destroy herself?"

"She may and in doing so may also cause much suffering for others. But will it change the course of history? Not in a meaningful way."

"So what humans do does not matter?"

"Oh, it matters. Humans are on the front line as co-creators of reality in the physical world. You make choices that determine what potentialities become 'real'; that is, manifested in the world of ordinary reality. For example, you have learned to control energy for healing, energy that flows through you and the earth at all times. We know the energy as cosmic rays, while humans in the future will use words like gamma rays and neutrinos. Each culture rediscovers universal energy and gives it a new name."

"So we humans gain more and more power through our discoveries, and we are free to choose how we use that power."

"Yes, on both an individual and a cultural basis."

"But if we knew this in advance, we would recognize the importance of our choices, and that we were being tested. We would automatically make the correct choices! It would be like having the answers in advance of the exam! You must place a great deal of trust in me not to reveal this insight to other humans. It would change the course of history!"

"It does not matter if you reveal it."

"But...why not?"

"Because they will not believe you."

CALEB APPROACHED SHANNI'S quarters and saw the two armed guards outside the entrance. He stopped as they closed ranks, blocking his way. "I wish to see my wife," he said.

"I am sorry," one of the guards responded. "We have orders that she is not to be disturbed."

Caleb fought back anger. No point in taking his frustration out on the guards. "Then give her the message that I wait outside to see her."

The guard looked at the other, who nodded. The guard walked back to the door and knocked, conveying Caleb's request through the partition.

In a moment the door opened and Shanni's face appeared. "Come in," she said, holding the door open for Caleb to enter. Two servants stood near her dressing table, hands folded, waiting.

"Could we have some privacy?" Caleb asked. "So we can talk."

Shanni dismissed the servants, who filed out quietly. Caleb studied Shanni's face in the dim light cast by candles set in lanterns along the walls. Dark circles of fatigue under her eyes made Caleb want to reach out to her. *Why don't I?* He thought. *Why do I no longer feel comfortable touching my wife?*

"How are you?" he asked tentatively.

"All right, except for the headaches. They keep me from sleeping."

"Did you have headaches before?"

"Never, until we came to the Yucatan. My attendants say it is caused by the heat, and that I will adjust to it."

"Maybe you're ill. Maybe you should see a doctor."

Shanni smiled at the irony. "Seen any around here?"

"No, and that's why I'm here. We need to get out of here, and back to civilization; back where we belong before it is too late!"

"Where is that, Caleb? Where do we belong?"

"Back at my ranch. I can make a good living, and we can grow with the times. We can have a comfortable life and raise our children in peace."

"Do you think that is how we should spend our lives, quietly and in comfort?"

"What's wrong with that?"

"That would only be self-indulgence while others suffer. Here we can use our lives in a worthy cause. Here we can make a difference! Don't you see?"

"Shanni, I could see it if we could make a difference. But if we stay here we'll all be dead soon. The danger signs are all around us, starting with Crescencio and Cen, who have their own motives and their own agendas. We'll die for nothing and be forgotten."

"You, maybe, Caleb. Somehow you've just never understood. Even if I die, it will be in a noble cause, helping to alleviate my people's suffering."

Caleb felt the strength go out of him. Shanni was lost to him.

"I guess that's it, then," he said.

"Remember I offered you the chance to sit beside me on the throne. Together we would be unstoppable. There is no limit to the good we could do!"

"No, Shanni. I'm not a king. I'm a man who wants to live a normal life. I want to sleep without fear in my own bed, and when the day comes, watch my children play in the sun."

"It is a nice dream, Caleb, but not very responsible. When destiny calls, we must answer."

"I guess I'll be going then. Nothing to hold me here."

"And the others?"

"They'll have to decide for themselves."

"All right. But Caleb, if you oppose them, Crescencio and Cen will come after you and I won't be able to stop them."

"You can't stop them now! Tell me you're not here by choice, and I'll move heaven and earth to get you out of here!"

"It is my choice, Caleb."

His eyes flashed as he paused at the door and turned. "Then know this, you're the only woman I've ever loved. I want nothing more than for us to be together and happy. It is your choice that is driving us apart."

He pulled the door open and stepped out past the guards. In the plaza, columns of armed Indios were assembling, their squad commanders gathering around General Crescencio, who stood on a platform inspecting the troops. Mule trains from Chetumal, in the British colony to the south stood loaded with rifles and ammunition. The revolt was coming to pass, and Caleb was powerless to stop it. He turned and walked to the barracks where he and the Huastecs were quartered.

Matal met him as he stepped up on the porch. "General Crescencio's men were here," he said grimly. "Said they're requisitioning all the weapons for the battle. They took our rifles and ammunition."

Caleb pushed by him to enter the barracks where Aurel and the others stood quietly in the shadows. Even their knives and machetes were gone! They were defenseless, and for all practical purpose, they were Crescencio's prisoners.

Chapter 27

AFTER YEARS OF political in-fighting, Porfirio Diaz had risen from humble beginnings in Oaxaca to the presidency of the huge and chaotic country of Mexico, which had recently thrown off the shackles of Spanish colonial rule, and later that of France, to shape its own destiny.

Porfirio had moved fast to consolidate his power, eliminating or exiling any who opposed him. And then his attention turned to the Yucatan.

Like a spoiled brat, the Yucatan had thrown repeated tantrums, first swearing allegiance to Mexico and its government, and then seceding on a moment's whim. The time had come to tame the Yucatan and bring it permanently into the fold, and General Vincente Mariscal was just the man to do it. Mariscal was ruthless and often his methods were messy, but he got the job done. The hue and cry of survivors reporting the atrocities of his men in the subjugated villages were drowned out, in Porfirio's ears, by the applause of the cabinet when Mariscal put down revolt after revolt, providing the power needed for the Porfirio Party to govern.

Porfirio turned as the door opened and Mariscal was shown in. Mariscal was of average height, with swarthy face half-hidden by a drooping mustache. His sleepy eyes belied the mind that could cut like a rapier. Too many had underestimated Mariscal and died as a result.

Mariscal bowed slightly. "You sent for me, Excellency?"

"Yes, it was good of you to come on short notice."

"It is my privilege. How can I be of service?"

Porfirio paused, thinking quickly how to best phrase his request. He wanted Mariscal's commitment, but did not want Mariscal to think that he was desperate.

"You have done well in your campaigns," Porfirio began. "Your service to our country has not gone unnoticed."

"Thank you, Sir. I consider it an honor to serve my country."

"You do honor to your family and to yourself. I know from experience that it is not easy to lead in such troubled times."

Mariscal nodded agreement, waiting silently.

124

"Ordinarily," Porfirio continued, "I would give you the reward you deserve - land, power, and position - and relieve you of the discomfort of another campaign. But there is a need; one last campaign to be fought, and I dare not trust it to lesser generals."

Mariscal's eyes brightened with interest. "What is it, Sir?"

"The Yucatan."

Mariscal drew in his breath. Everyone knew of the chaos in the Yucatan, state fighting against state, armed rebellions by the Indios, and gun-running by the British from their colony to the south. The Yucatan had repeatedly failed to govern itself, and had been unmanageable from Mexico City. "It is a tall order," he observed.

"Yes it is. That is why I only offer, rather than direct. Due to your illustrious service, you may pass on this one if you wish. I shall not hold it against you."

Mariscal studied Porfirio, thinking. They had fought many battles to reach their respective positions of power. Their respect for each other was deeper than friendship. Porfirio was paying him the greatest honor by giving him the choice. "And if I accept?"

"I will provide the army, the money, the transportation, and give you a free hand."

"They've fought among themselves for thirty years," Mariscal observed. "Subduing them will be brutal. Our political opponents will howl."

"I'll take care of that. You just get the results, as I know you can."

Mariscal smiled. "I love a challenge!"

He bowed and turned to leave the room.

CALEB AND MATAL walked across the plaza and approached Crescencio, who stood on a platform inspecting the troops. Crescencio flashed a steely smile as they approached.

"You are here about the weapons," Ccrescencio greeted before Caleb could speak. "Look!" Crescencio swept his hand in an arc over the Indios lined up in formation. "This is our army of liberators, yet most are armed only with machetes. In battle, they will risk their lives to capture a rifle or a revolver and fight on. Your weapons are an important addition to our arsenal."

"But we need them for our defense," Caleb protested.

"Against what?" You are under our protection here."

"If you start a war, we'll be held accountable by the authorities, whether we participate or not."

"The war has already started. It is time for you and the Huastecs to take sides. If you join us, I will gladly give you your weapons. With your skills, I will appoint both of you captains."

"And if we do not join you?"

"You will remain here where it is safe, under our protection. But in that case I am afraid I will have to keep your weapons. They will be needed for those who fight."

Caleb fought down the impulse to attack Crescencio and force him to return their weapons. But Crescencio's men were all around. He wouldn't stand a chance.

"I'm asking for the return of our weapons," Caleb repeated.

"And I'm asking you and the others to join our army and fight for our cause. When you decide, I will decide." Crescencio turned and stepped off the platform, leaving Caleb and Matal standing alone.

"Come on!" Caleb said, stepping off the platform to walk to Valencio Cen's headquarters. Cen was relaxing in his hammock in the shade of the porch when Caleb and Matal drew up before him.

"Crescencio has taken our weapons and ammunition against our will. I'm asking you to direct him to return the weapons to us."

Cen sat up, hanging his legs over the side of the hammock. "I'm afraid I cannot do that," he answered quietly. "I am the politician, and Crescencio is the general. I cannot interfere with his methods."

"But you are in charge! You are the supreme leader!"

"Our ways are not your ways. I will not interfere."

"Then we will be forced to take our own measures."

Cen blinked, pausing at Caleb's words. "My friends, you are in no position to make threats. General Crescencio is the law here. If you oppose him, you will be killed!"

Caleb turned to Matal. "Let's go," he said, leading away toward the Huastecs' living quarters where Aurel and the others waited.

"No good," Matal responded to their expectant looks. "Crescencio is keeping our weapons, and wants us to participate in their war on the Spaniards."

"If we do that, we'll become outlaws, enemies of the state," Aurel replied. "We'll be hunted by the authorities until we are captured or killed. Even Senor Fuentes will not be able to help us."

"Maybe Shanni can help," Aurel continued. "She has authority over Crescencio. She can direct him to return our weapons."

"It's too late for that," Ambria broke in. "Crescencio has ordered that none of us is to be permitted to see her."

Caleb turned and leaned on the wooden column supporting the thatched roof, thinking rapidly. They could not brave the jungle without weapons. "We'll have to pretend to go along with Crescencio," he said. "If we refuse, we will be left here helpless, or worse, pinned up as prisoners. I don't trust Crescencio to leave us free. We'll have to hope it is not too late to escape when we get our weapons back."

Matal looked at the others who stood silent, reflecting on Caleb's suggestion. "It's a poor choice," Ambria agreed. "But it is the only one we have."

"And Shanni?" Aurel asked.

"She's a prisoner, too!" Caleb said bitterly. "Only she doesn't realize it."

Chapter 28

GENERAL MARISCAL'S SHIPS arrived at the port of Campeche and began off-loading men and material. Meanwhile, the General himself assembled the local generals appointed by the Yucatan officials and placed them under the command of his colonels. One who objected, citing Yucatan autonomy, was taken outside and summarily executed. Within twenty-four hours, Mariscal was in charge of the Spanish government of the Yucatan. Now he could devote his full attention to subjugating the Indios.

On the dawn of the second day, Mariscal's army marched southward and eastward, rolling like a leviathan over the land.

Crescencio smiled at Caleb and the Huastecs, who stood in a lose group at the edge of the parade ground. "I knew you would see it my way," Crescencio said. "After all, you Huastecs are fighting for your queen and your homeland. But you, Caleb, what are you fighting for?"

"My wife, and our freedom."

Crescencio was silent a moment, studying Caleb's face. "That's enough then, for now."

Crescencio doesn't trust us for a moment, Caleb thought. *And I don't trust him. He'll be watching us, and time is running out.* "When do we get our weapons back?" Caleb asked.

"When we march, and prepare to engage the enemy." Crescencio's eyes glinted, as if he could read Caleb's mind, and he turned and walked away.

Crescencio's army marched at dawn the next day, flowing out of Chan de la Cruz like a rapids-filled, multi-rivulet stream as the leaders found their way through the dim hunting trails of the forest. The Indios had already sacked Valladolid, and were attacking and burning the dzul villages north of the Puuc hills. This time Crescencio and the Indios would not stop until they had destroyed Merida and Campeche, and driven the whites and mestizos into the sea.

Unarmed, and loaded with the gear in their backpacks, Caleb, Matal and the others struggled to keep up with the men born to silent travel through the jungle.

KUXUL STOOD AT the top of the pyramid, watching the crowd assembled below move apart to let Chah-neh's palanquin pass. The bearers stopped at the base of the pyramid and her honor guard helped her ascend the steep stairs. Kuxul swung his gaze to the other priests who stood in a semicircle, awaiting his reaction. Chah-neh had embarrassed him, but soon she would learn about true power, and who was really in control of the world of the Maya. The priesthood had spent a thousand years gaining ultimate power over the people, and now Chah-neh would see the importance of power, and come to love it and bow down to it.

"Your throne awaits, Anointed One," Kuxul bowed as Shanni reached the top of the stairs and paused for breath. Without waiting for an answer, Kuxul waved to the priests who lifted her onto the throne as her honor guard turned to descend the pyramid.

Shanni felt light-headed and disoriented, and her headache had returned. Was it the altitude, or the heat? She felt the edge of nausea rising in her stomach. *I must get hold of myself,* she thought. *My people are watching!*

Kuxul moved in front and stopped to look up at Shanni, spreading the sleeves of his robe like wings as he spoke. "The sacrifices we made to the gods were received with favor. Now the gods have returned to watch over us, and they are thirsty. We can only assure their blessing will continue if you, Chah-neh, lead us back to the magnificence our people once knew, and lost."

Shanni waited, uncertain. How was she to respond?

"You have but to watch and support us," Kuxul continued, "As we utilize the ancient power to restore you and our people to greatness."

The other priests began to chant, their voices a low rumble that washed across the heads of the throng below. The people began to weep and shout, caught up in the fervor of the sight of their queen restored to the throne of power.

Kuxul paused, watching Chah-neh's face. Soon the sacrifices would not repulse her. She would grow inured to the sight of blood, for after all, it was the victim's fate to die, was it not, so that others might live? And today, Chah-neh would witness the ultimate power, the ability of the priests to persuade their own people to volunteer for the sacrifice! By shaping the mind of a child, the priests could convince them that a ritual death meant honor and glory in the after-life! With such control, anything was possible.

Shanni watched as the crowd quieted and a couple dressed in ceremonial robes led a little girl slowly up the stone steps. Shanni leaned forward, uneasy. What was this all about?

As the threesome reached the flat top of the pyramid, two priests joined them, raising the parents' arms in salute to the crowd below. A roar of approval welled up, reverberating from the stone buildings that lined the open area below.

The two priests turned the adults to face Shanni. Their faces were dreamy, as if they were detached from the reality of their surroundings. "The child has volunteered, with the blessing of her parents, to sacrifice herself for the good of all the people. It is a great honor. She and her family have enjoyed great luxury since she was chosen, and her name will be engraved in the stone to immortalize her gift to her people."

Shanni leaned forward to stare into the brown eyes that dominated the child's face. The child gazed back serenely.

"Do you realize what is about to happen to you?" Shanni asked.

"Yes. I will go to live with the gods."

"Why do you want to do that?"

"It is a good thing to do. My mother and my father told me."

Shanni turned her gaze to the parents. "How can you consent to this?"

"She was chosen by the gods. It is a great honor," the father replied.

"Who told you that the gods had chosen her?"

"Why, the priests, of course!" The man cast a puzzled look at his wife. Did the god-queen not know how the child was chosen? The wife remained silent, casting her gaze downward.

Shanni turned to Kuxul. "So you chose her?"

"I am a conduit of the gods," he replied, unmoved. "I only relay the gods' wishes. It is up to the people to accept or decline."

"So you take no responsibility for this child's death?"

"We all must die. How much better to be instantly transformed into a state of perfection than to endure a lifetime of suffering. Many volunteer, but few are chosen."

"I will have no part in this! I forbade human sacrifice when I attended the last ceremony!"

"But at that time you were uninformed of our ways. Look at the people. They would be in terror if the gods were not appeased. It is our sacred duty to carry out the sacrifice. The very existence of the Maya depends upon it!"

"But I..."

"Enough talk! Be still and watch. This is beyond you or me now. Watch and see the power of the gods over the people!"

The priests separated the child from her parents and lifted her onto the stone altar. They held her arms and legs as Kuxul opened the robe to bare her chest. He reached into the niche and removed the obsidian knife, holding it high for the multitude below to see. Another roar of approval welled up from the crowd, rising in intensity to push Shanni back against the cold stone throne. Shanni looked down and her gaze locked with that of the child, who looked up unconcerned.

"No!" Shanni shrieked as horror and revulsion swept over her. Her body recoiled, concentrating her life-force into a tight beam of blue-white light that flashed from her eyes, shattering the knife into shards that fell, glistening like glass, toward the crowd below. She felt a tremor, as if the earth were quaking, and her vision dimmed. The scene shimmered and then flashed back into sharp focus. The crowd below had disappeared, along with the child and her parents. Only Kuxul and the priests remained. For the first time Shanni saw the thin blue light that emanated from under the altar and pierced her forehead.

She drove her *will* forward, pressing the beam back down into the hidden chamber where a multi-faceted crystal focused the light. And standing over it, directing the beam, was the Sentinel Huntal.

I have been here before, Shanni thought as she detached from all emotion. She focused her intent and saw the fear in Huntal's eyes just before the beam pierced him and he disintegrated in a brilliant burst of multi-colored sparks.

In an instant, her awareness returned to the pyramid as Kuxul turned to flee. "The Sentinels pay in their dimension!" she shouted, jumping down from the throne to confront him. "And you must pay in this one!" She grabbed his robe and swung him wide, to fall screaming down the side of the pyramid to the crowd below.

"And you!" she turned to the others, who ran terrified, stumbling and falling down the steep stone steps.

Shanni reached out and lifted the child from the altar and handed her to the bewildered parents. "Never again!" She ordered. "Do not be deceived by the priests! If the gods want her, let them take her themselves. The gods do not work through the hands of priests!"

The parents turned silently to descend the pyramid, leaving Shanni alone, looking out across the canopy of green rain forest. Her mind cleared and she felt as if she had awakened from a bad dream.

"What have I done?" She asked. "I've been out of my mind! I must find Caleb before it is too late!"

Chapter 29

CRESCENCIO AND HIS army occupied the town of Peto without resistance. Recalling the previous occupation during the Caste War, the inhabitants had fled when they learned of Crescencio's approach. One of Crescencio's scouts returned to report that an army of the Spanish, commanded by a General Mariscal, had advanced to Ticul, to the west. Crescencio set his men to building rock fortifications along the road to Ticul, to permit ambushes when Mariscal's army advanced. Crescencio's men were experienced guerilla fighters, seasoned in the battles of the Caste War, and they knew the terrain. Crescencio planned to cut Mariscal's army to pieces.

Caleb was assigned a company of men to lead when the army charged Mariscal's line, but he knew the Indio sergeant, who was loyal to Crescencio, was really in charge. Caleb was little more than a figurehead, and being out in front, likely the first to die. Matal and the other Huastec men held similar positions. Crescencio had refused to use the Huastec women as combatants, and left them behind at Chan.

Caleb walked along the road, attempting to keep track of Matal and the others. He recognized Aurel among the men who were piling stones for a crude battlement. "Have you seen Matal?" Caleb asked.

Aurel, stood up from placing a stone and unconsciously rubbed his back. "Farther down the road," he answered.

"When Crescencio returns our weapons, wait for the battle to start. Then slip away to the south. We'll rendezvous at the Puuc Hills and then head to Palenque."

"Why Palenque?"

"That will remove us from the field of both armies. They'll likely fighting back and forth through the state of Merida for some time. At Palenque, we can raft down the Usumacinta river to the coast."

"What about Ambria and the others?"

"We left word for them to meet us there. If they do not, we'll have to decide whether to return for them."

"It's a desperate plan," Aurel observed.

"Not much of a plan, more like a reaction to our circumstances. I think Crescencio means for us to get killed in battle, one way or the other."

Aurel nodded, and Caleb turned to seek out Matal.

Matal saw Caleb approaching and stepped away from the Indios to meet him. "Word among the men is that Mariscal is on the move, and expected to approach Peto before nightfall. For sure the battle will be joined then."

"I've alerted Aurel. Keep your pack handy and be ready to slip away. Maybe you can reach the Puuc Hills before nightfall."

"And you?"

"I'm going to Crescencio to find out when he intends to return our weapons. The enemy could be upon us within hours!"

Caleb continued down the road, his eyes scanning the forest and ravines that provided perfect cover for an ambush by Crescencio's men. Scores of Indios, urged on by their company commanders, worked feverishly to complete their work. Caleb could feel the intensity of anticipation. Soon the battle would begin!

Crescencio was surrounded by officers as Caleb approached, gesturing as he issued last-minute commands. He was not pleased at Caleb's interruption. "You should be with your men, getting ready!" he growled, between instructions to the commanders.

"We are ready. The battlements have been completed. We need our weapons."

"Issue him a machete," Crescencio ordered.

"Won't do! You said we'd get our rifles and ammunition."

"Half of my army is armed with machetes. They will fight until they capture a rifle or revolver. You can do the same. Your weapons have been distributed among my officers where they'll do the most good."

"Facing Mariscal's army with machetes is suicide. They're from Mexico, not Merida. They're a real army!"

"I don't have time to argue. Get back to your men and prepare to fight!"

"Another broken promise," Caleb bit out. "We know how to fight effectively with our weapons. We could have been of much help to you."

Crescencio's eyes flashed. Caleb had dared to question his judgment in front of his officers! "Our time will come," he said ominously. "But now I have more important things to do. Get back, or I'll have you arrested."

Caleb glanced at Crescencio's officers, who stood silently with hands resting on the revolvers at their hips. *Our guns,* Caleb thought grimly, *being used to hold us hostage.* "As you say," Caleb replied, turning on his heel to start back down the road.

"Your machete," one of the officers called out. Caleb turned and took the machete, hefting it in his hand, the heavy blade glinting in the sun.

"To a warrior, everything is a weapon," he said softly, looking at Crescencio. One of the officers glanced at Crescencio and then quickly looked away.

Caleb turned and retraced his steps down the road, Crescencio's reaction burned into his memory. He had gotten Crescencio's attention, and for once Crescencio had not smiled!

Caleb reached Matal first and informed him of Crescencio's decision.

"By the gods!" Matal swore. "He expects us to face Mariscal's troops with machetes? That's suicide!"

"That's what I told him."

Matal looked at Caleb. "He wants us dead, doesn't he?"

"Yes. The battle is a convenient way to dispose of us. Now they only want Shanni alive as a figurehead to legitimize their rule of the people."

"Then we'll have to escape before the shooting starts!"

"Crescencio will expect that. His officers are watching. They will shoot us in the back."

"What can we do, then?"

"Play along until the attack, and then fall and play dead. In the confusion, grab any weapon you can and disappear into the forest."

Matal nodded as Caleb hurried off to find Aurel. It would be over soon. They would be free, or they would be dead.

Chapter 30

SHANNI HAD ABANDONED the palanquin, moving fast on foot with her honor guard back down the road to Chan. The officer in charge had followed her commands so far, but she had seen the runner he dispatched who could only be going to Crescencio for instructions. She must free the other Huastec women and escape before the runner returned. Her mind was clear now, and she saw how Crescencio, Cen and the priests maintained their hold on the people. If Crescencio thought he could not control her, he would destroy her for rebelling against them.

They reached the village, the plaza deserted now that Cen's army had departed. She entered her quarters and dismissed her servants, ordering one to bring Ambria to her. She retrieved her backpack and began loading it with essentials for travel.

There was a knock at the door, and the servant showed Ambria in. Ambria stood quietly, studying her. Shanni dismissed the servant and eased close to Ambria, whispering, "I don't trust anyone here. We must leave at once!"

"Why this sudden change of heart?" Ambria asked, suspicion in her voice. "I thought you had abandoned us in order to become queen!"

"I was out of my mind, not myself, and I have no time to explain."

"How do I know you're not setting us up? Crescencio's men know the jungle and we don't. They'll slaughter us if we try to escape."

"Trust me!"

"That's the problem! We don't trust you! We don't know who you are anymore!"

Tears welled in Shanni's eyes as she faced Ambria. "You're right," she said softly. "I have betrayed all of you. How could you ever trust me again?"

Shanni sat down on the edge of her bed, her face in her hands, sobbing softly. "I've been ill," she murmured. "The evil beings, the Sentinels, somehow gained control of my mind. It was only after I broke their hold on me that I realized what was happening."

"What broke the hold? If you did not realize it was there, you could not resist it," Ambria observed doubtfully.

"A sudden shock! A shock so severe that I could not bear it! It broke the hold the Sentinel had on me, and I saw what was happening."

"What could cause such a shock?"

"The human sacrifice of a little girl."

"My God, Shanni! You condoned that?"

"I was expected to, but I couldn't do it. Now my credibility is gone. The priests and the people see me as human, not a god. The priests will destroy me if I stay."

Ambria stooped to cradle Shanni's head in her arms. "You are back," she whispered. "You are the real Shanni, returned to us! I'll go and tell the others that we must leave at once, before the men return!"

It was mid-afternoon when Shanni, Ambria, Niika, and Iika emerged from the barracks clad in their jeans and blouses, and carrying their backpacks. Shanni had secured supplies and an old machete from the servants. At least until Crescencio returned, she commanded some respect from the villagers. Very soon that would change; very soon she would be a fugitive.

Women and children came out to watch as they set out across the plaza. A few of the old men joined the group, but made no attempt to stop them. As always, the people watched and waited. They would leave it up to Crescencio to tell them what to do.

Shanni stopped at the edge of the village and took a last look around, seeing the dismal village and its inhabitants with new eyes. *They deserved better*, she thought sadly. *They deserved real leaders who could give them hope.*

With a sigh she turned and followed the others into the jungle.

MARISCAL'S MEN HAD advanced swiftly. They hammered Crescencio's advance guard and drove them back, bleeding and dying. Crescencio's shocked officers tried to rally and make a stand, but Mariscal's army rolled on ruthlessly. The officers realized with near-panic that they faced a real army, not the poorly-trained local militias they were used to fighting.

Crescencio raced back and forth along the road, sending runners with instructions to the front while he consolidated his troops strung out over a mile along the road to Peto.

Caleb survived the first onslaught, tucked in behind a stone battlement as a fusillade of bullets dropped Indios all around him.

He watched as the sergeant appeared, running back to escape the advancing troops. Caleb ran to the shelter of a tree, and reached out to grab the sergeant as he ran by. He snapped the man's neck, and removed the revolver and gun belt, hastily strapping it around his waist. He grabbed a machete and began running, crouched low, zigzagging deeper into the woods. He could hear the roar of battle, the whistle of bullets, and screams of dying men grow fainter as he stood up to run, pushing through the dense undergrowth that reappeared away from the road.

After awhile he outran the sound of battle and knelt on one knee to catch his breath. He could see only a few feet in any direction due to the dense undergrowth that closed in around him. And if he couldn't see them, they couldn't see him! Now he had to reach the Puuc Hills before nightfall, and find Matal and the others.

MAYAPAN EASED OUT of his cave and stretched, enjoying the afternoon sun baking quietly over the silent ruins. A condor soared in the distance, riding the thermals that rose from the day's heat.

"Ah, humans!" Mayapan said quietly.

"Created by the gods for their amusement.

Like a stream, they twist and turn, never straight.

Meandering, wandering, diverging.

But sometimes they find the Truth, after all!"

He smiled and waved at the condor. "Soon," he said. "Soon I will have a message for you to carry." Mayapan sat on a rock, tending the broth cooking over the campfire. He glanced at the edge of the forest expectantly. "Ah, humans! Soon it all would be coming together."

Chapter 31

CALEB PUSHED HARD through the jungle vegetation that almost obscured the hunter's path that wound through the forest. His eyes detected movement ahead, and he raised his right hand for the others to pause. They held their breaths as the sound crept closer. Was it *el tigre*, a jaguar?

Cautiously Caleb lifted his revolver and parted the broad leaves blocking his view. "Don't move!" he ordered, leaping forward. "Or you're a dead man!"

Startled, Puco threw up his hands, jabbering in Huatl. "Don't shoot!" he finally managed in Spanish. "I came to find you, to help you!"

"Like you did last time? You tried to get us killed!" Caleb fought to hold his temper as he gazed at the wizened figure clad in loin cloth and cotton shirt. A dirty headband held his coarse black hair out of his eyes. In addition to the usual bow and arrows, he held a shotgun loosely in one hand.

"Hand over that scatter-gun!" Caleb commanded as Matal and the others gathered around.

"What do we do with him?" Matal asked.

"We ought to shoot him after what he did!" Caleb retorted, waving his revolver in Puco's face.

"It wasn't my fault!" Puco protested. "I was beset by evil beings from the spirit world!"

Puco's words struck a cord of truth in Caleb. *What if the Sentinels were still trying to destroy them, only taking a different tack?*

"Explain!" Caleb ordered. "What beings? What did they look like?"

"Priests, dressed in robes. They sent out a blue beam of light that took over my thoughts. I was powerless to resist them!"

"Why didn't you warn us?"

"I was no longer myself. I could not reason."

"How do we know you are free of them now?"

"I will show you. Mayapan sent me to guide you to him."

"Who's Mayapan?"

"The keeper of the secret knowledge of the Maya. The knowledge that Chah-neh sought."

"Why would he reveal it to us?"

138

"He follows the ancient prophesies, and the time has come to reveal the knowledge. We must hasten to him."

"Where?"

"Palenque."

Caleb looked at Aurel. "What do you think?"

Aurel shrugged. "We planned to go there anyway."

"Let's go, then!" Caleb ordered, motioning to Puco with his revolver. "You lead. Any false move, or attempt to escape, and I'll shoot."

Puco nodded and set off down the trail at a trot, slapping the leaves and vines out of his way. Soon Caleb and the others were sweating, pushing hard to keep up. What good would the knowledge do them now? Caleb wondered. Without Shanni to interpret, the hieroglyphics would be meaningless. And now it was too late. Shanni was lost to them. The quest for a homeland for the Huastecs had failed, and now they were fighting for their lives.

SHANNI, AMBRIA AND the others skirted the village of Tikal and paused to study the solid wall of green vegetation that faced them. "How do we get through that?" Ambria asked, looking at Shanni.

"We'll have to keep our direction by the sun, and go north-west over the mountains. If we can reach the Usumacinta, we've got a chance."

"We could wander around in there forever without a trail to follow," Iika broke in.

"Maybe there is a trail, and maybe we'll find it."

"Maybe..."

Reluctantly they donned their backpacks and started forward. As they neared the wall of jungle, Tamil suddenly stepped into view. "Come with me," he said. "I will take you to Mayapan."

"What's Mayapan?"

"Not 'what', 'who'. He is the keeper of the secrets of the Maya."

"I've already seen the inscriptions."

"There is more, much more."

"Why reveal them to us? And why now? Why not when we were in Palenque?"

"There is no time to explain. All is being fulfilled according to the prophesy. Now we must go. We have far to travel."

Shanni shook her head with misgiving. Was this yet another attack, another obstacle thrown in their way by the Sentinels? "Why should we trust you?" she demanded.

"Because Mayapan sent you a sign."

"What sign?"

"He said to tell you that you and he together would stack the stones."

Shanni caught her breath and looked at Ambria. "Only a sorcerer would know about that."

"Is Mayapan a sorcerer?"

"More than that. He exists in two worlds. I do his bidding in this world, the world of ordinary reality."

"Lead, then. We will follow."

Tamil turned and pushed into the jungle. Soon he reached a game trail and picked up speed. The humid heat of the rain forest enveloped them in sweat as they wrestled with their packs. Shanni heard the labored breathing of Ambria and the others as they concentrated on maintaining their footing on the slippery forest floor.

One way or another, things are coming to a head, Shanni thought. *If only she had Caleb and the others here to help them. But were Caleb and the others even alive?*

Soon the numbness of fatigue enveloped her and she concentrated on her breathing, putting one foot in front of the other as she struggled to keep up with Tamil's receding back.

The morning of the third day of travel they struck the bank of the Rio Usumacinta and turned west, following it until they saw the ruins of Palenque to the north. Tamil used his machete to fell trees for a crude raft and they poled across the river, reaching the ruins in mid-afternoon.

They crossed to the silent palace and dropped their packs where they had camped before. *Somehow it seems like years, rather than a few weeks, since we camped here,* Shanni thought, looking around sadly. *By now Caleb, Matal and the others might be wounded or dead, and it is my fault!* Shanni wondered how she could bear the responsibility for the pain she had caused. With all her psychic gifts, she had proved to be all too human.

Ambria broke Shanni out of her reverie. "You're far away, and seem sad!"

"I've made a mess of things. Now we're back to Palenque, but what good does it do? Everything has changed."

"We have no time for self-incrimination. What's done is done. Now we continue to fight, or we die. Our men will be doing the same thing."

"Dare we hope...that they're still alive?"

"We must. Without hope, without faith that we can still battle our way out of this madness, we'll surely fail. Now buck up! Show that warrior spirit we learned from Walpi!" Ambria's eyes blazed as if she were chastising a spoiled child.

Shanni blushed, anger replacing self-pity. "I'm not sure I deserved that! I'm not a child!"

"Then don't behave like one! There'll be time enough for that after we're safely away from here. Find your old self, the one that freed us from the mining camp!"

"You're right. I'm still not myself. The Sentinels' attack has left me confused and unsure of myself."

"It can happen without the Sentinels. Our cause seemed noble when we started out, and we felt trained and ready. Then life began to test us. As the struggle increased, and we experienced hardship and death, we all began to doubt. That's when we had to learn to reach inside ourselves and find the courage to go on despite our fear. And it is not over! The gods watch to see if we give up and quit."

"If the gods are watching, I would expect them to help!"

"Perhaps they are," Ambria said. "Look!"

The wizened form of Puco emerged from the jungle far across the meadow containing the stone ruins. He paused a moment, blinking in the sun, a muddy bedraggled figure in loin cloth and dirty shirt. *Puco the traitor!* Shanni thought involuntarily. She started to protest to Ambria when a tall form appeared and pushed his way past Puco. Shanni's heart leapt! Caleb! She would recognize that tall form anywhere.

Caleb and the others started forward. As they approached, Shanni made out their muddy faces and the dark circles fatigue under their eyes. They had come far and fast, but they were alive!

Caleb stopped as Shanni ran toward him, wiping his eyes in bewilderment.

"Oh, Caleb! You're alive!" Shanni threw her arms around him.

"Is it really you? Or are the Sentinels attacking me again?"

"It is really me!"

"The real you, I mean. Not the Chah-neh of the legend!"

"The real me."

"How?"

"No time for that. I'll explain later. Now just hold me, and appreciate that we are alive!"

"Reckon I can do that!" He hugged her to him as Ambria, Matal and the others embraced in greeting.

"First we must eat," Matal said, "And then get ready to defend ourselves. Our troubles are far from over."

Puco was standing to one side, watching the reunion, when Tamil walked up to him and stood silently, staring. Puco returned the gaze, shifting uncomfortably. "It wasn't my fault," he said finally. "I was bewitched by the evil sorcerers."

"And now?"

"They've gone away."

"Then you will do as you're told until we decide whether we can trust you. If you turn on us again, I'll kill you!"

"I understand. You can trust me."

"Then hunt us some game to eat. Be back before nightfall."

"My shotgun?"

"Too noisy. Use your bow and arrows. Now go!"

"Is it wise to let him out of our sight?" Caleb cut in.

"Crescencio will kill him on sight for helping you escape. Puco's only hope now is with us. Isn't that right, Puco?"

Puco nodded slowly, and then he turned to walk back into the jungle.

"Come," Tamil said, leading back to camp. "I will take you to Mayapan."

They followed Tamil past the palace, toward the Temple of Inscriptions. Shanni remembered the encoded messages and realized events had kept her from sharing what she'd learned with the others. Maybe soon they'd have a respite, a chance to compare notes.

Tamil led with a sense of urgency, moving past the pyramids to ancient stone walls now fallen into disarray, tangled among the roots of the many trees that had encircled the ruins as the silent forest reclaimed the works of man.

Tamil stopped and pointed. The entrance to a cave stared blackly from the ruins of a wall. Someone had replaced the stones, forming a doorway accessible only by bending forward to clear the low portal. In front of the cave was a campfire. Over the fire a charred copper kettle simmered with broth.

"Eat!" Tamil commanded. "And then we will meet Mayapan!" He picked up crude clay bowls stacked nearby and passed them out to the Huastecs. The broth was strangely invigorating, restoring strength to tired and over-used bodies. Shanni's mood improved, and she noted the dark circles under Caleb's eyes disappeared. He and the others stopped to watch the entrance to the cave expectantly.

"Food for the body,

"Nourishes the spirit.

"And the spirit moves the body.

"The time is right.

"It is good that you are here."

Caleb and the others turned, startled, at the voice behind them. Seated on a boulder was a small, toad-like man, his body contrasting to an oversized head dominated by large, wet eyes that blinked slowly.

"Mayapan." Tamil said.

"Tell me," Mayapan said. "What did you learn from the Inscriptions?"

How does he know? Shanni thought, flustered. *And even I am not sure I was able to decode all the inscriptions.* "I had only begun to decode..." she began.

"I know. But tell us what you already learned."

"The inscriptions are a chronicle of the lives of the kings, their battles and the kingdoms they conquered."

"Go on."

Who is this man? Shanni thought. *Can I trust him with the deeper meanings, the encoded messages?* "There are other interpretations, deeper meanings, encoded in the apparent interpretations."

"Tell us about them."

Shanni glanced at Caleb and then Tamil. *It's time to get all the information out in the open*, Shanni thought with a sigh of relief.

"When interpreted using the deeper meanings, the scribes record how the priests turned away from the teachings of the Ancient Ones, who had set in motion the processes that built great nations. The priests usurped power for themselves and implemented increasingly bloody human sacrifice to maintain their power over the people."

"And what resulted?"

"The prosperity did not continue. Instead, people became selfish and uncivil. They forgot that wealth and prosperity must be shared so that each individual can received his fair share for his contribution. Illicit groups formed and attempted to take more at the expense of their neighbors. The priests fomented the divisions by singling out individuals for 'punishment'. Soon the priest had the populace believing that punishment and sacrifice were good things - good for the community, and pleasing to the gods. Compassion and understanding were lost. The civilization reached a turning point where no amount of torture and sacrifice was repulsive to the people."

"And?"

"The society fell. The people returned to barbarism and a stone-age culture."

"And the priests?"

"I don't know. The hieroglyphs referred to more knowledge, knowledge feared by the priests, that was hidden away for the benefit of future generations of mankind."

"Hidden away?"

"A vast depository of ancient learning, put in place by the Ancient Ones, who evidently preceded the priesthood. The inscriptions did not tell where the knowledge is hidden. Perhaps I did not get far enough into the decoding."

"Or maybe the knowledge is so powerful that the Ancients could not risk revealing its whereabouts, even in the codes," Mayapan finished.

Shanni remained silent, unsure of how to respond.

"Look out at the ruins, at the Temple of Inscriptions, and tell me what you see," Mayapan added.

Shanni, Caleb and the others looked back across camp, their eyes scanning the ruins they had studied as well as the ball court that lay along the stream. The complex had been magnificent once, but now only worn stone monuments gave testimony to a dead civilization.

"I don't see anything but ruins," Shanni said finally.

"Be patient. Soon all of you will *see*!"

The landscape shimmered and the stone ruins seemed to tremble as if shrugging off millennia of silence. And then the Temple of Inscriptions was transformed. Pristine and new, its sharply-carved inscriptions seeming to leap from the smooth stone. The land fill from hundreds of years of decay was gone, revealing the original structure built underneath the temple to support it. The base was a broad low building of white marble, the seams perfectly fitted, with a long shallow ramp that ended in giant doors giving access to a hidden vault.

"It's beautiful!" Shanni breathed, looking around at the rapt attention of Caleb and the others. "Do you see it?"

"I see it," Caleb agreed. "But it's otherworldly. It cannot be real! We must be perceiving it in the world of nonordinary reality!"

"Precisely," Mayapan confirmed. "The Ancient Ones attained the power to master both worlds, power the priests attempted to keep only for themselves."

"Now I understand," Shanni responded. "Tonah told me of the Dark Times of the Huastecs, when powerful warriors came from the south. At first they were friendly, and our people welcomed them. But then they turned on us, killing our leaders. As chaos followed, they also began killing and cannibalizing our people. Survivors were forced to seek refuge in the mountain niches, building cliff-dwellings in an attempt to escape them."

"They were trying to break the chain of knowledge, to stamp out the ancient learning that could be used against them," Mayapan said. "But somehow the knowledge survived, did it not?"

"You mean Tonah?"

"The same, who taught you about nonordinary reality, and the codes to the true meaning of the stone inscriptions."

"But why? Why would such responsibility be trusted to only one man? What if he had died too soon to pass it on?"

"Creation is a complex matter," Mayapan continued. "While we cannot understand, there is a plan, a Benevolent Consciousness that sets events in motion according to certain principles. When these principles are violated, the potentiality of creation moves to restore balance and harmony."

"Why us?"

"Events set in motion a thousand years ago created the reality of Tonah, and of you and your friends journeying here at this time, into this place. We are at a critical node in the matrix of the evolving universe. Now events set in motion a thousand years ago are coming together to restore balance."

"And bring retribution to the Sentinels?"

"To the Sentinels and beyond, into many dimensions of creation."

Shanni looked at Caleb, trying to absorb Mayapan's strange explanation. Was all that had happened to them fore-ordained?

"No wonder the Sentinels attacked us," Caleb observed. "Unknowingly, we are a threat to the world they put in place a thousand years ago, and all that has transpired as a result."

"Yes. In their eyes, you are the horsemen of the apocalypse, surfacing from a hidden place to destroy them."

"Then they have failed!" Caleb concluded. "Despite their efforts, we are here."

"You have destroyed those entities that the Sentinels sent against you by being able to resist their attacks on your minds. And you were only able to resist by the secret powers that Tonah had taught you. But now the Guardians, who are at a higher level than the Sentinels, will be forced to intervene. Now you will engage the beings that are behind it all!"

"Why now?"

"They are the ones with the secret, hidden for a thousand years; the secret that will destroy them if it is revealed and overturned."

"How can we withstand them?"

"By revealing the truth."

"But what is the truth?"

"The Temple of Knowledge, the vault that lies before you, will reveal it to you."

"And then what happens?"

"You will all know what to do."

Chapter 32

Returning to the earth-level required an enormous compression of energy. And energy was the real material of creation. Once a soul had made the transition from the earth-life, it re-entered the world of nonordinary reality, the existence level known as Sentinels, and began to apply enormous personal power to the unfolding of the universe. After success in an assigned sector, the entity moved to the next level, a higher dimension far removed from earthly concerns, and joined the ocean of consciousness that dreamed multi-universes into being. With awesome power came enormous responsibility. And the power sprang from compassion learned in the earth-plane.

Thus it was that the Guardian known in lower dimensions as 'Agora' was compelled to reincarnate at the Sentinel level. To accomplish this, he selected a small galaxy in an alternate universe and compressed its energy into a black hole that warped his essence back into the first dimension, the world known on earth as nonordinary reality.

Agora appeared to Huntal and Popol in the chamber containing the power crystal. "All your efforts have failed," he said. "Even now our enemies stand on the threshold of the Temple of Knowledge. If they enter, all is lost!"

"But we are still trying!" Popol answered. "We can send earthquakes, wild animals..."

"Useless! The Temple is in the world of non-ordinary reality. Physical events cannot touch them there."

"What, then? We've tried mind control, utilizing the crystal..."

"Ineffective against adepts. Someone taught them how to use Power in the fourth dimension, and now they are here."

"The shaman, Tonah, curse him! At least he is gone."

"Where?"

"Died. Passed on."

"Fools! Don't you see that when he moved to the higher dimension, he gained more power to interfere with our plans?" Agora paused, considering. He would have to look into Tonah's actions after he had dealt with the threat of the Huastecs. "And the others?" He finished.

"They seem to have acquired his powers. They weaken and seem to succumb to our control, and then at the last moment they rally and break free."

"Then we must hit them in both dimensions simultaneously, and split their strength so that they cannot concentrate. The three adepts must be destroyed at once. We must stop them before the access the Temple and use the ancient knowledge against us! Activate the crystal and focus it on the entity called 'Crescencio'!"

"And then?"

"I will tell you what to do."

THE BATTLE RAGED along the road to Peto. Driven by their faith in the prophesy of *Balam Chilam*, the men fought like demons, fighting and dying without regard for their lives. But this was not another militia they faced. Mariscal's army was well-equipped and battle hardened, and it mowed the Cruzob crusaders down like fields of wheat.

Crescencio raced back and forth, rifle in hand, directing his captains to keep the lines together, to fight in force, as he strove desperately to keep his troops from being routed.

He spun around as a blue flash of light blinded him, knocking him to his knees. He gasped for breath as he climbed to his feet, and stood trembling. And then without a word he turned and raced on foot into the forest, slashing wildly at the foliage with his machete.

PUCO RETURNED IN late afternoon carrying a fresh deer carcass over his thin shoulders. He and Tamil constructed a spit over the campfire near the ruins, and soon had the venison roasting for the evening meal.

For the first time in weeks, Caleb and Shanni had brief moments alone together. They walked down the long veranda of the stone palace away from the others. Shanni turned and leaned against a stone column, looking searchingly into Caleb's eyes. "I don't know what to say," she said simply. "There is no way to justify what I did."

"I thought we said it all. Back there, I mean..."

"Can we ever find our way back to each other?"

"I always thought that love was forever. Now I'm not so sure. You became a different person; someone I didn't know."

"I got caught up in the legend, in the power of becoming a god to the people. I know now that the Sentinels were trying to control me, but I cannot blame them for what I did. If I had not been willing, they could not have taken me so far."

"What stopped you?"

"Compassion. The priests made the mistake of moving me along too fast. I had not yet hardened to the point that I could accept the human sacrifice as normal, let alone that of a child."

"My God, Shanni! It had come to that?"

"And with more to come. Self-mutilation to draw blood, and brutal slaughter of human beings with no feeling for the victims and their suffering. Even the crowd in the plaza was screaming for blood!"

"What did you do?"

"When they attempted to sacrifice the little girl, I used my mental powers to stop it. Then I broke away and escaped with the other Huastecs."

"They'll want you dead now...the priests, I mean. You're a threat to them and all they stand for."

"I know, but what about us, Caleb?"

"We've got to defeat the Sentinels and get out of this country. We've got to get away from all this and let our minds clear. Then we'll see if we can pick up the thread that drew us together. I thought it was broken. I'd given up hope!"

"And I had become heartless...almost! Something deep inside snapped and brought me to my senses. Now I understand, Caleb. Each of us has areas of weakness we don't know about until we are tempted. My pride blinded me, and led me astray. But the experience made me understand your weakness when Nerial wanted you. I can forgive you, and hope that you can forgive me."

"Thank God!" Caleb drew Shanni close, kissing her tenderly. He drew back, shaking his head. "Both of us were almost lost!"

"I..." Shanni paused as Caleb raised his hand for silence, tilting his head to listen. There was a faint rustle in the brush and suddenly Crescencio rushed out, rifle thrust out before him.

Instinctively Caleb threw Shanni behind him as the firing pin snapped on an empty chamber. "Run, Shanni!" He commanded, as Crescencio raised a machete and hurtled forward.

Caleb stepped in and blocked upward, deflecting the machete as it descended. He grasped Crescencio's wrist and whirled back, using Crescencio's momentum to throw him into a forward roll. Crescencio's massive wrist slipped out of his fingers and Crescencio broke free, rolling to his knees, his eyes dilated and wild, his mouth frozen in a grimace of hate.

He's insane! Caleb thought, turning to charge off the stone walkway into the jungle. Vines tangled him as he fought to get clear. He could hear Crescencio's coarse gasps, fighting for breath as he closed behind him.

Caleb's eyes searched frantically for a weapon, anything he could use against the madman overtaking him. He rounded a tall tree and came up against a low stone wall. He leapt to the top and stooped to pick up a stone. He hurled it as Crescencio crashed clear below him, knocking Crescencio half-around to his knees. But Crescencio recovered, rushing the wall with his machete held high. Caleb grabbed another stone and backed up, holding it over his head. He gauged the distance and leapt forward as Crescencio reached the wall and attempted to climb up. A blinding blue flash caught Caleb in mid-stride, momentarily disorienting him. With his last ounce of will, he smashed the stone down into Crescencio's upraised face and then he stumbled off the stone wall.

Caleb's body crumpled into the soft leaves as his awareness shot out, riding the blue beam to its source. He recognized the stone vault with the crystal, and knew he had been here before when the Sentinels had attacked Shanni. But they had been killed! Was there no end to these evil entities?

The beam of light encompassed him, attempting to drive him back. He did not fight it, instead he absorbed its power, feeling it building up inside him like an electric charge, and then he spun it inside his body, down his back to the ground where it recoiled up and out of his eyes in twin beams of focused energy. The Sentinel's body flashed into multi-colored sparks that fell twirling into dust. Behind him Caleb sensed the form of a human body and he turned. A chill of shock and terror ran up his back as he saw the ancient human body suspended in mid-air, a projection that molded energy together into a mist-like solid.

Caleb felt the hate radiating from the sunken eyes and he knew. At last he was face-to-face with the Guardian, the real enemy! Only when he had defeated the Guardian would he and the others be free.

But there was Crescencio to deal with first! In an instant his awareness returned to his body and he opened his eyes. Too late! Crescencio already stood over him, machete held high above his bloody face. Caleb started to roll when he heard a thud and Crescencio stiffened, turning to face Puco who stood on the wall, reaching over his shoulder to retrieve another arrow.

With a scream of rage, Crescencio leapt forward, swinging the machete downward in a wicked arc. Too late Puco spun to get out of the way. The heavy machete sliced through his frail body and he fell without a sound.

Caleb gained his feet and charged Crescencio, trapping his legs to throw him head-first into the muddy ground. Crescencio's hands involuntarily opened to break his fall, allowing the machete to fall free. In a flash, Caleb rolled to his right, seized the machete and sprang to his feet.

"Don't...!" Caleb commanded, but Crescencio was beyond reason. He fought to his knees and launched his powerful body toward Caleb as Caleb swung the machete.

Crescencio blocked the blow with his left forearm, almost severing it, but he kept coming as Caleb stepped back and swung the machete. Crescencio's momentum crashed forward as the machete chopped downward, smashing the side of Crescencio's neck with a sodden blow. Crescencio froze, eyes glazing, as blood spurted from the severed artery. His lungs expelled a long gasp as his head, nearly severed from his body, tilted crookedly and he crashed forward to lie still.

Caleb leaned against the wall for support, catching his breath. He could hear the sound of the others scrambling through the underbrush towards him. He remembered Puco, and hurried to check the limp body, but Puco was dead. *Who would have thought that Puco would help?* Caleb thought. *He died saving my life, after trying to kill me a few weeks ago! Who could ever understand Puco?*

Matal, revolver in hand, broke through into the clear, followed by Tamil and Shanni. Shanni rushed into Caleb's arms, holding him tightly. "It's over," Caleb said. "But others may follow. Let's get back to camp!"

They dragged the bodies to the edge of the clearing and covered them in preparation for burial. Afterwards, Caleb returned to the campfire and sat down, exhausted. "I was careless," he said to Shanni. "I left my revolver behind, thinking we were safe. From now on, we keep our weapons within reach, even when we sleep."

The Huastecs nodded agreement as Caleb swung his glance around the campfire. "I saw the Guardian who has been attacking us from the spirit world," Caleb continued. "Where is Mayapan? Maybe he can tell us how to defeat the Guardian."

"Mayapan moves back and forth between the worlds," Tamil responded. "He disappeared a couple of hours ago, when we decided to wait until morning to explore the Temple of Knowledge."

"Call him back. We can't wait. We must seize the initiative and keep it until we're free of the Guardian, the Sentinels, and anyone else arrayed against us in the spirit world!"

Tamil stood up and led them across the grass-covered plaza to the cave at the edge of the jungle. Mayapan's campfire had died to embers and the large stone that Mayapan used for a seat was empty.

"I've never had occasion to call him before," Tamil said uncertainly. "He's always been waiting when I arrived."

"Find a way," Caleb urged.. "We need him now!"

The air over the stone shimmered and then Mayapan appeared, sitting just as they had left him hours ago. "You called?" he asked.

"Come, lead us into the Temple of Knowledge. We must learn how to fight the Guardian!"

"Follow me!" Mayapan said, as the air shimmered and he again disappeared.

Chapter 33

"WE MUST ALL make the shift to nonordinary reality," Shanni said. "That is how the Ancients hid the Temple from humans all these centuries."

"How?" Ambria asked. "We're not all sorcerers!"

"You saw the Temple earlier with Mayapan's help. He adjusted the vibrations for you. Just repeat the process, and trust yourself. It is lack of belief that holds you back. Concentrate on the ruins and wait. The Temple will come into view."

They waited until the Temple appeared and saw Mayapan standing on the marble stairway, waiting. Caleb, Tamil and the Huastecs walked across the plaza to the stairs and ascended to the massive doors at the top. Mayapan swung the doors open and they entered. A sensor hummed faintly and the interior lighting came on, emanating indirectly from the ceiling tiles.

Murals lined the wall, depicting in full color a civilization built on an island continent surrounded by the sea. Vast canals reached out like the spokes of a wheel, permitting sea-going ships to sail into man-made harbors busy with loading and off-loading of trade goods. Immense buildings with white domes dominated the horizon in back of an immense city that covered the land.

As Caleb and the others walked along, they "heard" a narration, like a soft voice in their heads, that explained what they were seeing. They learned of the advanced civilization known as Poseidius, later to become Atlantis, that exerted its influence as far east as Egypt, south to the Americas, and north and west to advanced civilizations in the orient. While the Poseidians shared their knowledge of organization and adminis-tration, they jealously guarded the secrets of their technology, which gave them vast and unlimited energy to power their machines.

Caleb and the Huastecs reached the end of the hall and entered an alcove, a circular room with a table waist high in the center. As they cleared the portal, a door slid closed silently behind them and the lights dimmed.

The projection of a man, clad in a white robe, with silver hair combed carefully down his back, appeared in mid-air above the table. He began to speak in a strange language that somehow they each understood, translated automatically in their minds.

"Greetings. We are happy you have found us. The fact that you are here indicates that humankind has again advanced to the point where you are rediscovering the knowledge that was lost. When we learned that Poseidius would be destroyed by a massive meteor, we elected to preserve our knowledge in seven temples scattered around the world, one in each major cultural center. Our technology was too advanced to be transferred, although we have included principles and blueprints in the archives.

"We also permitted our scholars to emigrate, to rebuild in the host civilizations. Some unfortunately smuggled out machines to take with them, crystals to capture the power of the sun, and lasers that could cut stone to exact fit.

"As the host cultures flourished through the magic of the machines, the scholars and their apprentices in the priesthood, became like gods to the populace. But then the machines began to wear out and the scholars lacked the technicians, and the industrial infrastructure, to replace them. Craftsmen in stone attempted to duplicate the work but of course fell short.

"As the scholars aged and died, the priesthood wished to preserve its enormous power over the populace. They resorted to evil sorcery, and trickery, to awe the people and keep their allegiance. As time passed, the priests substituted fear and paranoia for compassion and understanding, to convince the people only the priesthood could intervene with the invisible gods.

"As goodwill and compassion were lost, the people became self-centered, turning against their neighbors, and forming into groups whose selfishness and greed attempted to dominate those less fortunate. In time internecine warfare destroyed each of the advanced civilizations

"Some people of goodwill remained. Even in the priesthood, a few remained who understood that the destruction resulted from the loss of compassion and cooperation. But they were powerless to intervene. Any dissenters were summarily sacrificed, to the roar of approval of the people. So they could only set plans in motion, using secret codes that would be detected only in later times, after the evil societies had destroyed themselves. And that is why you are here, to use our knowledge and our mistakes to build anew. And in some cases, to right ancient wrongs. Go now. View the murals and read the inscriptions and you will know what you must do."

The projection dimmed and slowly disappeared as the light came up in the room and the door opened.

"By the gods!" Matal exclaimed. "Can this be real? I feel that I am dreaming!"

"It is a reality among many that are still unknown to you," Mayapan answered.

"Now I know what a burden of responsibility Tonah carried," Aurel said. "He was trying to pass enough knowledge on to us in the world of sorcery that we could absorb this knowledge when the time came."

"I'm still not sure what the secret is, and how we're supposed to use it," Caleb said.

"Caleb's right," Ambria agreed. "Something is still missing."

"Maybe there's more," Shanni suggested. "We haven't explored all the rooms."

"Let's finish," Caleb agreed. "We still have the Guardian to deal with."

They toured the other rooms, listening to the murals 'talk', but only learned more about the continent of Poseidius. When they finished, they left the temple and gathered around Mayapan.

"Well?" Mayapan asked.

"We learned how the Mayas, and other advanced civilizations, prospered with the knowledge of the Poseidians. But we did not learn how to defeat the Guardians."

"But all was set in motion, a thousand years ago, for you to prevail."

"We know," Shanni agreed. "But we're still missing something. Maybe if we sleep on what we've learned, something will come to us in the morning."

"When the apprentice is ready, the master will appear," Mayapan added.

"What did you say?" Aurel spoke up sharply. Mayapan repeated his words, looking expectantly at the group.

"That's it!" Aurel said, his voice rising with excitement. "That's who we need to tie this all together!"

"What?" Shanni almost shouted.

"Tonah, I must speak with Tonah!"

Chapter 34

THE NEXT MORNING Shanni was up early, returning to the Temple of the Inscriptions in the world of ordinary reality. She had only begun to decipher the glyphs, weeks ago, when they had been forced to leave and go meet with General Cen. Somehow she felt there was a mystery here yet to be solved, and she must find it. Caleb and Aurel had come with her while Matal and the others set up sentry posts and rotated guard duty. Aurel was assisting Shanni, making notes on thin bark with a charcoal marker.

"Their numbering system used these symbols," Shanni explained, pointing out each one as she described it. "The 'rabbit ears' symbol represented zero, while the hollow dot, or circle, represented '1'. The hollow horizontal bar stands for '5'. As a result, they could write any number using combinations of these symbols."

"That seems easy enough," Aurel agreed, scribing quickly.

"It is. Then they combined numbers with words to indicate dates; months, years, and so forth, reading downward, right to left. So this column," Shanni pointed to a long column of glyphs, each line containing two characters, "Gives the date as II Imax, 9 Vayeb, and describes feats of the ruler, called '18-Rabbit'."

"Odd name for a ruler," Aurel observed.

"That's just it," Shanni explained. "That's the surface translation, the one obvious to all who could read back then, which apparently were the priests and the rulers themselves. But with the codes that Tonah taught me, there are different meanings!"

"You mean the same glyphs can be read different ways?"

"Yes. Two and sometimes three levels of meaning that I know of. Maybe there are more."

"That required a very sophisticated ability, to write on three levels at the same time." Aurel shook his head.

"Yes. They were very clever. I can't imagine that anyone was actually called '18-Rabbit', but it had to make sense back then, or the priests would have become suspicious. I suspect it refers to the eighteenth generation of a ruling dynasty, with the rabbit as its totem."

"That would make sense," Aurel agreed.

"But when I apply the codes, I get a very different meaning," Shanni continued. "Now the glyphs describe an ancient sage, Agora, who came from the east and founded the priesthood. He possessed great knowledge and what the Mayas saw as magical powers. He became the source of power for the ruling dynasties he chose. But the real power resided in the priesthood which Agora created and controlled."

"That could lead to abuse of power," Aurel observed. "Too much power residing in one man."

"Yes, I ...wait." Shanni frowned, her fingers moving rapidly down the columns carved on the face of the stone. She pondered a moment. "Now I see!"

"What?"

"The reason for the code." Shanni breathed. "The authors are explaining what really happened - the horrors instituted by the all-powerful priesthood!"

"Who, if they realized the coded message, would have executed the authors and destroyed the glyphs!"

"Exactly. Some number of honorable priests risked their lives to preserve the truth. But why? Why take the risk?" Shanni shook her head.

Hours passed as Shanni deciphered the long columns of glyphs with Aurel dutifully recording her findings.

She reached the final group early in the afternoon and paused, wiping perspiration from her brow. She sat down and took a drink from the canteen. "It's all there," she said to Aurel. "The tragedy of the Mayan civilization."

"I'm afraid I don't follow you. I've been concentrating on getting the words down, not their meaning."

"Let's go back to camp," Shanni replied. "The others also need to hear what we've learned."

The sun hung low in the west, casting long shadows over the camp as Caleb and the Huastecs gathered for the evening meal.

Shanni looked at Tamil who sat quietly, eating. "Mayapan may want to hear what we found."

"He already knows," Tamil said.

Shanni and Aurel exchanged glances. "How could he?"

"The prophesy. He trusts that all is unfolding as planned by the ancients."

"But these glyphs are nearly a thousand years old. How could anyone possibly plan a thousand years ahead?"

"In the spirit world, time has a different meaning. Things happen simultaneously, not sequentially."

"But only a shaman could know that," Aurel said. "I thought you said you were not a shaman."

"I said I was neither a shaman nor a sorcerer. I never said that I was not a man of knowledge."

"If you and Mayapan knew what the glyphs reveal, why didn't you act? Why wait for us?"

"We did not have the power to act alone. The prophesy states that only those with the secret knowledge of the ancients can right the wrongs and put the evolving universe back on its rightful course."

"But we don't have the knowledge," Shanni protested. "If it was passed on to my people, it was lost generations ago!"

"What about the codes?"

"Our shaman, Tonah, passed the codes along to me, but reading the glyphs only tells us what happened, not what to do."

Tamil shrugged helplessly. "I do not know how to answer. The prophesy states that you will arrive at the propitious time and know what to do."

Shanni looked at Caleb, who shook his head. "Maybe they've got the wrong group," he said. "Maybe the prophesy refers to others that haven't arrived yet."

"No," Tamil objected. "Look at the context. In those times, the Huastecs' ancestors were at the furthest reach of the empire. Something happened, and the Huastecs were cut off from communication with the Center, but not before some of the knowledge was shared with your most trusted priests."

"I remember the legends of the Dark Times," Shanni agreed. "When warriors from the south invaded, killing many of our people, and forcing the survivors to seek sanctuary among the cliffs, where they built their dwellings in hidden places. Our enemies hunted them down and slaughtered all they could find. Only a few escaped."

"And why would they try so hard to exterminate your people?" Tamil asked.

"To assure that the knowledge could not be passed on!" Aurel said as realization struck him like a bolt.

"That means that the priests in power suspected a plot," Caleb added. "But if they did, why didn't they destroy the glyphs?"

"That explains it!" Shanni broke in. "The final column of glyphs refers to ritual sacrifice of some of the priests! The ones killed did not have time to pass all their knowledge on to our Ancient Ones before they died. They left it here in the glyphs for us to find!"

157

"But we haven't found anything helpful!" Aurel protested. "Only the history of what took place."

"But I can see it now!" Shanni replied. "Looking with fresh eyes, I understand what the glyphs reveal. The Mayan people were hard-working and prosperous in the beginning. There was a shared cultural faith in a positive future based on productivity and cooperation. The priesthood made great advances in administration, astronomy, and mathematics. Their expertise was used to expand the cities, build roads and canals, and other public projects to benefit the people. But something changed, causing the priesthood to lead the people into evil practices. They introduced the people to the shedding of blood, that of captives at first and then eventually their own blood. The people were led to believe that the shedding of blood was a sacred act pleasing to the gods, and necessary to sustain their world.

"As the acts became more bizarre and evil, the people lost their feeling of revulsion, of compassion for the suffering of a fellow human being. Increasingly barbarous methods of torture and blood-letting were witnessed by men, women and children without remorse. Indeed, they came to revel in it. As the people became cold and unfeeling, they followed the priests without question, becoming totally in their power. Death and destruction became the religion until they destroyed themselves."

Ambria shivered, rubbing her arms with her hands. "What a horrible story!" she whispered.

"All their energy, their greatness in building these magnificent temples, reduced to rubble!" Iika added.

"Now that we know what happened," Matal interjected. "The question is why? And who was responsible for this terrible change in the culture? Surely the priesthood should have known better. That information may be the final bit of knowledge we need to know what to do."

"Those answers are is not revealed in the glyphs." Shanni answered, sadness in her voice. The glyphs only reveal that a priest named 'Agora' was in charge of the priesthood during this period."

"We must journey to Tonah," Aurel said. "Maybe with what we've learned, he can supply the missing link."

"We?" Caleb raised his eyebrows.

"You, Shanni, and I. We've had the training; now we must use it. There has to be a reason that Tonah completed our training in the world of nonordinary reality before his death."

Shanni nodded, not waiting for Caleb to respond. "Let's go to the temple, and attempt to reach Tonah."

Chapter 35

CALEB, SHANNI, AND Aurel sat quietly on the flat top of the Temple of the Inscriptions, gazing across the green canopy of the rain forest as the sun set, casting a stillness for the coming night. A faint breeze whispered through the stone archway, rustling Shanni's hair.

"Close your eyes and clear your minds," Aurel said softly. "Send out your awareness to join mine, and I will lead us to Tonah."

How can he lead...? Caleb thought, and then caught himself. If he had learned nothing else from Tonah, he had learned how disbelief sabotaged possibility. He relaxed his mind and expanded his awareness, trusting the process. He knew now that all things are possible, but belief was necessary to bring their potential into the world of reality.

Aurel's awareness hung over the forest like a mist, a cloud of blue that wavered gently as if rocked by a current. Caleb's awareness joined Aurel's and he "felt" Shanni's perception linking up.

Aurel's perception coalesced into a blue column of energy that rose, pulling Caleb and Shanni along in its wake. There was a blur, a feeling of immense acceleration, and they were cast out as if from a funnel onto a field of white.

Caleb's saw Shanni and Aurel as luminous balls of light, floating nearby. Then he turned his awareness toward another ball of light that materialized in the distance and floated toward them. Caleb felt a sense of warmth projected by the light as compassion flowed wave-like over and through him, and he "knew" the presence was Tonah.

"Ah, my children!" Caleb "felt" the words from the entity deep inside his mind. "I sense your urgency. What brings you?"

"A matter of importance," Aurel responded mentally. "Shanni has deciphered the message in the stones."

Aurel paused. Tonah instantly read Shanni's thoughts as she recalled what she had learned.

"So Evil displaced Good," Tonah concluded.

"Evil?" Aurel asked.

"Men's words," Tonah replied. "The more correct terms are 'positive' and 'negative'. To evolve positively, the universe must have a balance of positives and negatives."

"But the balance was destroyed. Why did the negative destroy the Maya?" Aurel asked.

"There is much that I am learning here in the higher dimension," Tonah replied. "Here we become apprentices again, applying the lessons learned in our lives on earth."

"The Sentinels have attacked us repeatedly in the world of non-ordinary reality," Caleb added. "Why?"

"Shanni has found the key. It was not known here that the being known as 'Agora' in the earth plane was head of the priesthood when it turned toward violence and bloody rituals among the Maya. He now has great responsibility as a Guardian."

"How can that be? He led the Mayas away from compassion and cooperation," Shanni objected. "How did he become a Guardian?"

"I am investigating, but he is elusive," Tonah responded.

"I think I know," Shanni said, suddenly remembering. "When I became 'Chah-neh', ruler of the Maya, I did not have to act. The events were already set in motion by the culture. All I had to do was go along with it."

"That must be the answer," Tonah agreed. "Any leader must understand human nature in order to be effective. Agora must have encouraged the people to accept, and even demand, the bloodletting by playing on their belief that the acts propitiated the gods. The violence would gain momentum without him taking responsibility for it."

"How do we find out for sure? And what happens if we are correct?"

"The priests' coded inscriptions reveal to us that Agora was using his hidden abilities to lead the Mayas into evil," Tonah said. "That is the key information we need to deal with the results of his ancient actions. The upright priests in that time must have correctly feared that Agora would use his evil powers to ascend to a higher level after his reign on earth, where he would be able to perform evil on a much greater scale. They were powerless to oppose him. Any hope they had of a positive future for the descendants of the Maya depended upon Agora eventually being found out and brought to justice."

"With the information now revealed, I will pursue Agora in our dimension. In the meantime beware! He is very powerful. Until I can expose Agora's wrongdoing to my superiors, he will continue to have free rein."

"My guns and knives won't stop him!" Caleb added.

"They are of no use," Tonah agreed.

"We must return now," Aurel said. "The battle with Agora has been joined all along, we just didn't know it! We must defeat Agora and the Sentinels he controls before we can defend ourselves in the world of ordinary reality."

"I will take the Truth that Shanni has revealed in the coded glyphs to my superiors. They will sit in judgment on Agora for the evil he allowed when he was on earth."

Aurel turned and entered the blue pool of sparkling light, followed by Caleb and Shanni. In a flash their minds joined and accelerated downward in a blinding flash.

Caleb felt a cold breeze ripple past his body, and he opened his eyes to the night sky filled with silent stars twinkling overhead. He turned and watched as Shanni opened her eyes in the ordinary world, the "real world" that Caleb understood. *Now we know what we must do*, Caleb thought. *We must defeat the Sentinels, and then fight our way past Pich and the Cruzobs to safety.*

Chapter 36

AGORA FELT A tremor in the matrix of potentiality as Aurel, Shanni, and Caleb made contact with Tonah. Despite his efforts to stop them, they had used the knowledge of the Ancients to push aside the curtain of energy that separated the worlds. He and his predecessors had thought they had stamped out the knowledge long ago, but now the crisis had come to threaten the world he had helped create a thousand years ago.

Since his ascension to the higher dimensions, Agora had learned that the physical universe was made up of pure energy, vast and uncontrolled in its primordial state. But energy could be focused and controlled by conscious effort. The Universal Consciousness had begun the process when it had congealed the energy into a primal ball that congealed and then exploded into being, creating the stars and galaxies that made up the world of ordinary reality. But the galaxies were held together by forces that connected in nodes to make up a vast matrix that ebbed and flowed in balance. If a node was disturbed, then that portion of the universe became unstable. And the node that Agora had set in place was based on a false foundation. He had hidden the truth, the character flaw that had permitted him to manipulate humans to achieve ultimate power over them on earth. His success had resulted in his rapid promotion to greater power in the higher dimensions. Now he was being forced to utilize his powers openly to stop the humans who had become capable of exposing his wrongdoing to his superiors, the only ones strong enough to remove him from power.

The threat had become so imminent that Agora had expended the force necessary to compress his energy and return to the physical dimension, where he could bend the forces of nature to his will. He stood in his physical body at the apex of the stone temple in the place known as "Tikal" by the humans. He flexed his muscles, feeling the power flowing through him, power fed by the blood of past human sacrifice. And then he projected his awareness across the rain forest like a bolt, seeking Caleb, Shanni and Aurel, the sorcerers that Tonah had left behind. He would destroy them, and then he would deal with Tonah.

SHANNI LOOKED UP as she, Caleb and Aurel descended the steep steps of the Temple of the Inscriptions. "Looks like a storm is coming," she observed.

Caleb scanned the sky and then looked at Aurel. "Looks bad," Aurel agreed. "We'd better get inside the palace."

"And tie everything down," Caleb added. "The sky has a strange appearance that fills me with foreboding."

Matal, Tamil and the others had already moved their gear inside when Shanni, Caleb, and Aurel crossed the open meadow to join them. The group turned to watch in silence as the dark clouds rolled forward like surf across a stormy beach.

"I've never seen anything like it," Matal said quietly as the wind rustled his hair.

A blast of rain whipped across the roof, forcing them to duck inside where they could see only dimly in the sudden gloom. Lightning rippled across the sky, charging the atmosphere with static electricity. Caleb felt a tingle, and then a burning sensation as a bolt of lightning curved around a stone column as if seeking him out, snake-like, to strike. Instinctively he threw his hands up to block the flash and found himself deflecting the energy like water across an oar, upward and outward. His awareness shifted and he saw the Being standing at the top of the pyramid, hurling the lightning that sought to destroy him.

Caleb levitated, driving himself forward to strike at the being he recognized as Agora. Agora laughed and hurled a fresh lightning bolt that sent Caleb reeling.

"We're here," he heard Aurel say out of the darkness. A loud crash of thunder signaled that Aurel and Shanni had joined the battle, deflecting the lightning bolts back upon Agora. But Agora had surrounded himself with a protective wall of Sentinels, each adding their power to the blue streaks of lightning that writhed and crashed in the cloud-covered space that separated Caleb, Shanni, and Aurel from Agora and the Sentinels.

The lightning changed from blue to white-hot, searing Caleb with its heat. He heard Shanni's cry of dismay and then they stood defenseless in front of Agora's onslaught. A look of triumph crossed Agora's face as he braced for the final strike. Such Power he had! And these humans had dared to oppose him!

A white orb of light flashed into existence in the space separating Caleb and his friends from Agora. Agora paused, confused, his hand raised high to hurl the final strike.

The orb expanded, forming a luminous ball of blue-white energy that Caleb recognized as Tonah. Tonah's spirit expanded to enclose Caleb, Shanni, and Aurel, the pyramid, and then Agora and the Sentinels in a giant bubble of light. The clouds overhead vanished, revealing the clear, night sky.

"It is over," Tonah 'said' to Agora. "I have come to bring you before the Council."

"No!" Agora screamed. "You have no authority over me! You cannot interfere!"

"After a thousand years, the truth of your evil has been revealed. There are nine levels of the Underworld. The Council will decide to which you will be banished."

"No!" Agora screamed again as a smaller bubble separated from Tonah and contracted, removing Agora from the world of ordinary reality in a flash of light.

The Sentinels stood stunned as their leader disappeared, and Shanni, Caleb, and Aurel flashed forward to confront them. Huntal stared in horror as Popol kneeled in front of Aurel, Caleb and Shanni and bowed his head. Huntal and the other Sentinels followed until all knelt in a half-circle.

"We cannot trust them!" Caleb said. "But how do we destroy them?"

With a howl of anguish, Popol was enveloped in a cocoon of flame that crackled and disappeared. One by one, cocoons of flame engulfed the other Sentinels until only Caleb, Aurel and Shanni were left standing alone on the pyramid.

"The Council has acted," Aurel replied. "Without Agora's power to support them, the Sentinels reverted to the Underworld."

"Forever?"

Aurel shrugged. "In human terms, I suppose."

TONAH AND THE Council watched as the star exploded into a supernova, spewing a stream of intense light and energy across the galaxy located in Agora's sector of the universe. The explosion set off a chain reaction across the galaxy that set it crashing into a sister galaxy in a cosmic collision. But Tonah concentrated on holding the remainder of Agora's former sector together and it steadied.

"It is good," a Council member said. "The transition could have been much worse. Agora's sector is now combined with yours. You have done well."

Tonah nodded, acknowledging the praise. Now he had much to focus upon, and much to do. Soon he would have no more time for the world of men. He must say good-bye to Aurel and Shanni.

Chapter 37

Early the next morning, Caleb and the others broke camp, packing their backpacks in preparation for departure down the river to safety, and then overland to Fuentes' haciendado.

"Travel as light as you can," Caleb advised, concern in his voice. "There'll be rapids in the river that we'll have to portage around, fighting the jungle all the way."

They hoisted their packs and hurried across the open meadow to join Tamil, who waited by a freshly-constructed raft. Caleb tossed his backpack on board and stepped back as the others loaded their gear. Caleb and the others climbed into the dugout canoes that Tamil had lashed on either side of the raft, and Tamil pushed the assemblage off from shore, jumping in to take his seat and join in rowing down the tributary that led to the Rio Usumacinta.

Dark clouds hovered overhead, portending rain and adding to the foreboding of their surroundings.

"If we can just get free of all this..." Ambria whispered, speaking the thought that focused all of them on the task ahead.

"We'll go quickly once we reach the current of the river," Tamil responded.

"Not too quickly for me!" Aurel added.

The raft was unwieldy, and tended to drift sideways in the current. Caleb, Shanni and Aurel concentrated on matching strokes with Matal and those in the other canoe in order to keep the raft on course, perspiring freely with the effort.

"We'll join the Usumacinta around the next bend," Tamil said, pointing.

They rounded the point and turned slowly into the river where they began to pick up speed. The water was brackish from the silt and leaves it picked up as it descended from the mountains to the south. The current took them in a northwesterly direction as the river twisted through the uneven foothills of the Sierra Madre del Sur.

Tamil stood up, listening, and pointed toward shore. "Rapids," he warned, as Caleb heard the roar of white water intensifying ahead. They angled toward the muddy bank of the river until

Tamil was able to grasp the branch of a fallen tree. With an effort they swung the raft and canoes around and tied them off.

Caleb gazed up the steep bank with misgiving. They would never be able to lift the raft up that muddy slope. They would have to carry the canoes and build a new raft on the other side of the rapids.

They untied the canoes and dragged them up the bank, and then returned for their packs. The slippery slope fought their efforts to climb back up with their burdens. As he reached the top, Matal dropped his pack and sat down, trying to catch his breath from the exertion.

"I hope there aren't many rapids," he said as the others joined him. "We'll never make progress this way!"

"We hadn't counted on this," Caleb agreed, looking at Tamil. "I thought the river would take us all the way."

"It gets better farther downstream where the land evens out into a long plain," Tamil replied. "Few rapids there, but the current slows, which will require more rowing."

"I'll take rowing over this any day!" Ambria answered, still trying to catch her breath.

After a brief rest, Tamil pushed into the dense undergrowth, leading the Huastecs who dragged the canoes with the packs inside.

They were making slow progress in the sweltering heat when Tamil suddenly paused. Caleb stepped up behind him and listened, but only the low roar of the rapids reached his ears. What had startled Tamil?

Tamil waved a hand silently, motioning for them to kneel as he eased back to join them. "I glimpsed men ahead, moving through the underbrush. I suspect an ambush."

Caleb looked around, taking a quick inventory of their weapons. They had machetes, Puco's shotgun, and the revolver. Not enough if their enemies had rifles. "We need to know how many," he whispered to Tamil. "If we can surprise them, we'll gain the initiative."

Tamil nodded and eased away into the brush and then returned after a brief absence. "A small force, stragglers from Crescencio's army."

"Weapons?"

"Machetes, maybe a rifle or two."

Caleb nodded. "We could use the rifles."

They developed a quick plan of attack and then spread out to advance toward the unseen enemy. In seconds Caleb's line of sight was cut off from the others by the dense foliage. *We're all proceeding blindly*, he thought. *There's no way to coordinate our attack. It will be a free-for-all.*

He heard the thud of a machete striking flesh, followed by a wild scream. Shots rang out, sending bullets spatting through the foliage. Yells followed and the sound of machetes clanging on steel rifle barrels.

Caleb spun as a tall body broke free from the underbrush and raised a rifle. Reacting reflexively, Caleb threw his machete with a hard swing of his arm. The machete clanged against the rifle barrel, knocking the rifle out of the man's hands. As he stooped to recover it, Caleb lunged forward, knocking the man off his feet.

The man rolled on top and hammered blows at Caleb's face. Caleb struggled to break free, but the man's weight pinned him to the slippery ground. In desperation, Caleb grabbed the man's shirt, yanking him forward as Caleb shifted his hips and twisted over on top. The man lashed out, knocking Caleb backward, and rolled to his knees. He grasped the machete and climbed to his feet, a triumphant gleam in his eyes. As he raised the machete, Caleb lashed out with his feet, striking the side of the man's knee, breaking the bone. The man fell backward with a scream of pain as Caleb clawed through the underbrush for the rifle. He heard the man thrashing toward him as his hands grasped the rifle and he turned, half-blind from the blood seeping into his eyes. The man broke away with his arm raised to slash down with the machete, as Caleb thrust the rifle forward and pulled the trigger. The man's face exploded in a flash of blood as Caleb fell back unconscious.

He heard voices through throbbing pain as he slowly regained his senses and raised his hand to his head. He felt a bandage on his head, and explored his face. His eyes were swollen shut, burning from perspiration in the heat.

"Rest, Caleb," Shanni whispered in his ear. "We're free of them. Tamil says we'll soon reach safety and ride for Campeche."

Caleb drew a deep breath as Shanni grasped his hand. He squeezed tightly and then lapsed back into unconsciousness.

Chapter 38

CALEB GINGERLY EXAMINED his face in the mirror as he prepared to accompany Shanni down to dinner at the Hacienda Fuentes. The days on the river had been a blur, but he had healed fast. "There'll be scars," he observed. "Won't help my looks any!"

"Stop admiring yourself and let's go!" Shanni admonished. "I can't wait to sit down at a real table and eat real food!"

"If you can stand to be seen with me..."

Shanni grasped Caleb's shoulders and turned him toward her. "Seeing you here in front of me, alive, after what we've been through...Well, you're just handsome to see, scars or no scars!"

Caleb started to respond but Shanni touched his lips and steered him out of the door and down the stairway.

They joined Matal and the others and soon were enjoying the food and wine as Senor Fuentes smiled his approval. "After thirty long years of bloodshed," Fuentes ventured after polite conversation, "the Caste War of the Yucatan is over. General Mariscal broke the back of the Indio resistance, and Crescencio Pooled signed the peace treaty. The provincial governor, with Mariscal's support, is setting up a council to assist the Indios in reclaiming land to rebuild their villages. As long as they remain peaceful, they will be assisted in regaining their ability to raise their crops and live free. Cen's captains, the ones who survived, were captured and imprisoned, but may be considered for pardon after serving a prison term. The British have signed a treaty with Mexico closing their border and agreeing to cut off the flow of guns and ammunition. After all the destruction, it appears that peace and normalcy will return to the Yucatan.

"You, my friends, are very, very lucky to have survived the chaos. Perhaps the prophesy was right after all. In a way you have brought peace to the Yucatan."

"We feel grateful to be alive," Caleb agreed. "Now Shanni and I just want to go home."

"Back to the United States?"

Caleb nodded.

"And what about you?" Fuentes turned his fatherly eyes to scan Matal and the others.

"I guess we'll return also," Matal responded quietly. "We failed in our quest to find a homeland for our people."

"A homeland that no longer exists," Fuentes observed, shaking his head.

"We expected to find a thriving society, the legacy of our ancestors. Instead we found only ruins. Now there is nothing to keep us here."

"Have you considered rebuilding?"

"The ruins?" Ambria broke in, brow furrowed.

"No. Your civilization. After all, the Mayas still exist, albeit in a present state of disarray. But with the Commission there is hope for the future of the Indios. At the same time, we landowners are threatened as the market for sisal, made from our 'Yellow Gold', or henequen, dries up. Already some of the hacienda families have moved to Cuba. All of us in the Yucatan must now lay aside our old ways and work together to restore prosperity."

"How would that help us rebuild?" Matal asked.

"If you have the means, you can buy hacienda land and return it to raising corn, the crop that is natural to the soil. Bring your people here to live and work with their cousins, the Maya."

Aurel looked at Caleb, and then at the shocked stares of Matal and the others. "But the haciendas..." he stammered. "You said that they were large, many square miles! They must cost a fortune!"

"Not anymore. With the crash of the sisal market, those forced to move away will consider any offer to recoup their losses. There will never be a better time to buy in our lifetime. My former neighbor, Augusto Orlina, has authorized me to sell his hacienda of forty-eight thousand hectares for any reasonable offer."

Caleb calculated mentally. "That's nearly one hundred and twenty thousand acres! What would be a reasonable offer?"

"The equivalent of fifty cents an acre, U.S.," Fuentes replied.

Caleb shook his head in amazement. Nearly two hundred square miles of land for about sixty thousand dollars! "How much would be needed to place a deposit to hold the land?" he asked.

"One thousand U.S. dollars," Fuentes replied. "And I'll advance it to you on your signature."

Caleb was taken aback. "I'm grateful, but that's a lot to offer to a person you hardly know. Why would you do it?"

"My life is here, and that of my family. At last peace has a chance in the Yucatan. I believe that you and the Huastecs can be a positive force in leading the Mayas, and us along with them, into a prosperous future."

Caleb looked around the table at Matal and the Huastecs. "Sam and I deposited the last of the silver in the bank at Denver before I left. There should be enough funds there to purchase the hacienda if that is what you want to do."

"It gives us the homeland we sought, and a future," Matal said. "I suggest we accept Senor Fuentes' kind offer."

"I agree," Ambria seconded. "We can give our people a choice. Emigrate here and build a new life, or remain with our friends, the Navaho."

"It won't be easy," Fuentes reminded them. "You must learn the language and customs of the Maya, and how to work the land to make it productive."

"The people have been successful in the past, and we can learn to be successful again!" Matal responded. "We'll be free to build our own future!"

"Is there anyone who is not convinced that this is the right thing to do?" Aurel asked.

"It is the opportunity of a lifetime," Ambria said. "How could it not be the right thing to do?"

One by one the others nodded their assent.

"It's settled then," Matal said.

"Both Matal and I will sign the advance," Caleb said, turning back to Fuentes. "To pledge the good faith of your new neighbors, the Huastecs, but Shanni and I will be returning to the U.S. The hacienda will belong to the Huastecs."

Fuentes grinned broadly, his dark eyes twinkling as he raised his glass of wine. "That is as it should be. I propose a toast to a prosperous future for all!"

"To a prosperous future!" Caleb, Shanni and the others raised their glasses in gratitude. Despite their hardships, the gods had shown favor. At last they had found their homeland.

Chapter 39

Caleb nudged the sorrel stallion up the slope of the meadow and reined to a halt, breathing deeply of the pine-scented air. In the distance his herd grazed peacefully, scattered across the hundred of acres of valley split by the tributary that fed the Mancos River.

He removed his hat, feeling the cool breeze rustle his hair as his gaze swept to the north and east, up the pine covered mountains that terminated in Hesperus Peak.

The two years had passed quickly since he and Shanni had returned to the United States with Matal and Ambria. After getting the funds from Denver, Matal and Ambria had returned to the Yucatan with more than fifty Huastec families to join Aurel and the others who had remained. The latest correspondence from Aurel had indicated that all was progressing satisfactorily on the Huastec hacienda. The Huastecs were safe at last building their new homeland, with Matal and Aurel as their leaders.

Sam had done a masterful job of maintaining his and Caleb's herds, and the combined roundup this fall was expected to yield more than ten thousand dollars each, to be banked in Denver. The Territory was moving rapidly toward statehood, and property values were rising steadily.

Shanni and I, and little Caleb Tonah have much to look forward to, Caleb thought with contentment as he nudged the horse up the path that led to the stone house that, at last, had become home.

As he dismounted in the courtyard, Shanni opened the door and walked out with Caleb Tonah on her hip.

"Hey there, big guy!" Caleb lifted "Tony" up, smiling and hugging him close. Tony's bright eyes studied Caleb's face as his mouth tried to form words. He managed "da-da" and lapsed into laughter.

"Why, I think he's trying to talk!" Caleb said, drawing Shanni close with his free arm.

"I get the sense that he already understands our words," Shanni replied, tickling Tony's chin. "He gets frustrated when his baby mouth cannot yet form the words."

"It will come soon enough," Caleb said to Tony. "You cannot rush life; you have to learn to flow along with it!"

They walked into the house and Caleb sat Tony down on the warm rug to play. "How was your day?" Caleb asked, turning his attention to Shanni as he hugged her close. She leaned on his chest, savoring the peace they had fought so hard to find.

"My day was wonderful. I enjoyed playing with Caleb Tonah, prepared food for our dinner, and then looked out the window at the beauty of our land. I cannot imagine a place more beautiful in all the world!"

"I knew all along that you would love being here, but there were times when I despaired of ever seeing it again!"

Shanni stood back, looking full into Caleb's eyes. "So many times events went wrong for us. I tremble to look back on how tenuous the thread that brings life instead of death!"

"I suppose it is life's way of teaching us what we're born into this world to learn."

"What is that, Caleb? What did we learn?"

"That after all the fighting and struggle to seek happiness somewhere out there, we found it inside ourselves. It's not where we are, but who we are, that brings happiness."

"And who we're with," Shanni corrected. "Without love there can be no happiness."

Caleb nodded. "Somehow I had come to believe that the world was against us. I felt that I had to fight it at every turn. But after the vision quest, I understood that the universe cares about us and wants us to be happy. It is the sum total of mankind's poor choices that creates so much havoc in the world."

"I hope from now on we can focus on our lives and our little corner of the world. We did our duty, and now maybe the gods will let us live in peace."

"I'll be content if I never have to engage in shamanism again in this life!" Caleb laughed.

"With our psychic abilities, and what you learned during your spirit quest, I worry that we will be called upon again. I'm not sure we'll ever be able to shut out the world out there."

"Nor should we," Caleb replied. "Plenty of ordinary men and women are meeting the call to build this country and make it a better place for their children. We can do no less. But for now, let's enjoy the opportunity to be ordinary people, living on our ranch, sleeping in our own bed and raising our children. Now we know that we're not missing anything 'out there'! All we need is right here."

Shanni moved into his arms and held him close. Tony giggled and crawled toward them, getting their attention. Shanni looked at him and smiled. "We have an interesting life ahead of us!" she laughed. "Today I peeked in on Tony and he was stacking his blocks one on top of the other."

"What's so special about that?" Caleb asked.

"He wasn't touching them. He was stacking them with his mind!"

"Well, I suppose that's to be expected. After all, he has shamans for parents!" Caleb chuckled. "I no longer fear the paranormal; in fact I embrace it. Now that I understand, I consider it part of this wonderful and mysterious world!"

Shanni returned to the kitchen as Caleb sat down in his chair in front of the fireplace. He stared at the flames, savoring their warmth, and sighed with contentment. At last he was home.

Epilogue

AUREL FLASHED UPWARD at lightning speed, riding the blue column of light to the pristine white plain where he knew that he would meet the being formerly known as Tonah, the shaman on the earthly plain who had been his mentor and surrogate father.

Tonah had long since discarded the 'props' of human form he had used to avoid frightening Aurel on his prior visits to the higher dimension. Now Tonah appeared in his true form as a bundle of pure energy that floated above the surface of the plain. Aurel noted that the energy bundle seemed thinner, less opaque, than in the past.

As if reading his thoughts, Tonah responded telepathically. "As one progresses through the dimensions of higher consciousness, one's energy bundle becomes diffused, spreading out and merging with the ocean of reality. Memory of the earth life dims as new experiences engage one's awareness."

"I am grateful that you could still meet me," Aurel responded. "We prevailed in the earth plane, but there is so much that I do not understand! Why were we so ineffective against the Guardian?"

"Guardians cannot be overcome in the earth plane. They exist beyond the reach of ordinary reality."

"Then how did Agora attack us?"

"Through his intermediaries, the Sentinels, who can move back and forth between ordinary and nonordinary reality."

"But we defeated the Sentinels repeatedly!"

"Yes. And when he became desperate and reincarnated into the physical world, he joined his Sentinels in defeat. Now he is banished to the Netherworld, the nine dimensions of purgatory."

"Why purgatory?"

"As punishment for his misdeeds on earth, the Council cast him out."

"But how could he do evil and rise to such a high dimension of responsibility?"

"He was very cunning. He used the ancient knowledge of the Poseidians against the people. He knew that each soul is given life in the earth plane to learn to differentiate good from evil, and to experience the pain caused by one's evil choices. From earthbound struggle, the entity develops understanding and experi-

174

ences compassion. Agora knew that if he acted overtly to cause evil, the Council would send him to the lower worlds to suffer greatly until he was allowed to return to the earth to redeem himself.

"So instead of causing evil directly, he played on the hates and fears of other humans, covertly encouraging them to commit evil acts in the belief that they were appeasing the gods. He ascended to the higher dimension, leaving his priests to foster even more bizarre and hideous acts of sacrifice. That is why he set the Sentinels against us in the physical world."

"I don't understand," Aurel replied.

"He knew that if he were found out, his part of the universe, the node in the matrix that he had created, would be ripped up by the Council, and he would be cast out.

"What kept him from succeeding? He had covered his tracks well."

"He was found out after all this time because some in the ancient priesthood retained their sense of humanity. They abhorred the evil and risked their lives to leave the truth behind, to be discovered in a later time when the knowledge could be used to correct the evil course that Agora and his priesthood had set in motion."

"The knowledge that you handed down to Shanni!"

"That, and the coded inscriptions the priests left in the Temple of Inscriptions, identifying Agora and revealing his treachery. They could not risk placing all the knowledge in one place, lest it be found and destroyed. So they created a system, a process, that would come together in due time, far in the future."

"And that's where we came in; you, Shanni, Caleb and I."

"A unique combination of internal skills and external forces came together to unite us in a common cause, a quest to find the 'Center'. The journey triggered the threat to Agora and his Sentinels, and all that they had carefully put in place."

"And we, without realizing it, fulfilled the plan to stop Agora. We carried out the plan left behind for a thousand years by the good men of the priesthood! They must have been very wise to conceive and execute such a plan right under the noses of Agora and his evil priests!"

"Yes, their contributions are great and they have moved on to greater responsibility in the higher dimensions."

"But what I don't understand," Aurel continued, "Is why all that evil was permitted in the first place. Mankind could be limited, and made so that they could only make good decisions. They could be precluded from doing evil."

JAMES GIBSON

"Then they could no longer be co-creators of the universe. They would become like the animals, programmed at birth to behave a certain way. Men were allowed to evolve in order to carry creation to the next level. Potentiality had been pushed to a point of diminishing returns. By evolving humans, creation made a species that could make new choices and then act on the physical world to influence its evolution. Man studies the world of ordinary reality and creates new and different ways of utilizing its energy. Some choices bring great good into the world: medical advances that relieve illness and suffering, machines that reshape the world for safety and comfort, manipulation of nuclear forces for energy and medical advancements. But man can also make choices that result in great destruction and suffering: murders, wars, pollution and disease. But without the free will to make choices, there could be no progress."

"So there is no limit to what man may invent in the future?"

"It is more correct to say that all things are possible, but sometimes we are forced to impose limits on man's choices."

"How?"

"Some entities, referred to as 'souls' in the earth plane, volunteer at great personal sacrifice to return to earth form, to endure pain and suffering on behalf of the world in order to correct the false course that mankind's choices have caused, a course that would lead to total destruction."

"Those become our martyrs, prophets, and sages." Aurel suggested.

"Yes. In the earth plane we revere them without a real appreciation of what they do for mankind."

"So there *is* a plan for the universe, after all!"

"Not a plan, a purpose. The Universal Consciousness cares about its creation, and has a purpose for the universe to evolve in a positive, constructive manner fostered by mankind's free will. Often man disappoints, and corrections must be made."

"Why are you telling me all this?"

"Why? Because you asked."

"But now you must trust me not to divulge this knowledge. If I go back and relate what I've learned, mankind will know how the world is supposed to work. There will be no reason to guess, or to make bad choices. It is like knowing the answers before you take the test!"

"It doesn't matter if you reveal what we've discussed. It won't change anything. Man will not change his ways."

"But how could it not change mankind's choices once they know their purpose, what they're supposed to do?"

"Because they won't believe you."

176

TIME HAD PASSED and Mayapan had watched as the strangers fulfilled their mission and righted the flaws created in the matrix of evolution by the evil one, Agora. Now the strangers had gone, leaving Mayapan one last mission to fulfill. He looked up at the sky, watching the condor circling overhead. He reached out with his *intent,* merged his consciousness with the raptor, and then he exercised control and directed it to fly southward, its strong wings beating effortlessly as it swiftly covered the miles. Below the forested slopes turned to raw rock outcroppings and then to tall snow-covered peaks. The land below narrowed to an isthmus, and then widened into a vast continent marked by a backbone of massive mountains that man called the Andes.

Through the condor's eyes, Mayapan looked far ahead at dark forms that rose to meet him. As the forms neared, he recognized condors from the mountains circling as if they expected him. They turned to guide him down among the mountain valleys. As he followed, Mayapan saw the hidden city set high on a barren ridge, surrounded by the river gorge that cut deep into the stone foundation of the mountain. The condor set down on smooth wings, where Mayapan disengaged his consciousness and stood waiting.

Three men emerged from a temple made of stone that had been fitted too perfectly for human hands. Mayapan let his gaze sweep over the stone buildings and terraces that wound in geometrical precision to the stone observatory that dominated the complex, the sacred place known to the Incan nobility as "Machu Picchu".

"You came far," the leader said. "I trust you bring favorable news." He was an ancient man, his lined face framed piercing eyes that seemed to be focused on a distant place.

Mayapan bowed. Many earth years had passed since the leader, Aztlan, the last of the Poseidians, had left Mayapan as his trusted observer of mankind's progress in the north.

"Strangers came, ones who embraced the ancient knowledge," Mayapan answered. "I believe they foretell a change in human development, away from external focus on technology and war, toward inward reflection to reconnect with the knowledge of the ages."

"All is proceeding as foretold in the Mayan calendar, which dates from the dawn of civilization," Aztlan replied.

"The Long Count of the Sacred Calendar, you mean?" Mayapan said.

Aztlan nodded. "All is on course. The Long Count encompasses over five thousand earth years, and completes the thirteen-batun Grand Cycle in the year mankind measures as 2011."

"And what will happen then?" Mayapan asked.

"The consciousness of mankind will evolve from the cycle of the Galactic Underworld into the Universal Underworld cycle. Consciousness will evolve from the individual to the group; the whole earth will be embraced in a global consciousness. There will be a fundamental shift in the way mankind views the world."

"That will be a great step toward reconnecting with the Universal Consciousness. I had almost lost hope," Mayapan said.

Aztlan turned to the others. "Soon our work here will be done and we can return to the higher dimensions."

The others nodded, smiling.

"And you, my friend," he said, turning back to Mayapan. "Well done. Now you can return with us and watch our efforts come to fruition. In 2011, a new world will rise from the ashes."

Acknowledgments

I AM GRATEFUL FOR the reader feedback, and for the new friends I have made through my books. I started with a vision, and soon found there is an enormous learning curve in the writing and marketing of books. While errors and omissions are my own, many people have come to my aid with expertise, encouragement and support. Tom Davis of Old Mountain Press was one of my first contacts. He soon realized he had a total novice on his hands. With the patience of Job, he led me through the steps to get my first book, *Anasazi Princess,* ready for publication, and he kept my spirits up until at last *Anasazi Princess* came off the press. Since then, he has been a staunch supporter, and helped to bring *Anasazi Journey, Anasazi Quest, Anasazi Desolation,* and now *Anasazi Triumph* through the publication process. I cannot say enough to express my gratitude for his help and support. He also writes and publishes books, I treasure my copy of *The Life and Times of Rip Jackson.* His latest book, *The R-Complex,* just came off the press as I write this, and I can't wait to read it.

Chris Day, Ph.D. is a long-time supporter who sets an example for what one can accomplish with boundless energy and keen focus. Her insights on my books are incisive and valuable. Julie Keating graciously proofreads my manuscripts, pointing out typos and syntax errors, but more importantly, pointing out areas where the concept works, or doesn't work. She often reminds me that the writer is incapable of effectively proofreading his own creation! Ralph and Mary Gillum share their interest and knowledge of similar books, and give me helpful suggestions while proofreading my manuscripts. Soon Ralph will enter the ranks of published authors himself, with *The Brace Beagle Forum,* on the breeding of championship beagles. Mary's familiarity with the books of Sharyn McCrumb helped me to incorporate the "Second Sight" concept into *Anasazi Quest,* my third novel. Alan Stuart attended my book signings, and shared his experiences during a three month sojourn in Mesa Verde in the 1940s. Alan provided documentation of Dark Canyon, a hidden enclave with water that validated my premise that the Huastecs could have remained in Mesa Verde until the 1870s. Dale Eckerty, a friend and former business associate, utilized his unique talents to point out inconsistencies in time, place, and other errors of fact in my manuscripts.

Our son Mark is particularly helpful in providing technical support to keep my computers operating, and in handling the digitalization of photos and maps. His ability and willingness to put my computer back in business after a catastrophic hard-drive crash is deeply appreciated. In addition to cover art, Lee Flamard provides visual arts expertise and creative ideas that help me to visualize new and better ways to improve my books. Artist Cindy Falle created the Anasazi Princess oil painting, which has become the centerpiece of our marketing visuals. To Betty, Chris and others at the "Little Book Shoppe on the Park", special thanks for being the first to stock my books and to support my book signings. I also acknowledge and appreciate Ron Gibson's support at my book presentations. Kay Gibson, Mom and others in the family have all been most supportive and helpful. Special appreciation to my wife, Cathie, with love, who seems to find a way to support all my schemes and dreams. I also acknowledge and appreciate the support of other family, and friends, whom I will not attempt to name for fear of leaving someone out.

And to you, the reader, thank you for your continued support. I feel that we are in a partnership, on a journey together through the characters in my books. I hope you find the journey stimulating and rewarding

James Gibson
Northville, Michigan
June 29, 2005

GLOSSARY OF TERMS

Anasazi (AH-NAH-sah-zi): Modern Navaho word for the "Ancient Ones", the Basket Weaver-Puebla culture of Native Americans who inhabited the region of what is now northern Arizona-western Colorado from CE 100-1300. They are noted for their elaborate pueblo and cliff dwellings (e.g., Chaco Canyon, Mesa Verde.)

Caleb (KAY-leb): Biblical name, representing "courage". In Numbers 14:24, Caleb is allowed to enter Canaan, the "Promised Land" because of his faithfulness in spite of great adversity and threats from his own people.

Caste War of the Yucatan: An actual historical event that occurred in the 1840s, lasting formally for seven years and continuing as guerrilla warfare for decades thereafter, resulting in over 200,000 casualties. In *Anasazi Triumph,* the time is fictionally shifted to the 1870s, and some of the historical characters and events are also utilized fictionally. *The Caste War of Yucatan* (Nelson A. Reed, Stanford University Press, 2001) does a great job of depicting the history of the war, and grateful acknowledgment is made of using it as a background resource.

Huastecs (Hu-AZ-teks): Descendants of the Mayas living in the Yucatan region of southern Mexico. The term is used fictionally in the Anasazi Princess series of books to assume a connection between the Anasazi of western Colorado and the Maya, which becomes the motivation for Shanni and her people to attempt the hazardous journey back to their mythical "Center".

Palenque: (PAH-lahn-ka): Ancient city-state of the Mayas, located along the Rio Usumacinta in the state of Chiapas, Mexico. It is used fictionally as the "Center" of the ancient Mayan civilization that the Caleb and the Huastecs seek in the *Anasazi Princess* series.

Shaman (SHAH-mon): From the Tungusic word 'saman' in Siberia; one who actively enters into an altered state of consciousness ("nonordinary reality") in order to gain knowledge, harness power, and gain other nonordinary ability to solve problems and to heal sickness in the ordinary world.

Shanni (SHAH-nee): Princess of the Huastecs, a fictional sect of the Anasazi, who possesses paranormal powers.

Sorcerer (SOR-SIR-er): In the Anasazi Princess series context, a shaman who goes beyond healing to use paranormal powers in nonordinary reality to gain knowledge, increase power, and fight battles. Sorcerers are referred to as "brujos" (male) and "brujerias" (female), and "healers" are sometimes referred to as "curanderos", in Mexico.

Tonah (TONE-ah): Shaman, sorcerer, and spiritual leader of the fictional Huastecs of Mesa Verde; despite his age, he is considered "grandfather" by Shanni.

Vision Quest (VEZ-YON KWEST), also called "Spirit Quest": A rite of passage common to many aboriginal and /or shamanistic societies in which the initiate goes into the wilderness alone and faces physical death. The belief is that the danger taps into latent survival abilities and mystical knowledge deep within the psyche that is only activated to save the person's life when death is imminent. Caleb is forced to survive a Vision Quest in the third book of the *Anasazi Princess* series, in order to deal with his enemies in the world of nonordinary reality.

BOOKS BY JAMES GIBSON
at
www.pentaclespress.com

ANASAZI PRINCESS: A Fable of the Old West. *Anasazi Princess* combines traditional Western romance with Native American shamanism to create a "New Age" Western in which Caleb Stone returns to Mancos, Colorado to avenge his father's murder and reclaim his family's ranch. After he is ambushed, the Huastec Tonah and his granddaughter Shanni rescue Caleb and take him away to their hidden enclave in Mesa Verde. Tonah uses his shamanistic powers to save Caleb's life, and as Caleb recovers, he falls in love with Shanni. As a result, he is caught up in their dangerous journey to return to their ancient homeland, the fabled Mayan "Center" far to the south. (Published 2001, 193 pages.)

ANASAZI JOURNEY: A Novel: The *Anasazi Princess* saga continues...Anasazi princess Shanni and her people, the Huastecs are lost and suffering in the desert of New Mexico as they journey south in an attempt to reach the "Center" of their ancient Mayan homeland. Seeking help to find food and water, they fall into the hands of renegade leader Kaibito, who takes them prisoner. The Huastec shaman Tonah realizes that a more sinister force in the spirit world threatens the Huastecs and the life of Caleb Stone, the Anglo who has joined the band to help Shanni and the Huastecs complete their journey. The sorcerer Jorge Tupac utilizes ancient Mayan occult arts in an attempt to murder Shanni, which forces Caleb and Tonah to risk their lives to rescue her and deliver the Huastec nation from a strange and perilous world. (Published 2002, 178 pages.)

ANASAZI QUEST; A Novel: As the *Anasazi Princess* saga continues, the Huastec nation escapes from the clutches of renegades and forges southward from the Territory of New Mexico to enter Mexico during the turbulent times of the revolution of the 1870s. Despite their peaceful intent to return to the mythical "Center" of their ancient Mayan civilization, the Huastecs are attacked, and princess Shanni and her women warriors are carried off into captivity. At the same time, a sinister force of Mayan sorcerers attempts to attack, forcing Tonah, the Huastec shaman, to send the Anglo, Caleb Stone, on a spirit quest to learn how to save his own life and that of Shanni. As they face their individual crises, both Caleb and Shanni learn to use the latent powers of the human mind to survive strange and hostile worlds. (Published 2003, 224 pages.)

ANASAZI DESOLATION: A Novel: The fourth novel in the *Anasazi Princess* saga carries a small remnant of Huastec warriors deep into Mexico in the search for their homeland centered in the ancient Mayan civilization in the Yucatan. With the loss of her grandfather, the shaman Tonah, the Huastec princess Shanni is forced to deal with the strange and sinister attacks by sorcerers in the spirit world who threaten her life and that of her husband, the Anglo, Caleb Stone. As the attacks intensify, Shanni is forced to probe the depths of the human psyche, and to fight an imposed paranoia that threatens to destroy her sanity and her love for Caleb. (Published April, 2005, approximately 200 pages.)

ANASAZI TRIUMPH: A Novel: The concluding novel in the Anasazi Princess series brings the Huastec warriors into the Yucatan, and face to face with their tormentors, the Mayan sorcerers who have made repeated attempts to kill Caleb and Shanni, and prevent them from uncovering the horrible secret of the Mayan priesthood that has remained hidden for a thousand years. (Publication planned for 2005, approximately 180 pages.)

Order Form

To order additional copies, fill out this form and send it along with your check or money order to: James N. Gibson LLC, P.O. Box 51, Novi, MI 48376.
Or order online: www.pentaclespress.com

Cost per copy $14.95 plus $2.50 P&H. (MI residents add 6% sales tax)

Ship _____ copies of *Anasazi Triumph* to:

Name_____

Address:_____

City/State/Zip:_____

___ Check for signed copy

Please tell us how you found out about this book.
___ Friend   ___ Internet
___ Book Store   ___ Radio
___ Newspaper   ___ Magazine
___ Other _____